ALITA
BATTLE ANGEL

THE OFFICIAL MOVIE
NOVELIZATION

Also available from Titan Books

Alita: Battle Angel – Iron City (The Official Movie Prequel)

THE OFFICIAL MOVIE NOVELIZATION

BY PAT CADIGAN

BASED UPON THE GRAPHIC NOVEL ("MANGA") SERIES "GUNNM" BY YUKITO KISHIRO

SCREENPLAY BY JAMES CAMERON AND LAETA KALOGRIDIS

TITAN BOOKS

Alita: Battle Angel – The Official Movie Novelization
Paperback edition ISBN: 9781785658402
E-book edition ISBN: 9781785658396

Published by
Titan Books
A division of Titan Publishing Group Ltd
144 Southwark Street
London
SE1 0UP

First edition: February 2019
1 3 5 7 9 10 8 6 4 2

This is a work of fiction. Names, characters, places, and incidents
either are the product of the author's imagination or are used
fictitiously, and any resemblance to actual persons, living or dead,
business establishments, events, or locales is entirely coincidental.
The publisher does not have any control over and does not assume
any responsibility for author or third-party websites or their content.

A CIP catalogue record for this title is available from the
British Library.

Printed and bound in the United States.

Did you enjoy this book?
We love to hear from our readers. Please email us at
readerfeedback@titanemail.com or write to us at
Reader Feedback at the above address.
To receive advance information, news, competitions, and exclusive
offers online, please sign up for the Titan newsletter on our website
www.titanbooks.com

In Memory of:

Susan Casper
Georgina Hawtrey-Woore
Geri Jeter

Battle Angels live forever

And as always for The Original Chris Fowler,
whose kind, loving, generous heart
makes everything possible

 CHAPTER 1

The floating city of Zalem was most beautiful at sunset, or so most people said. Or so most people *thought* most people said. In fact, Zalem was impressive at any hour of the day or night, hanging in mid-air like a good magician's best trick. It could have been some mythical realm—El Dorado maybe, or the Kingdom of Prester John, distant Thule or Camelot—except it wasn't lost. Everyone in Iron City could find it. All they had to do was look up and there it was: a perfect circle five miles across, wearing its skyline like a crown, ever present and ever out of reach.

Other than that, there were only three things the ground-level population knew for certain about the place: 1) the Factory in Iron City existed to support Zalem, sending food and manufactured goods up through long tubes that extended from it like graceful spiders' legs; 2) you couldn't get there from here—only supplies went up, *never* people; and 3) you never stood directly below the centre of Zalem unless you wanted to be crushed under the trash, junk and general refuse that suddenly and without warning rained down from the large, ragged hole in the underside of the disc.

This was just how the world worked, and no one now alive remembered anything different. A very long time ago there had been a War against an Enemy, and it had left the world in its current sorry state, where people on the ground had to scrounge around for whatever they could repair, revamp or remake, while Zalem sucked up anything worth having. No one had the time or inclination to wonder how people had lived before the War; the daily effort of survival kept them too busy for history.

Dr Dyson Ido, Cyber-Surgeon, MD, was one of the very few people in Iron City with a detailed knowledge of the past—the War, the Fall, and why Zalem was the only one of the original twelve floating cities to remain aloft. Right now, however, as the sun set on another long day of treating patients at the clinic, he wasn't thinking about history. He was picking his way through the sprawling pile of Zalem's refuse in search of anything salvageable, taking a circular path halfway between the centre and the edge.

The continual addition of new rubbish and regular scavenger activity meant the contents of the mound were always shifting; things buried deep in the centre were eventually pushed outwards and upwards. The area Ido was searching often yielded items that could be repaired or rebuilt, or sometimes just cleaned—Zalem's people were a wasteful bunch—while being far enough from ground zero to let him hunt without risk of being flattened by new arrivals. Assuming no one flushed a house down the chute, of course; so far no one had, or at least not all at once.

Ido spent the end of many days on the trash pile, using a hand-scanner to catch any stray electronic or biochemical signals from some bit of rechargeable tech. An observer with an especially sharp eye would have noted that although his long coat had seen a lot of wear, it had been nice once, too nice for Iron City. Then there was that old-fashioned hat— on anyone else it would have been a sad affectation, but it belonged on him, mostly because of his bearing. The way he carried himself suggested he was an educated man of some importance who'd taken a wrong turn off the open road and ended up in Iron City. But no observer would know he had once lived a life of privilege and gentility and, after losing everything, was now reduced to picking through the dregs and dross of a better world.

His previous existence felt as distant to him as the War nobody knew very much about any more. Nobody knew very much about him, either, except that he was a highly skilled cyber-surgeon who offered his services to Iron City's cyborgs at whatever price they could pay. For them, this was as miraculous as a floating city, only a hell of a lot more useful. They were grateful for his skills and he was grateful they never asked how he had come by them, or where he was from, or even how he'd got the small pale scar on his forehead. Everybody in Iron City had scars, as well as a past they didn't want to talk about.

Ido stooped to pick up a corroded metal hand, peering at it through his round spectacles. As he dropped the hand into the bag slung across the front of his body, he caught sight of a single glass eye nestled in the socket of a burned metal skull. The eye was perfect, without even a small crack. How had it escaped damage when the skull had been fried? Ido bent down to have a closer look and decided the eye didn't belong to this skull but had rolled into it by chance. All sorts of things happened by chance. If he hadn't come along at the right moment both the eye and skull might have sunk back down into Zalem's broken, unwanted crap, never to resurface. Or some nearby movement might have caused the eye to roll out of the skull as accidentally as it had rolled in and, unnoticed, would be mashed underfoot by an endless parade of scavengers.

Ido pushed himself to his feet and looked around, trying to decide whether he should continue while there was still enough daylight for him to see where he was going or quit while there was still enough night ahead for a few hours of sleep. Most of the other scavengers had given up and gone home, leaving only the desperate and the hardcore, the ones who were secretly hoping to find a real treasure. It was possible, for example, that a diamond ring had fallen off some Zalem aristocrat's hand into the trash by accident. Highly improbable, yes, but not *physically* impossible.

Selling it in Iron City for even half its worth—*that* was impossible.

Ido permitted himself a small chuckle and turned his thoughts back to the question of where to go next. Zalem had dumped a load about fifteen minutes ago; while there was no set schedule, there was usually at least twenty minutes between deliveries. *Usually*, however, didn't mean *always*. He was trying to decide whether to tempt fate in ten-minute increments—scavenge for five minutes, then stand back for another five. Normally he didn't take chances—he was the only doctor most of Iron City's cyborgs could afford and he took his duty of care seriously. That, however, was why he was weighing the risk. The centre hadn't already been picked over, which gave him a better chance of finding something usable, particularly servos. He needed more servos. He *always* needed more servos.

He was still deliberating when two things happened at once: his gaze fell on something half buried in the slope about three metres ahead of him, and he felt the scanner in his hand pulse ever so slightly. For a moment, he didn't dare move. If his eyes weren't playing wish-fulfilment tricks on him in the dying daylight, and if the scanner wasn't reacting to the last gasp of a dying circuit under his feet, he was looking at something worth more than a thousand diamond rings.

Keeping his eyes fixed on the shape, he moved towards it slowly, willing it to stay real and not turn into an illusion produced by a chance arrangement of junk. Then he was standing over it and, no, it wasn't a scrapyard mirage, it was a real thing that was really there, and he had found it by chance. But as any self-respecting, if outcast, scientist knew, chance favoured the prepared mind.

He knelt down and began gently excavating it from the trash, working as carefully as an archaeologist who had come across the find of the century. After a few minutes he sat back on his heels and stared at what he had uncovered. It was the face of a young girl: beautiful, angelic and completely impossible except in dreams of an especially pleasant, magical kind. He could tell he wasn't dreaming now by the sharp edges and lumps poking into his knees and lower legs, and the ache in his back.

This wasn't *her* face, either, not the one he wished so intensely to see again, but it could have been. She looked so utterly serene with her eyes closed and her mouth on the verge of a smile, as if she were dreaming of something wonderful. Only the rips in her skin—at the base of her neck, along the right side of her jaw, above her left eye— gave her away as synthetic.

Ido leaned forward and began clearing away the detritus below her neck. The work progressed more slowly because his hands were trembling now and he had to stop sometimes to steady himself. After what might have been a minute or an eternity, he had uncovered her cyber-core: upper chest, one shoulder, her metal spine and the ribs caging her perfect white heart, which shuddered with each slow beat.

Hesitantly he put the scanner to her temple and watched, mesmerised, as the waveform on the readout confirmed that a person was still present.

"You're alive," Ido said, unaware that he'd spoken aloud.

He couldn't let her lie there a moment longer. He manoeuvred his hands around the broken fragment of her form and lifted her out of the trash, holding her up in the fading daylight, wondering how anyone could discard her as if she were no more than a broken doll, and feeling something he had not felt since the birth of his daughter, and had thought he would never feel again when she'd died.

CHAPTER 2

Nurse Gerhad had swapped the surgical instruments on her cyber-arm for a normal hand in preparation for going home when she heard the basement entrance open and close. After a busy day treating patients and trading for parts, Ido had insisted on going out to see what he could find in the trash heap and hadn't minded when Gerhad said she was too tired to go with him. She wasn't as good at it as he was anyway, even when she wasn't tired, because of her personal feelings. The mere idea of picking through the discards of some unattainable and supposedly better world made her lose the will to live; actually doing it made her want to die.

Not that she'd ever known anything different. Her family had always lived in Iron City and most of them still did. One or two adventurous sorts had taken off in search of something better in parts unknown, and had never been heard of since. Gerhad didn't think this meant anything good. She had never considered doing anything like that herself; as far as she knew, the Badlands weren't hiring nurses, or anyone else for that matter. And even if they were, she doubted there were any other Dyson Idos out there. There sure weren't any others in Iron City, unless you counted the ice queen, and Gerhad most certainly did not.

Thinking of Ido's ex was something she preferred not to do, ever, and she wouldn't have, if it wasn't for what Ido had brought back. The way he'd come running up the stairs, Gerhad thought he had a bag full of servos. They needed more servos. They *always* needed more servos. But instead—

The cyber-core now locked into the stereotactic frame was the last thing she had expected him to bring back, right after a bag full of diamond rings. Well, if she'd found a discarded cyber-core showing the existence of a person, she'd have done the same. But she recognised the face; it was impossible, it could not be. And yet it was, big as life, and a heartbreak for sure. She wasn't certain how that would work since the doc's heart was already well and truly broken, but life could be very inventive.

After securing the cyber-core in the frame, he'd run back down to the basement for something. She'd known what he was after but she still caught her breath when he reappeared, carrying what looked like a child's body in his arms. In fact, it *was* a child's body, one that Ido had made. But the child had never used it and Ido had put it into storage, all those heartbroken years ago. Gerhad's feelings were mixed as she watched him lay it gently on the operating table next to the cyber-core in the frame.

It was beautiful, a work of art and an expression of

profound love. She understood why Ido had packed it away unused, but she had also felt there was something inherently wrong about letting something so extraordinary go to waste. For a while, she'd hoped he might someday reach a place where he could let someone else benefit from his creation. But that would have meant he was healing, and healing was the one thing Ido would never, ever allow himself to do.

Ido had been jumping around the room, making preparations for surgery, shooing Gerhad away when she tried to do anything more than sterilise her own instruments. He was in the midst of recalibrating the micro-surgical robot arms when he suddenly turned to look at the slumbering cyber-core. After two hours of soaking up a pre-op infusion of brain nutrients, the cyber-core's eyes were now moving restlessly back and forth beneath the closed lids. Correction: *her* eyes, *her* closed lids; as the revival process went on, she looked more and more like the girl in the holo that Ido stared at countless times a day, every day.

Now he went over to the frame and reached out to touch her cheek. "What are you dreaming, little angel?" he asked with a tenderness Gerhad hadn't heard in a long time. He turned to her and she was shocked to see tears in his eyes.

Abruptly, he was jumping around again, setting up the micro-surgery workstation, running diagnostics, rechecking the robotic arms. He never said a word to her but he didn't have to. Gerhad was a registered nurse trained in cyber-surgery. She always knew what to do.

It wasn't the longest twenty-four hours Gerhad had ever spent in an OR but it was definitely the most intense. Ido had been a man in a fever, or a man possessed, working the micro-surgery arms and demanding she read data outputs from half a dozen different screens to him continuously, only because he didn't have six extra pairs of eyeballs to read them himself. She had no idea how he kept all the figures straight while he guided the micro-surgery instruments through all the tiny connections. He was just that brilliant—there were still times when she was awestruck by the breadth and depth of his intellect.

Like now, she thought as she watched the spidery surgical arms dancing in a delicate ballet choreographed by Ido. He didn't *have* to hover over the instruments while they worked—he'd designed and built them himself and his surgical machines never malfunctioned unless you hit them with a hammer, and sometimes not even then. But it was more than his making sure nothing went wrong. The micro-surgery instruments carried out procedures that his own steady and practiced hands were simply too big to accomplish; as such, they were extensions of himself, and he had to witness every connection of every blood vessel, every muscle fibre, every nerve.

Ido turned to her, nodded almost imperceptibly. She fetched two bags from the fridge. One was filled with standard biological human blood, heart's-blood; the other, twice as large, contained iridescent celestial-blue cyber-blood. The term "blood" wasn't quite accurate, as the latter had a lot more to do in a cyborg body, using nano-machines instead of white or red blood cells. Having only one cyber arm, Gerhad didn't need as much as this girl would require for a Total Replacement body, even one smaller than an average mature adult.

Gerhad placed the bags in the transfusers and set the rate of flow for each; all Ido had to do was trigger them. He grunted his thanks and dismissed her by way of a head jerk, though only temporarily; he expected her to remain handy and alert until further notice. At one time, Gerhad wouldn't have tolerated grunts and head jerks from a doctor. She still wouldn't, except for Ido.

The day Gerhad met Dyson Ido, she had been lying in a bed in post-op, mourning for the career she had lost along with her arm. She'd known who he was—everyone at the hospital knew Dr Ido for his work with cyborg patients. Gerhad herself had referred people to his clinic.

When Ido had told her he could not only save her nursing career but enhance and improve it, she'd thought he was a hallucination generated by some rather iffy painkillers—not an unreasonable assumption. She was on staff at the hospital, and the Factory had been shorting their supply of meds. The pharmacy had become desperate enough to seek out alternative sources; as a result, in the last couple of weeks, people who came in with broken bones went out tripping balls, and migraine sufferers spent their nights going to raves and kissing everyone. Oddly enough, there wasn't a single complaint from anyone, but it was no solution.

The Factory had promised to make things right, but they'd taken their sweet-ass time about it. The Head Nurse told them there was nothing any of them could do except pray for rain and, *For God's sake, don't get hurt.*

Three hours later, her shift over, Gerhad walked out of the front door of the hospital just in time for an out-of-control gyro-lorry to sideswipe the front of the building, taking out all the windows, half a dozen newly installed hanging plants, a few No-Parking signs, and her left arm.

Somehow, she had remained conscious, although there were a few bad splices in her memory. One moment, she'd been stepping out on the sidewalk with the door of the hospital closing behind her; the next, she was lying on the ground amid broken glass, chunks of cement, clots of damp, dark dirt and torn-up flowers. She remembered knowing her arm was gone and, with it, her nursing career, such as it was.

Nursing wasn't always everything she'd hoped it would be—there was an awful lot of repeatedly patching up people who couldn't stop making the same mistakes, feet that hurt all the way up to her hips, and more vomit than she could ever have imagined. But there were good days, too, when she encountered someone who refused to be beaten down by circumstance, or at least weren't their own worst enemy. And there were the kids, the ones who had not yet begun to grow up too fast.

The pay was crap and sometimes it got crappier. They couldn't lay anyone off because they needed every warm body they had, so there were pay cuts. Always with the Factory's *sincere* apologies, played over the background noise of shipments travelling up to Zalem via the tube that arced right over the hospital from a nearby distribution annexe. Making ends meet required a lot of double shifts—not at overtime rates but at regular pay, sometimes less.

But being a nurse wasn't a *job*, it wasn't just a way to make a living while you looked for something better, it was a profession—a vocation. Nurses *wanted* to be nurses; it was the only thing Gerhad had ever wanted to be. Nursing had given her focus and discipline, which she discovered were crucial to surviving in a world that was shambolic and uninspiring at best and, at worst, pitiless and corrupt.

And now, thanks to a lorry driver who hadn't been qualified for a commercial vehicle heavier than half a ton, it was all gone. Compensation? She could whistle for it. The truck had been Factory-owned, and it hadn't been a kingpin like Vector behind the wheel, just some poor shlub who vanished without leaving a name. And that was the state of the nation, thank you and good night.

The next time she woke up, her upper body was locked into a stereotactic frame; Ido had her positioned so the nerves in her shoulder could most easily make the acquaintance of those in the cyber-arm. Ido was hovering over the robotic arms, his face set in an expression of intense concentration, as if Gerhad were the most important person in the world and he were performing the micro-surgery with his own hands.

She'd drifted in and out of consciousness, feeling no pain

and seeing nothing psychedelic—later she found out he made his own medications, including anaesthesia—until she finally woke up completely and got her first good look at the work of art that was now part of her body.

"I don't know if I'm safe having an arm like this," she told him, admiring the designs etched into the metal. It made her think of an antique silver tea service. "I might get jacked the minute I step outside."

His smile had been knowing and even a little gleeful. "This town isn't full of geniuses but pretty much everybody knows better than to mess with my work."

She nodded, still admiring her arm. "I've treated more than a few patients who had parts they couldn't possibly afford. And now I'm one of them."

"Oh, there's no charge," he said, enjoying the look on her face. "Of course, there *is* something *you* can do for me that none of my other patients can."

That would have rung alarm bells except he didn't sound sleazy. "What?" she asked, more curious than wary.

"Work for me. I need a nurse and I can pay better than the hospital."

To her surprise, she'd said yes immediately. Then she'd waited for *that* moment, when he put his hand where it didn't belong and she had to break his nose or dislocate his shoulder, but it never came. She had accepted purely for the money, thinking she could build up a nest egg and if the job sucked, go back to the hospital. But before long, she decided it would be just plain stupid to give up an opportunity to work with a genuine, no-foolin' medical genius.

She had gone to work for Ido shortly after his heart had been well and truly broken, but other than that, she knew very little about him. He wasn't from around here, but you only had to talk to him to know that. He wasn't just bright, he was educated far beyond anything available at ground level, unless there was an ivory tower in some faraway land beyond the Factory's reach.

But Gerhad was certain Dyson Ido had not travelled from some far-off land to fetch up in the dead end of Iron City. No, he was from somewhere much closer, a place everybody in Iron City saw all the time but was more remote than the moon and just as unattainable.

Travel from ground level to Zalem was strictly forbidden, a law the Factory's Centurians enforced by lethal means. No heavier-than-air flight of any kind was permitted, for any reason; just flying a kite could get you killed. The Centurians weren't programmed to distinguish between machines and living creatures; as a result, whole generations of Iron City residents had lived and died without ever seeing a bird except in photos.

No one knew if Zalem's residents were equally restricted or whether the view from on high convinced them to stay where they were. Gerhad suspected it was the latter. Not that it made any difference—there was no way for anyone in the floating city to get to the surface.

Well, no way save one, and that was one hell of a long fall.

Gerhad didn't think many people could survive something like that. A parachute was out of the question—the Centurians would blast it into confetti and make mincemeat out of the person attached to it. The trash heap below would hardly provide a soft landing; at terminal velocity, a person was likely to pile-drive through several layers of accumulation, and the scrap metal would be like shrapnel.

You'd have to be some kind of batshit genius to figure out how to come out of that alive—and not just you but your wife and kid, too. And if the kid was kind of fragile, say, disabled—Gerhad had thought about it for years and she was still baffled.

Nonetheless, all three of them had survived. The girl had died a few years after that, in circumstances that were as brutal as they were pointless. Which, in Iron City, was unremarkable.

The real puzzler, though, was why Zalem had let someone so brilliant leave. Or had they? Gerhad wondered. They might grow the population a lot smarter up there but she doubted there was anyone who'd have made the doc seem dull by comparison. He was—she looked for a word other than *intense* and came up empty. Because that was what he was: intense. Everything he did for his patients mattered as much to him as it did to them, and she was sure he had always been this way. By all rights he should have gone crazy long ago but somehow he'd stayed sane. Or just sane enough.

Maybe Zalem *hadn't* let him go, Gerhad thought. Maybe leaving had been *his* idea. He certainly hadn't tripped and fallen over the edge by accident.

Ido turned to Gerhad, about to say something, and saw she had fallen asleep in the chair, head resting on her cyborg hand. He considered waking her, then decided not to. The embodying procedure was almost finished. He turned back to the girl on the table, to the white ceramic-and-titanium heart in her open chest. It was beating more quickly now, at a rate normal for a girl fast asleep and lost in her dreams.

She was alive.

CHAPTER 3

Waking was like drifting up from the depths of a warm, dark ocean. It was gradual, requiring no effort on her part, proceeding at its own rate. Time passed, or maybe it didn't, or it stopped and then started again. After a while—an hour or a week or a century—she opened her eyes.

The ceiling above her was blank except for a few cracks. There was nothing distinctive about it or even familiar—it could have been any ceiling anywhere. She was certain, however, that it wasn't the same ceiling she'd gone to sleep under. If there'd been a ceiling at all.

She yawned, enormously and deeply, her eyes squeezing shut as her lungs expanded to their limit. She had half a second to think her chest felt a little strange before she opened her eyes again and saw the hand she had reflexively covered her mouth with.

The hand wasn't hers. It wasn't even human.

Like that, she was awake; looking at the hand, turning it this way and that, wiggling the fingers. This wasn't *just* a hand. Someone had *envisioned* this hand, then brought it into existence, made it something that could move, that could touch and be touched.

And it was *beautiful*, decorated with designs of flowers and leaves and curlicues rendered in perfect, delicate lines. The metal inlay in the centre of her palm was etched with similar designs, only much smaller. She closed her hand slowly, then opened it again, watching the way all the sections worked; it had the same range of movement as a flesh-and-blood hand. Where there would have been pads at the base of each finger, she had small rounded sections, each one decorated with an exquisitely intricate sunburst. The metal shining in her finger joints was the same as that inlaid in her palm.

She even had fingerprints—but, oh, what fingerprints! The curved lines etched into the top two joints of each finger were a glorious riot of crashing waves that morphed into impossible flowers, clouds, arcs and spirals, dancing and swirling in a way that was exultant, even defiant.

On the back of her hand was a flower so complex she would have to study it at length to see all of its details. The thought that someone would give her something so beautiful was a surge of light and warmth inside her.

Her wrist was mechanical, its articulation and segments even more complex than her hand. Past that, more flowers blossomed in symmetry along her outer forearm, the lines delicate and perfect, some of them spilling onto her inner arm, right up to her mechanical elbow. The design resumed all the way up her bicep to a gold inlay etched with lines very much like her fingerprints. The segments that made up her shoulder were outlined in silver and gold. She'd never seen anything like this. If she had, she'd have wanted it immediately.

And her left arm?

She pulled it out from under the covers and was relieved to see that, yes, she had the set. She stretched her arms out so she could admire them both. With arms this beautiful, she might never wear long sleeves again.

The rest of her—what was that like?

Nervously she pulled the covers back. For a long moment she could only stare at herself in wonder. The whole body—*her* whole body—every bit of it, was a work of art. She stared at the—at *her*—creamy pinkish "skin" and the beautifully etched silver and gold inlays. How long had she been asleep?

And while she was at it, where had she woken up?

The bedroom was no place she knew, but she got the impression from the funny little figures on the shelves, the pictures on the walls and the stuffed bunny on her pillow that it belonged to a young girl. A *smart* young girl who loved to read—there were shelves and shelves of hardcopy books. But other things in the room didn't seem to belong—a shabby briefcase bundled with a stack of old file folders, for instance. Young girls didn't go for briefcases, not even smart young girls. A stuffed animal maybe—she picked up the bunny and ran a finger along its floppy ears. The fur was soft with comfort under her fingertips; she could practically feel the pattern of how the little-girl hands had petted and stroked it countless times. The bunny was old, too, just like pretty much everything else she could see. The very smart young girl who'd lived here must have been long gone by the time Alita had been tucked into her bed.

Who had brought her here and how had they done it without waking her? Because she had the strong feeling she had gone to sleep in a place far away. She couldn't remember where that had been, or what she had been doing there, or, now that she thought of it, anything at all.

But even if she didn't know where she was now, she was sure of one thing: it was safe. The place was old and a bit shabby, but it was intact. There was no visible damage from heavy munitions or explosives. Nor could she see any weapons stashed in convenient spots where they'd be easy to grab in an emergency, not even—she checked— under the bed.

She didn't wonder why that last thought had crossed her mind. It seemed only natural to think about safety after waking up in a strange place, not to mention in an unfamiliar body. Yes, the body was pretty, but was it useful? Was it able enough, fast enough, tough enough?

Her gaze fell on the full-length mirror across the room. She walked over to it on her unfamiliar but very beautiful legs and stood holding her arms slightly away from her body so she could see everything: the silver and gold inlays at her collarbone and the ornate but delicate artwork just below them and in the centre of her chest; the complexity of her segmented torso; the etched gold inlays at the tops of her thighs and the designs that curled along the front and sides of her legs above her complicated knees; the perfect symmetry of the fantasy flowers on her calves, mirror images of each other. She could actually imagine the work in progress, someone bending over each part in turn, working under a bright light, never looking up until it was perfect. The person in question was a dark blurry shadow with an impossibly steady hand and eyes that didn't see only surfaces—they saw all the way *through* the world, into its essence.

But the beauty she was admiring was a doll's beauty. The realisation brought her back down to earth with a thump. She was a toy girl, lacking the crucial anatomical features of a real person. There were pretty flowers along the line of collarbone, and gold and silver inlays just above the place on her chest where her breasts began, and more inlays below them. But her breasts were blank, featureless.

She pressed a finger to one of them, expecting it to be as hard as the rest of her, and was surprised to feel it give. Her body wasn't completely hard metal; there were some soft places.

Moving closer to the mirror, she touched her face. That was soft, too, but she was certain it was her own, not something that had come with the body. She looked down at herself and made a slow turn, looking over one shoulder and then the other. She was pretty in back, too; her behind also had some give, though it wasn't as soft as her breasts. But like her breasts, it wasn't real. She moved closer to the mirror, looking into her own eyes, but the toy girl in the mirror didn't seem to know anything more than she did. Some impulse made her tap the mirror with her fingers. She heard a quiet *tik*, metal on glass.

"Well, hell," she said, just to hear her own voice. It

didn't sound strange to her. Whoever had given her this work-of-art doll body hadn't messed with anything above her neck. Or so she hoped.

As she turned away from the mirror, her gaze fell on some clothing folded up on a chair. She picked them up—a sweatshirt and some cargo pants.

Cargo pants were back in style? She must have been asleep for a *really* long time.

The door of her room wasn't locked, she discovered, and it was an immense relief to know she wasn't a prisoner. Of course, a young girl's room made a very unlikely prison cell, but as she didn't know where she was, she couldn't be sure of what was unlikely and what wasn't. Plus, cargo pants were back in style; all bets were off.

Careful to move soundlessly, she stepped into a short hallway, where she saw a flight of stairs. This was a private home. Did it come with her new body? If so, it didn't match; the place was clean but it was as old and shabby as the room where she'd awakened.

As she moved to the top of the stairs, she heard voices from below. Listening for a few seconds, she determined there was one woman and at least two men down there, although she couldn't make out the conversation. The voices didn't sound hostile, though. Time to see what she had landed in, she thought, and crept down the stairs, still moving silently, listening as the voices grew clearer.

When she got to the bottom, she found herself looking

into a room that seemed to be some kind of clinic or laboratory. Was this place actually a hospital?

"Well, that's the best I can do for now," one of the men said. He was bending over something on a tray in front of him while a tall, dark-skinned woman in blue scrubs stood nearby; a nurse. "They don't make parts for this model any more."

The man moved back and she saw he'd been working on a piece of machinery that had obviously seen a lot of use. The metal was scratched and dented, with a few parts clearly taken from something else and adapted to fit. It looked heavy and clumsy and it was attached to the shoulder of a second man sitting in a chair beside the tray.

"I'm real grateful, Doc," the second man said, lifting the thing off the tray and testing its movements. "I'll be getting some overtime next week." He got to his feet and pulled up the top half of a greasy coverall, zipping it with his machine arm.

"Pay me when you can," said the first man in a kind voice.

The second man picked up a sack lying on the floor beside the chair. "Here, I got these for ya. My wife works out at Farm Twenty-two."

The woman chuckled. "Keep getting paid in fruit and we'll be pickin' these ourselves."

Just as she was thinking that she should look for a way out, the woman spotted her.

"Well, hello, sleepyhead." The woman smiled at her and she automatically smiled back. You couldn't assume someone was okay just because they smiled at you, but something told her this woman meant her no harm.

The man with the mechanical arm also smiled at her, but the doctor was startled. Maybe he'd thought she would still be asleep. He was pale with blond hair and round spectacles that gave him the appearance of a man who'd just been interrupted in the middle of reading something long and complicated. The woman—the nurse—ushered the man with the mechanical arm to a door across the room while she and the pale man stared at each other.

This was the man responsible for her beautiful work-of-art body, she realised. He had long fingers that seemed to move in a precise way even when they were just fidgeting with his lab coat and the small parts and tools in the pockets. Now that the surprise of her appearance had worn off, he was looking her over with the sharp, alert eyes of someone who knew so many things, far more than most people. She could also see he was a bit haggard, like he'd had a lot of long days and not enough sleep.

Unsure of what to do or say, she took a step forward and was briefly blinded by a shaft of sunlight coming in from a high window. The warmth felt good on her face.

"How do you feel?" the man asked her.

She sat down in the chair where the man with the heavy arm had been. "Okay."

Abruptly he reverted to his role as a doctor, grabbing a small flashlight so he could look into her eyes, then her mouth. He felt the area under her jawline and then the length of her neck, his long fingers expert and gentle.

"Any pain anywhere?" he asked, feeling her hands and bending each finger. "Numbness? Motor dysfunction?"

When he went into doctor mode, he went all the way, she thought. "Well, I'm a little… hungry."

He ushered her out of the laboratory or whatever it was and into a small kitchen. Seating her at the table, he reached into the bag his patient had given him and held out a round orange thing.

"Eat this," he said. "Get your sugar levels up."

She took it from him and examined it. The colour was pretty but she didn't think it looked terribly promising as food. A doctor wouldn't give her anything bad, she reasoned. She took a bite and immediately spat it out on the table.

"Taste receptors are working." Now he was an amused doctor. "You'll like that a lot better with the peel *off*." He took it from her and began removing the outer covering.

She watched him for a few moments, then decided it was as good a time as any to ask questions. "Um… I don't mean to be rude," she said, "but… am I supposed to know you?"

As if someone had flipped a switch, the doctor was gone and he was staring at her again, like he didn't know what to do. Finally, he said, "Actually, we've never met. I'm Doctor Dyson Ido." He nodded at the woman, who had just come in from the laboratory. "This is Nurse Gerhad." The woman's warm smile made her feel a bit less anxious about asking her next question.

"Okay, I don't quite know how to say this—" She took a steadying breath. "Do you happen to know who *I* am?"

The doctor and nurse looked at each other, taken aback by the question. Her heart sank a little.

"I was hoping you'd fill in that part. Since you're a Total

Replacement cyborg, and most of your cyber body was destroyed, I can't find any records."

They looked at each other again, and this time she had the distinct impression Nurse Gerhad was displeased about something.

"But your very *human brain* was miraculously intact," Dr Ido went on after a moment. "Theoretically, you should remember something."

"Oh," she said. "Well, uh…" She thought for a moment. "It's pretty blank." They were looking at her expectantly. Her heart—or whatever she had as a Total Replacement cyborg—sank a little more. "It's completely blank, actually."

She didn't have to be a doctor herself to know that wasn't right at all. There should have been *something*, even if it was only a vague image: someone she knew or a place where she'd been, or a few words someone had spoken to her—whoever *that* was, or had been. All at once she felt like the world was becoming less solid, like she was about to fall through it into nothing.

"I don't even know my name!" Tears welled up in her eyes and spilled down her face.

"I know this is all very new and strange," the doctor said in the warm, kindly voice she was already growing to love. "But you're not alone—I'm here with you. I'm going to protect you and everything is going to be okay. And let's look on the bright side." The doctor dabbed at her face with a napkin as he handed her the thing he had finished peeling. "Your tear ducts are working."

She couldn't help smiling a little. That was just the sort of thing a very kind doctor would say. Although how she could know that but not her own name made no sense at all. She bit into the thing he'd given her. This time, there was an explosion of taste in her mouth; the feel of the pulp between her teeth and a flood of liquid that overflowed and ran down her chin was delightful. Suddenly she no longer felt like crying, about anything.

"This is *good*!" she said, looking from Ido to Gerhad and back again. "What do you call this?"

She saw the nurse give Ido a wry half-smile. "It's *your* fee, *you* tell her. And make sure she knows it's not money anywhere else in town."

CHAPTER 4

"YEEEOOOW!"

Ido ran out onto the porch, thinking the little cyborg had managed to put her foot through a loose board and then torn off a finger trying to free herself. But she was completely unhurt. Nothing wrong with her yelling function, he thought as she grabbed his arm and pointed at the sky. "What's *that*?"

Gerhad, who had followed more slowly, gave him a knowing smile that told him he'd be answering a whole lot of questions and he'd better get used to it. He pretended not to notice.

"That's Zalem," Ido told the cyborg girl. "It's the last of the great sky cities."

She turned back to look at it. "What holds it up—magic?"

Ido thought if her eyes got any wider, they might fall out. "No, something much stronger. *Engineering*."

The girl ran down off the porch and into the street,

where she stood gazing up at it and the low clouds sailing slowly underneath the disc, unaware of the two-wheeled gyro truck honking its horn madly as it bore down on her. Ido yanked her out of the way just in time. As the truck blew past, the driver made an angry gesture, yelling *"Pinche cabrón!"*

Ido was about to scold her, then thought better of it. She hadn't even known what an orange was, so of course she didn't know better than to play in traffic. "And down here," he said, turning her to face the direction in which the gyro-truck had gone, "this is Iron City, with all its charms."

The girl gaped as if it were an exotic wonderland filled with the promise of adventure and excitement rather than a sad, dirty town that Zalem used as a toilet.

That last thought was a bit dark even for him, Ido thought and blinked, trying to see Iron City's street life through the eyes of a girl who had never seen a city before. At the moment, however, she was looking at the sign on the front of the house: DR DYSON IDO CMD, CYBER-SURGEON. She could read, it seemed, yet she'd never seen an orange before; one more thing to add to the growing list of oddities.

"While I'm learning names," she said, touching his arm tentatively, "do you have one for me?"

It was out of his mouth before he could think better of it. "Alita. Alita is a nice name."

The girl beamed up at him as if he'd just given her the best present in the world. "I *like* it!" she declared, and he knew it would be no use suggesting anything else. "Let's keep it, at least until I can remember my real name. Thank you!" She threw her arms around him and gave him a hug that took his breath away.

Ido gazed down at the top of her head, which came to the centre of his breastbone, then looked to see how Gerhad was taking it, but she had already gone back inside. She'd heard him, though—Gerhad heard everything—and she'd make him answer for it later. As if he'd ever stopped answering for Alita.

Alita. He stroked her beautiful dark hair and held her tight. Of course, Alita—that face, those eyes. No other name would do. "Well, then, Alita, let's get you back inside for some tests. I need another brain scan now that you're conscious, and a full neuro-motor calibration and—"

She looked up at him with an eager smile. "No, let's take a walk! Can we? *Please?*" Without waiting for an answer, she started pulling him down the street.

Gerhad reappeared on the porch. "Go on. She looks pretty calibrated to me," she said, laughing a little. "Shoes! You should get shoes!"

As soon as she had a name, the floodgates opened and she deluged him with questions. What was engineering and why didn't anyone use it to make Iron City float? How big was Iron City? Had there always been so many people? Who'd named it Iron City and why? What was outside the city? Who lived there, and what did they do?

Ido gave her a potted history of the last three hundred years, including the War and the Fall, thinking she would be distracted while she digested new information. Fat chance—apparently he had forgotten what a bright fourteen-year-old girl was like. Well, it *had* been a while; he was out of practice. He decided to take her for a walk through the city so she could goggle at all the street life. He just had to make sure she didn't wander into traffic.

Alita trotted along beside him, her wide eyes taking in everything and everyone—the standard, un-enhanced humans; cyborgs of all kinds, from those with only one or two machine limbs like Gerhad to Total Replacements like herself; as well as the kids weaving among the crowds, some running barefoot, others on motorised rollerblades. Even the street signs fascinated her, including the ones she couldn't read. Ido made another mental note: she was fluent only in English.

As if she had somehow caught the flavour of what he'd been thinking, she turned to him and said, "Why so many languages?"

Ido smiled, telling himself to be patient. "After the big war I told you about—"

"The Fall," she put in, looking pleased with herself for remembering.

"Yes, after the Fall, Zalem was the only floating city left. Many survivors of the War and from the other fallen cities came here from all over the world. Now everybody down here works for Zalem—the Factory, the Farms, the Motorball games."

"Does anybody down here ever go up to Zalem?" she asked.

He shook his head. "Nobody from down here can *ever*

go up. You can't get there from here—that's the rule, and it's never broken."

She looked surprised. "Why?"

Ido laughed a little. "We're going to have to put some kind of limit on how many times you can use the word 'why' in one hour." He waited for her to argue; when she didn't, he looked down and discovered that she was no longer beside him. He looked around frantically. If she had wandered into the street again—

No, she was safely on the sidewalk; her attention had been captured by a four-storey flatscreen on a building across the street. Then he saw what she was watching and all his good feelings fled.

Massive, heavily armoured cyborgs charged along a track at high speed, fighting each other and chasing a large motorised ball bouncing and tumbling erratically ahead of them. Alita was open-mouthed, enchanted by the sight of the cyborgs jumping and flipping through the air, delivering kicks and blows to each other, as if they were dancing some kind of brutal ballet on wheels at a hundred miles an hour.

Ido put a hand on her shoulder to usher her away from the screen and discovered that she would not be moved.

"What—what *is* that?" she asked finally. Her great big eyes were sparkling with excitement, as if she had seen something miraculous.

"Motorball," Ido said, letting his disapproval show. "It was created by the Factory so people can blow off steam. Everybody loves having heroes, someone to cheer for, idols to worship. So the Factory gave us Paladins. But it's nothing you need to be wasting your time watching."

They passed some kids in filter masks hawking cheap lube jobs. As soon as they saw her, they called out. "Hey, best-quality Teflon lube products! Fix you right up, only ten Cs!"

Ido put his arm around Alita protectively. "Never— *never*—get a street lube," he said firmly.

"Why not?" she asked.

He gave her a look. "You're over your quota, remember?"

She giggled and let him steer her up the street. But to his dismay, she kept looking back at the Motorball screen.

As sure as Alita was her name, falafel was *the* best food in the world, and oranges were second. Falafel was also the messiest. She licked hummus off her fingers while trying to keep the wrap from falling to pieces. Were all the best foods the messiest ones? She glanced surreptitiously at Ido to make sure he was too busy going through a bin labelled SERVOS to notice her wiping her hands on the seat of her cargo pants.

Ido had told her this was a marketplace, and it was *amazing*. There were so many people, doing all kinds of things. A lot of people were selling stuff, but there was also a guy with something called a double-necked guitar; his cyborg arm could play both necks at once, making wonderful music that made her want to dance instead of just walking.

But it was like Ido didn't even hear it. All he was interested in was those servo things. She didn't understand that at all. How could he not be excited in a place where so much was going on? People were selling all kinds of stuff—blankets, baskets, flowers (though none as pretty as the ones on her body), things to wear, things to play with, things for making other things, things that had uses she couldn't imagine.

And so many amazing items to look at—holos that tricked the eye, pictures made of shifting light, pictures that glowed *without* light. There were puzzles, games, dice with as many as twenty-one sides, although she wasn't sure how you were supposed to know which number was the right one.

She stopped in front of a rack of cages containing all sorts of birds. Some were little and flew around their enclosed spaces from one perch to another and sometimes to the bars, clutching them with their tiny feet like little prisoners.

"Please, can we buy some and let them out? Pleasepleaseplease?" she asked Ido.

"They wouldn't survive," Ido told her.

"But they should be allowed to fly free," she said.

"Anything that flies gets shot down by Zalem's defence system," Ido said. "There are no free birds in this city."

That was all wrong, Alita thought. *Someday, I'll find a way to free you*, she told the birds silently. *Someday.*

Now she moved on to the food area. So many wonderful smells! There were ingredients that sizzled in wide pans or bubbled in big pots, little meals in round bowls no bigger than her palm, and foods that came in big hunks on sticks. They even had foods that wrapped around each other or had other food stuffed into them, all served by smiling people who had replaced one hand with tongs or ladles or carving blades or even little torches.

But Ido had headed straight for a stall with nothing but machine parts, saying he always needed more servos—whatever those were. She was supposed to stay right by him and not wander off or even ask a lot of questions. Or any questions, for that matter. But how could he bring her here and expect her to do nothing when there was so much going on? She'd thought she was going to explode with frustration when he'd finally bought her the falafel.

Suddenly she realised she wasn't alone. A small dog of mixed pedigree was looking up at her hopefully and wagging his tail. She crouched down to pet him and he immediately began licking her face. Well, that solved the problem of how she was going to clean up.

"Here you go, buddy," she said, letting the dog have the rest of the mess in her hands. He was more than happy to finish it for her, licking every last trace from her fingers before he went back to washing her face. She enjoyed the feel of his warm tongue. Doggy kisses were great.

A gust of wind blew a sheet of paper against her ankle and she picked it up: WANTED FOR THE MURDERS OF SIX WOMEN. BOUNTY 10,000 CREDITS. There was no picture, only a black square labelled UNIDENTIFIED LARGE CYBORG.

That wasn't a whole lot to go on, she thought, frowning. Didn't anyone even know *how* large this unidentified cyborg was? He couldn't have been all that big if he'd got away with killing six women, otherwise someone would have seen him do it.

"What do you think, buddy?" she said to her new friend, showing the notice to him. "This sound like anybody you know?"

The dog sniffed the paper, smelled nothing delicious, and continued licking her face.

Hugo got out of bed that morning with no intention of doing anyone a good turn, much less saving a life. His usual schedule involved keeping his eyes and ears open for any opportunity to make some credits. He'd headed down to the market on his gyro, hoping to find some vendors with a pressing need for certain hard-to-find items and who were willing to pay for fast delivery of special orders, no questions asked, thank you and good night.

Finding the hard-to-find was, in fact, what Hugo was known for, and not just in the marketplace. He and his crew could have given up their marketplace customers and still made a good living. But the market was where he'd started out and where he'd built up his reputation. He wasn't going to forget where he came from—not yet, anyway. He glanced up at Zalem.

Bent low over the gyro's handlebars, he swerved through the crowds, occasionally taking a fast pass over the sidewalk to get around a truck or a slow-moving pedal-car. The gyro was built for speed but he spent a godawful amount of time stuck in traffic. He was going to have to take it out on the open road soon to blow out the cobwebs and keep the motor smooth.

At the moment, however, he was only thinking about meeting up with his crew, who would be hanging around in front of the CAFÉ café. Hugo had given the owner of this rather unimaginatively named establishment a break on some critical parts and now it was one of the few places in town where they could hang around without anyone complaining or trying to chase them off—well, as long as they didn't block the sidewalk or tie up tables during a rush. But that was only fair. Giving someone a cut rate on espresso-machine parts and then making it impossible for them to make a living was no way to do business. Tanji had argued that giving big discounts to cafés was no way to do business, either, but always having a place to hide out when it rained, or even when it didn't, had shut him up.

Tanji had absolutely *no* business sense; anything that wasn't just a straight money-for-goods deal always had to be spelled out for him; he was kind of a pain in the ass that way. But once he understood, he was good to go—and he'd go all the way, no second guessing or bailing at the last minute, which made him the kind of pain in the ass Hugo wanted in his crew. It was also why he was Hugo's closest friend.

Then he heard the sound no one ever wanted to hear, the metal clank and stomp of Centurians in the street ahead of him, and he forgot about everything else.

They were marching into the marketplace, which was never good. Centurian programming was specific and narrow to the point of stupidity. They existed to put a stop to illegal activity in one of two ways: bullets or missiles. Well, three ways if you counted the single warning Centurians gave to cease the proscribed activity under penalty of law. Unfortunately, their programming didn't allow for much time between the warning and the penalty. Worse, Centurians couldn't always tell the difference between cooperation and defiance.

But worst of all, they sometimes couldn't tell the difference between legal and illegal behaviour, especially in a place as chaotic as the market. There were always kids playing Motorball with jerry-rigged ramps and slopes. If a Centurian registered a kid doing a double somersault with a hot breakaway onto an overpass as an illegal flying machine, it would shoot the kid into hamburger and there wouldn't be a damn thing anyone could do about it. Unless they wanted to be hamburger, too.

The smart thing to do would have been to take off in the opposite direction and come back later; instead, Hugo followed them, albeit at a distance. They were definitely going to march right through the middle of the market, but why? Did the Factory actually *want* them to shoot the place up, or just make everyone crap their pants in terror?

Then he caught sight of the girl with the dog. She was crouched down directly in the path of the big metal bastards, looking at a flyer and patting the dog like she had no idea she was about to get trampled by three walking machine guns. And they *would* trample her and the dog both without missing a beat. Centurians weren't made to care about the safety of living creatures; they were executioners.

Before he even knew what he was going to do, Hugo shifted into high gear and zipped through the crowded street at a speed even Tanji would have said was whacko. And that silly girl was *still* petting that stupid dog! Was she crazy, or did she get dropped on her head too many times as a baby?

"Hey, you—girl with the dog! Watch out!" he yelled.

Somehow, despite all the noise, his warning got through to her. She stood up and looked at the clanking armoured gun platforms relentlessly advancing on her. But instead of running, she just stood there, gaping like she'd never seen a Centurian before. Rabbit in the headlights, thought Hugo, trying to go faster. The Centurian in the lead let out a warning siren. Anyone would run from that sound— anyone but *this* girl. This girl dropped into a crouch with her fists up, like she really thought she could fight Centurians and live to regret it. She wasn't just crazy, she was super-mega-*batshit*-crazy.

And so am I, Hugo thought as he launched himself off the gyro and tackled the girl. As they tumbled over and over on the street, Hugo closed his eyes, bracing himself for the feel of a Centurian foot crushing him into the pavement. But when he opened his eyes again, he and the girl were lying on the ground just out of the robots' path. The girl blinked at him in surprise. He had a second to think that she had the biggest eyes he'd ever seen before she pushed away from him and ran *towards* the danger he'd just saved her from.

To save the dog, he realised, the goddam dog. It was whimpering as the first Centurian passed over it. The girl dropped down in front of the second Centurian, grabbed the dog, and rolled away a heartbeat before the enormous foot came down on the spot where they'd been.

Hugo's jaw dropped. Had he just seen that? Had he *really* just seen that, or had he taken too many headshots playing Motorball?

Alita had no doubt she could reach the dog in time and get him out of the way. What she hadn't expected was the sudden picture show in her head. The images had flashed so quickly she couldn't really see what they were, although she had a very strong impression of weapons and combat. Whether these were flashes from one battle or several, she had no idea. The whole thing had been so fleeting she wasn't even sure if she were remembering a real event or a dream.

Then she was moving again, diving between immense mechanical legs with impossibly easy speed and fetching up on the other side of the street. She tucked and rolled into a sitting position, keeping her fists up, ready to defend herself.

"Outstanding!" said a voice beside her. She turned to see a boy sitting on her right staring at her with admiration. He was wearing a leather jacket and a bandanna over his dark hair, and he had the brightest, most wonderful dark eyes and the best smile she had ever seen. He leaned forward, looking past her at the retreating backs of the big stomping machines and yelled, "Hey, why don't you watch where you're goin'?"

Alita blinked at him, unsure of what to do or say. That

bandanna was just about the best thing anyone could wear, she thought as he stood up and brushed himself off.

"Gotta admit, I *never* saw anybody play chicken with a Centurian before!" He offered her a hand to help her up and she took it. "Whoa, you're heavy!" he blurted as he tugged her to her feet, then looked embarrassed. "Sorry, I meant—" He broke off at the sight of her hand in his. "Oh! You're a cyborg!"

Suddenly self-conscious, she pulled away from him and hid both hands under her arms.

"I was just admiring your hand," he told her. "It's great. Let me see. Please?"

Still feeling self-conscious, she extended one hand. He looked at it closely, turning it over so he could see all the designs.

"It's really nice work. Did Doc Ido do it?"

She felt a surge of pleasure. "He built all of me, except my core."

"He sure did a great job," the guy said as she offered him her other hand to examine. She hoped he would take his time because she really liked his face, especially when he was looking at her.

"What *were* those things?" she asked.

It took him a second to realise what she was talking about. "You mean the Centurians? *Seriously?* Jeez, what planet are *you* from?"

She shrugged. "Ido found me in the scrapyard."

"The scrapyard?" Now his wonderful face was incredulous. "But that would mean—"

Before he could finish the sentence, however, Ido

himself had materialised beside her, annoyed because she had wandered off and made him look for her. He'd been so busy finding servos, he had no idea what had just happened, she realised, which was a good thing.

"Hey, Doc," the guy said cheerfully. "I've got those driver-boards you were lookin' for."

Nodding at him, Ido put his arm around her shoulders in a way that felt both protective and possessive. "Alita is new here, and she's just learning about Iron City." He looked down at her, his face serious. "Centurians are Factory enforcers. You need to stay out of their way."

"Oh, so diving through their legs wouldn't be good?" said the guy, looking innocent.

Ido gave him a look. "Don't even joke about that."

The guy smiled at Alita and winked, and she felt a powerful surge of happiness run through her.

"Gotta go," the guy said to Ido. "I'll drop the boards off later. I need a rebuild on a quad servo." He paused and gave her a smile. "Maybe I'll see you around."

Alita watched as he ran to a machine lying half on, half off the sidewalk. There was a seat on it but only one wheel. He checked it over, then climbed on and fired it up. She stared after him, amazed at the way he could weave through the traffic on only one wheel.

"Who was that?" she asked Ido with a dreamy wistfulness.

"Hugo," Ido told her. "He's a hard worker, but..." He paused. "Well, it's a desperate city, Alita. Come on, let's go home."

She let Ido usher her in the other direction but she

couldn't help turning around for one last look. To her delight, she caught a glimpse of him looking back at her. "Hugo," she sighed.

Ido sighed, too, but in an entirely different way.

CHAPTER 5

All day long the kids in the filter masks called out to passing cyborgs, shouting themselves hoarse about the miracles they could work for a mere ten credits. Shadows lengthened, the day waned, and the kids were still at it when the sun went down.

The city was a different kind of place after dark but the kids hung in, promising Iron City's cyborgs a glaze to amaze that would make them slick as a magic trick, sleek on every peak and smooth in every groove, they could slip, slide and electro-glide the night away. This was royal oil, grease of the gods, only ten credits for the lube of a lifetime.

The Total Replacement cyborg who decided to take them up on their offer may have been thinking he'd give them a break so they wouldn't have to go home with nothing to show for all those hours of pitching. Maybe they reminded him of himself at the same age—too young for the Factory, but money for rent and groceries had to come from somewhere.

Or maybe he'd been meaning to get around to a lube but there was always something else he had to do first, and now he was due, possibly a little overdue. And then—son of a gun—a couple of kids pop up with exactly what he needed at a bargain price. Only a fool would pass this up. Or he may have been thinking something entirely different and unrelated.

What he wouldn't have been thinking about was his personal safety. He'd always been a big guy and now that he was a TR, he was even bigger. Tall and heavyset— emphasis on heavy—for a moment, he wasn't sure the chair the kids were showing him to would take his weight, but it turned out to be stronger than it looked.

He certainly would have noticed the kids eyeing the custom designs carved into his chrome overlay. People always stared at his body art and he didn't mind. Every design had a special meaning. The spiral above his heart was for those he had pledged himself to for life, while the stars in the centre of his chest were his family. The waves crashing on his shoulders represented the power of love, a burden he was willing to bear and was, in fact, what he was hoping to find tonight. Broken chains ran up and down his arms, showing that he had already overcome things that had tried to hold him back.

The chair was partly blocking an alley and he meant to move it a few centimetres to the left so there would be only a solid building at his back—it wouldn't have been hard, the chair had wheels. But the kids were fussing and flitting around him so that he could barely keep track of them. They looked so alike in their filter masks, he wouldn't have been able to tell them apart if one hadn't been taller than the other. The taller one was in front of him saying they had the highest-quality lube in Iron City while the shorter one messed around with cans or something behind him. He was starting to wish he'd just kept walking.

"Make it fast, muchachos," he said, grimacing at the taller kid. "I got a date. I need smooth moves tonight, you know what I mean?"

"Don't worry," the kid said. "We're so fast—"

The world exploded in a blinding light. He felt his body stiffen all over, his arms and legs bent at hard, awkward angles. *This must be what it feels like to be struck by lightning,* he thought. Then the lightning let go of him and he went limp.

"—you won't know what hit you," finished the tall kid as they wheeled him into the alley.

It was a rough ride over cracked, uneven pavement; he bounced helplessly in the chair, unable to move even though the other kid had removed the paralyser from his spine. They'd taken him right out on the street—in public—someone must have seen what happened to him. Why wasn't someone yelling, trying to help him or at least saying they'd call the Centurians? How could a person be attacked in a public place and no one would do anything?

The chair came to an abrupt stop and they tipped him out onto the ground. He still couldn't move a muscle. When he heard the sound of power ratchets starting up, however, he managed to find his voice.

"You little *maricons*!" he yelled. *"Hijos de todo tu pinche madre!"* But he could barely hear himself over the power tools. But they could. He knew they could.

The noise cut out and he saw the kids lifting his arms away from him. Bright-blue cyber-blood poured from the severed ends. He could sense it seeping from his body and pooling on the ground around him.

They didn't bother with ratchets for his legs; they used a circular-saw blade that sent more cyber-blood spraying in all directions. Nasty little butchers! They cut him up like he was a steer and now they were handling his arms and legs like they were nothing, like he had never freed himself from chains that other people were too weak to break, like he had never stood up for his people, his family, himself.

The kids were packing them into the carriers on their gyro-wheels when suddenly the alley was filled with the brilliant glare of a Centurian's spotlight. Someone had called for help after all—he was saved!

"Help!" he shouted. "Help me, I'm getting jacked!"

"Move along," the Centurian ordered him in its expressionless, mechanical voice. The light went off and he heard the thing clanking away from the mouth of the alley.

"Come back!" Desperation took his voice up a full octave. "Come back and help me, you *pinche madre* piece of shit!"

The kids burst out laughing. "Forget it, this ain't no crime against production," said the short one. "The Centurians only care about the Factory, and the Factory don't care about *you*!"

He felt the kid kick him. The little bastard actually kicked him when he was down! If he ever found out who these *maricons* were he would tear them limb from limb, just with his hands.

"Leave him alone," said the other kid. "Come on, we gotta go!"

The cyborg watched as they took off on their gyros, leaving him armless and legless in a pool of cyber-blood, and still unable to move, even just to roll over.

"*Auxilio!*" he yelled. "Somebody help me, dammit!" He was probably going to lose his voice, too, before anyone came along.

He was right.

The gyro-cab rattling along the dark, deserted street was dented and scratched and very much in need of a new paint job. The driver was saving up for that, or trying to, but these were awfully lean times. Times were always lean in Iron City but the driver tried not to think about that.

He'd actually thought he'd get more night-time fares with a vicious killer roaming around looking for ladies to slice up, and he had, but not as many as he'd hoped. Women went out at night in packs of four or five or even six. He wouldn't have thought that would be much of a deterrent—it wasn't like half a dozen women could overpower a large homicidal cyborg and pin him to the street with their stiletto heels while they waited for the Centurians to show up and blast him to death. But the killer didn't take on groups; the killer liked to pick them off one at a time. With all the warnings, you'd have thought it would be impossible to find any woman alone on the street at night.

Sadly, not everyone could get a group together when they really needed to. Like this poor soul who was his current passenger—he'd spotted her standing on the Factory's front steps, and known immediately that she was contemplating the prospect of walking home all by herself in the dark. He stopped in front of her and told her to hop in.

She'd looked pained and said, "Well… uh… I don't…" Universal code for *I can't afford to.*

Instead of driving off in search of a couple of party animals too drunk to know the fare was padded, he said, "Get in. Special low rate for the danger zone. Don't know if you've heard but there's a killer running around."

She'd hesitated, then climbed in, thanking him in a way that wrenched his heart. What the hell—his mother had always said a good deed was never wasted. Although he still couldn't help thinking how good the fare would have been if he weren't such a soft touch. On the other hand, if he hadn't been a soft touch, he'd be driving around empty. So, what the hell.

The trip was quick at this time of night, and when he saw where she lived, he was doubly glad he'd picked her up. The block was deserted at this hour—Murder o'clock, one of the other cabbies called it. The woman gave him half of what he usually charged and tried to add a tip. He pushed it back at her along with a couple of credits. She looked startled. It was probably a long time since anyone had cut her a break for anything.

"Go on," he said, chuckling a little. "Just don't tell

anybody or I'll never be able to make a living."

She gave a small laugh. "Your secret's safe with me. I'll take it to my grave."

Her words gave him a funny feeling and he wished she'd picked a different expression. He was probably over-tired, he thought, smiling at her. "Hey, a good deed is never wasted, right? Now get indoors fast, okay?"

She hurried off, and he waited until he saw her stop at what had to be her own front door before he drove away. It was just about time for the next wave of drunks to spill out of the Kansas Bar and that bunch *could* afford a padded fare. Not very nice of him, but what the hell— he'd done a good deed and even if it really wasn't wasted, it wouldn't do any harm to make up the loss.

She couldn't help feeling relieved when the cab drove off. All the way home, she'd been worried: what if *he* turned out to be the killer? Or what if he started talking about how pretty she was and if she *really* wanted to thank him for giving her a break on the fare, etc., etc., etc. Instead, he *was* a nice guy. Or at the very least, a guy capable of being nice.

But dammit, where had she put her keys? Why hadn't she opted for a keypad, or even an implant in her forearm? She was going to put the money she'd saved tonight towards something better and flush that stupid key down the toilet—

Just as her fingers closed on the key in her purse, she heard something stir behind her, and though she knew it was absolutely the wrong thing to do, that she should just stick the stupid key in the stupid lock, rush inside, and slam the stupid door behind her, she couldn't stop her stupid self from turning around to look.

Something enormous and darker than the night rose up and threw itself over her. She opened her mouth but her scream didn't last even a second. Blood splashed across a nearby wall with a noise like a slap.

The sound of the elevator woke Alita. Curious, she got out of bed, tiptoed to the door, and opened it a tiny crack to see what was going on.

For a moment, she wasn't sure it was Ido because he looked so different. It wasn't so much the long leather trench coat and the black gloves, although she'd never seen him wear anything like them before. It was the expression on his face. There was no trace of kindliness or affection. He looked positively grim, like a man who saw the world as a terrible, dangerous place where only the worst could happen.

Stranger still, he had a wheeled suitcase that he was pushing ahead of himself. She drew back a little as he rolled it past her door, one of the wheels going *squeak-squeak-squeak*. It was a very strange suitcase; there was something about the size and shape that made her think of a toolbox rather than something to pack clothes in for travelling. He went down the hall to a door at the end, then paused to slip his coat off one arm, wincing as he did.

There was a nasty gash on his forearm and it was still oozing blood; heart's-blood. It must have hurt like hell. It was all she could do to keep from bursting out of her room and running to him to ask what happened. But even though he was grimacing in pain, his face was still cold and hard. This was not the Ido who had made this lovely body with all the flowers and the silver and gold inlays, not the Ido who named her Alita. She didn't know who this Ido was, and she hoped she never would.

Ido unlocked the door, wheeled the suitcase inside, then shut the door. The lock re-engaged with a hard metal click.

The next morning, she wondered if Ido would say where he'd gone the previous night, but he didn't even mention the bandage on his forearm. Not that there'd been much time for conversation—their first patient came to them in a box outside the front door, missing his arms and legs. Nurse Gerhad said it was as good a time as any for her to begin training as Ido's assistant. She was nervous at first, especially with the limbless cyborg. What if she screwed up, and as soon as he got off the operating table he fell apart? Or what if she dropped a bag of cyber-blood and it splashed all over the place—or worse, heart's-blood?

Gerhad assured her there was very little she could do that would cause anyone to fall apart, and transfusion bags were too tough to break open easily because everybody dropped them. It was all just a matter of becoming familiar with the instruments and the procedures. Once Alita was more experienced, Gerhad said, she'd know which instrument to hand Ido before he even asked for it. As for the patients, Gerhad told her most of them barely noticed there was anyone else in the room besides Ido. This certainly seemed true of the first patient, who was immensely talkative.

"So there's the damn jackers that ripped me to shreds standin' right there," he was saying as Ido tinkered with the arm socket in his shoulder. "I'm lyin' there yellin' and that *vale madre* Centurian wouldn't do a thing. Not a single thing. If it'd had fingers, it wouldn't have lifted one to help me."

"Torque coupling," Ido said, holding his hand out without looking away from what he was doing. "Jackers want your parts on the black market to supply the Motorball games," he added to the cyborg on the table.

"*My* parts? That's messed up," the cyborg replied.

As Alita handed Ido the torque coupling, her gaze fell on his forearm and her happy pride over giving him the right part faded. The bandage looked fresh but a little blood had seeped through it already. What had happened to him last night?

"You were lucky," Gerhad was saying to the cyborg on the table. "Another woman was murdered last night, right near where you got jacked."

The cyborg gave her an incredulous look. "Oh, yeah, this is me, lucky. You know, I heard he carves them up and puts them in little metal—"

Ido gave him a nudge and looked reproachfully at both him and Gerhad before nodding at her. "Alita, I don't want you out after dark. Is that understood?" he said, pushing both hands into his lower back as he straightened up from the table. "And if you do go out, don't wander too far from this neighbourhood."

Now Gerhad and even the cyborg were looking at her expectantly. "Okay," she said.

"Promise?" Ido said.

She was supposed to think he was being stern with her. She might have, if she hadn't seen that grim expression on his face last night. "Okay, I promise," she said.

He looked pleased as he turned back to the patient.

After Ido replaced the cyborg's arms and legs, he told Alita there wasn't much left for her to do, and she could go out if she wanted, but she had to remember her promise to be back before dark. Alita nodded, barely listening as she took off the surgical gown and gloves and dropped them in the USED bin. The market, she decided, was a good place to look for Hugo.

She bounced out the front door and onto the sidewalk. Something good was definitely going to happen today, she thought as she brushed past someone. As soon as she found Hugo—

"Hey, you—kid!"

Automatically, she stopped and turned around. A tall woman with long dark hair, icy blue eyes, and what looked like a purple jewel in her forehead stood on the sidewalk, staring at her like she was some kind of criminal. Alita was about to turn away but the woman was on her in two big strides. She grabbed Alita's wrist and started manipulating her hand, as if she were a doctor like Ido. Only, she was more like the Ido from last night, cold and grim and pitiless.

The woman looked up from her hand and glared at her with intense anger. Alita twisted out of her grasp and took a couple of steps back.

"What the hell is *your* problem?" she demanded.

The woman just went on glaring at her. Standing as straight as she could, Alita made a show of deliberately turning her back and walking away, mainly so the woman wouldn't see how creeped out she was. She could all but feel that icy gaze boring into her back, and she had to force herself not to run, afraid that if she did, the woman would chase her. After twenty steps, she sneaked a glance over her shoulder. The woman wasn't looking at her any more; she was staring at Ido's clinic.

No, not at the clinic—at Ido, who was standing at one of the second-floor windows and staring right back at her.

It was bound to happen, Ido thought as he watched Alita march away from Chiren. He just hadn't expected it to happen so soon, before he'd had a chance to tell Alita about his estranged wife. Or rather, warn her. Of course, that would have meant telling her everything, and he wasn't quite ready for that. He wanted Alita to be more acclimated, more at home in the body he'd given her before he told her whom he had really made it for.

Abruptly, Chiren turned and looked directly at him, as

if she had not only sensed him watching from the window but caught the gist of his thoughts as well. He wouldn't have been surprised. There had been a time when he was sure she had known his mind better than he did, and that had been just one of many things he'd loved about her. But that had been a different time in a different world, before their own personal Fall. What they'd had was gone now, as if it had never existed.

The poster on the side of the building was enormous. Two people, one a TR cyborg, the other all-organic, both looking heroic and noble, stood shoulder to shoulder, eyes lifted up towards a bright future. Below their hopeful, optimistic faces were the words HARMONY, PRODUCTIVITY, SECURITY in bold letters as bright as the future that awaited them.

The message was more than slightly undercut by the splashes of paint as red as heart's-blood, an effect reinforced by the dripping letters that spelled out a different message: "The Factory does not own your soul."

Good to know, Alita thought. Then she turned the corner and found the kids skating on a makeshift course in the street, and she smiled for the first time since her encounter with the crazy woman. The kids had jerry-rigged a course with ramps and obstacles all around a plaza with a fountain in the middle. People were sitting at tables eating or drinking coffee and watching the kids swooping and spinning and skidding on motorised rollerblades as they chased a misshapen metal ball. Not as fancy as the real thing she'd seen on that big screen, and they didn't have armour, but they sure had the spirit.

Alita was wondering how to ask if she could get in on the game, or even if she should, when one of the players peeled off the track and skidded to a stop in front of her.

"Hey, Alita," Hugo said, taking off the bandanna covering his head and letting his hair fall free.

She beamed at him joyfully. "Hugo! This is Motorball, right?"

He beamed right back at her and she thought her heart would leap out of her chest and into the air. "Just a scrimmage. You want to join in?"

Her smile shrank a little as several kids rocketed past them. They might not be real Motorball players but they had a lot more experience than she did and they could leave her in the dust.

Hugo tugged at her arm. "Come on—*every* kid's gotta play Motorball!"

"Yeah," she said. Suddenly she had a yen to throw caution to the wind and jump into the game just to see what happened. "Why not?"

"Who's the girl?" Chiren asked.

As usual, she was overdone—fancy make-up, fancy hair, fancy dress, fancy fur jacket, fancy shoes, all vintage designs, possibly handmade by cyborgs who were paid extra for not sleeping or eating till the job was done. It was a desperate city full of desperate people, and Chiren was the most desperate of all.

She had a handkerchief pressed to her face, the way she always did when she was in this part of town. It wasn't remotely anything like an air filter; all it did was let everyone, especially him, know what she thought about everything around her. As they walked along the sidewalk together, Ido had an urge to yank it out of her hand and throw it into the street.

"She's my new assistant," he replied.

Chiren arched an eyebrow at him. "And you like her so much, you decided to give her our daughter's body. Needless to say, I was surprised, since you were supposed to have destroyed it years ago."

"I couldn't," Ido said. "I just—I couldn't."

"Clearly," Chiren said, not bothering to hide her scorn. She never had. "Did you tell your 'new assistant' whom you built that body for?"

"Our daughter is dead, Chiren," he said evenly. "You need to let it go."

Now she gave him an incredulous look. "Well, it's obviously not *me* that's clinging to something here."

He had no answer for that.

"You were the *best*," Chiren went on, "and now look at you. I suppose you think you're doing noble work, wasting your talent on the broken, mouldering masses while you angle for sainthood. Dyson Ido, patron saint of Iron City's rusted, wretched refuse. Don't you think it's about time to end your penance?" She stopped suddenly, her attention captured by a large screen over the taqueria.

Ido had no desire to watch the screen, but he couldn't look away as a gang of Motorball Paladins crashed into each other at high speed. Motorball fans loved those pile-ups. One huge hulk in bright chrome armour emerged from the tangle, holding the fifty-pound ball high in the air with one hand.

The waiter who appeared on Ido's left was a wiry older man with a single cyber arm and a big smile for Ido. The man had come to the clinic with no feeling in the cyber arm from his elbow to his fingertips. Ido had fixed the botched job and upgraded the controllers for him.

"What are you having?" Ido asked Chiren.

Chiren wrinkled her nose with disgust. "Nothing."

As if he had to ask, Ido thought. "*Dos tacos y una cerveza,*" he told the waiter.

"*Si, muy bien.*"

"Claymore regains possession!" shouted the announcer in Motorball ecstasy. "But Jashugan is coming up fast, looking for some payback at turn six!"

Back when they had first arrived in Iron City, Motorball had hooked both of them, and it had seemed like the city's one saving grace. Chiren had actually stopped talking about going back. That hadn't fooled him into thinking she'd finally come to terms with their situation and accepted reality. He knew it would be a very long time before that happened, if it ever did. He was well aware that she would still be awake for hours at night, trying to figure out some way to get their old life back, to regain paradise. It had never been any such thing, of course. But there was no point trying to remind her of just how short of paradise their old life had fallen, because she wouldn't hear him.

There were stretches of time when she was so engrossed in the work she did that she forgot to feel sorry for herself. Sometimes he thought she had even forgotten to be unhappy, although that may have been wishful thinking on his part. But it didn't matter now, not since it had all gone bad.

Chiren pointed at a juggernaut in black and gold on the screen who was now leading the pack. "He's one of mine."

As if that were a great accomplishment, Ido thought. It seemed to have slipped her mind that he also knew the Paladin in black and gold. He gave an irritated sigh. "What do you want, Chiren?"

To his surprise, she grabbed his hand and leaned forward, urgency large on her face. "I want us to be a team again," she said. "I've got a great new set-up. And equipment worthy of your skills." The hanky was no longer over her mouth because the hand holding it was stroking his arm from shoulder to elbow. "Work with me," she said, her invitation becoming a plea. "Together we can build Champions—the finest players the game has ever seen." She took his hands in hers. "And that can be our ticket home."

Ido pulled away from her. "When are you going to realise *there's no way back*?"

"*Vector* can make it happen," she said, almost snapping.

"I can't *believe* you trust Vector."

"He's got very high connections." There was a note of petulance in her voice. "He can get us back to Zalem."

Ido shook his head. "This is my home now."

Chiren's shoulders slumped, as if whatever was holding her up had started to give way. "Please. This is my shot. Help me. *Please*."

She sounded so desperate his already-broken heart almost broke again. She had that effect on him. He wished that he could take her in his arms and tell her that everything was going to be all right because he would help her, take care of her, do anything she wanted, find a way or a work-around. But if he did, he would be as lost as she was. He pulled away from her.

"I can't help you build monsters," he said. "I *won't*. Your so-called 'champions' have a nasty habit of turning into killers. They wind up living on the street, junkies with big hydraulic arms and bad attitudes. Or have you forgotten?"

Chiren spotted a cockroach crawling on the table and used a napkin to crush it. "I'm going to get back to Zalem," she declared, standing up. "I'll claw my way back up with my bare hands if I have to."

Ido stared after her as she walked away. She didn't have to walk far—before she'd gone even half a block, an armoured limo pulled up at the kerb. She got into the back seat, and as it drove away Ido had a glimpse through an open window of the man sitting next to her. Vector didn't look at him as the window went up.

Ido felt a sudden, intense rush of pity for Chiren. Her histrionic desperation, pawing his arm—it had all been about Vector and for Vector, not him. The son of a bitch was stringing Chiren along, playing her for a fool, promising her things he couldn't possibly deliver even if he wanted to. This had just been his latest ploy: if Chiren could bring him the genius cyber-surgeon and get him to work on Vector's Motorball team, Zalem was a done deal. No place like home, baby.

Ido waited for his tacos and beer, then took them back to the clinic.

CHAPTER 6

Skating was a hell of a lot harder than she'd imagined, Alita thought as she wobbled along the street in the wheeled boots Hugo had loaned her. There was a lot more to the boots than just wheels—there were motors, drive wheels, gears, breakers, suspension, even shocks. It was like wearing cars on her feet. She couldn't get a sense of how they were supposed to work, even with Hugo telling her what to do and holding her hands to keep her steady.

"That's it. Keep doing exactly what you're doing," he said cheerfully. She nodded, but she had no idea what she was doing or how she was doing it. "I'm gonna let go now and you just keep going like you are, okay?"

But as soon as he stepped aside, her feet began rolling away from each other and no matter how hard she tried, she couldn't get them back together. Hugo was keeping pace with her but, maddeningly, he didn't take her hands again. Couldn't he see that she *didn't want* to do the splits?

"Try the remote," Hugo suggested.

Alita had forgotten all about the control button strapped to the palm of her hand. She tried it now, but her arms were flailing as she tried to keep her balance and she clutched it too hard. Her feet accelerated forward suddenly and she went down hard on her butt.

Hugo ran to her and she glowered up at him from under her brows. "You laugh, you *die*," she warned him.

He didn't laugh as he helped her up (still an effort for him, she noticed). "Next time, keep your weight a little lower and more forward," he suggested, walking her over to the edge of the makeshift Motorball track. Several other kids were skating around the course, which was laid out around the trestles of a long-unused highway overpass. "Hey, everybody," he said, waving at the other kids. "This is Alita."

The kids came over to say hello. Hugo introduced her to Tanji, a skinny guy with wiry muscles and a halo of thick, curly brown hair. Alita thought his hair was more fun than he was; he didn't smile much—or at all, really. Maybe he was having a bad day.

The other kids were lots friendlier. There was a tall guy named Risotto, a solid-looking kid named Dif, and a pretty girl named Koyomi, who told her not to mind Tanji. Koyomi wore her hair in long, thin braids gathered high on either side of her head. Alita envied the style and wondered if her own hair would grow that long so she could wear it the same way.

"You know," Hugo said, turning to her as everyone skated back to the track, "sometimes the best way to learn is just to go in."

Alita pressed the palm control, careful not to do it so hard this time, but the wheels still took off faster than she expected. Her arms pinwheeled as she fought to keep her balance, and for a moment she was sure she was going down again. But finally, she straightened out, bent her knees and leaned forward the way Hugo had told her to.

"Hey, I think I'm getting it!" she called to Hugo as she steadied herself. She squeezed the remote and the wheels took off with her just as she realised she had no idea how to turn or brake. She slammed into a concrete pillar, but instead of falling, she rebounded onto the track where she rolled around in crazy loops and zigzags as the other kids zoomed past her in a blur. Still trying to straighten herself out, she hit a kerb, flew forward and flattened an old street sign, before finally coming to rest on her back with her feet in the air, wheels still spinning madly.

"Uh, you can let go of the remote now," Hugo said.

Alita unclenched her fist. "Crap," she said in a small, humble voice.

Hugo helped her up and got her going again, this time on the track. He ran along beside her, reminding her to stay low and forward, then beckoned to the other kids. She felt nervous as they all rolled up around her but Hugo kept talking to her, yelling encouragement.

Koyomi zipped past her, carrying the ball. Alita had a second to wonder what she was supposed to do now before Koyomi whipped the ball directly at her. She amazed herself by catching it without losing her balance or careening out of control. Maybe I really *am* getting the hang of this, she thought. A moment later, something slammed into her. The ball flew out of her hands as she went down in a clumsy belly-flop.

Alita looked up, blinking in confusion. Koyomi was glaring angrily—not at her but at Tanji, who now had the ball. Tanji leaped up, performing a showy near-split in mid-air as he hurled the ball into the goal.

"Sorry, princess," Tanji said to her as he sailed past, skating backwards and laughing.

"Nice one, Tanji," Hugo said, disgusted. "Thanks for that. She's never played before."

Still showing off, Tanji did an effortless figure of eight on a jerry-rigged banked slope. "If she ain't ready to run with the hounds, get her off the track," he said, gliding away.

Hugo offered Alita his hand. She ignored it, getting back up on her feet by herself and watching Tanji do a lazy victory lap back to the starting line. Hugo was saying something to her, probably giving her more advice about staying low and forward, but his voice seemed to come from somewhere far away. Power was gathering inside her, telling her body exactly what to do as she moved to the starting position with all the other kids and dropped into a crouch.

The ball snapped into play and she clenched her fist for full throttle, blasting forward with everyone else, although she was barely aware of them. She only had eyes for Tanji as she pushed herself to go faster. The wheels under her threatened to go out of control but she wouldn't let them, shifting her body weight every time they tried to run away from her, pushing herself to go faster.

The ball zoomed past her, right into Tanji's hands. He looked smug as he turned towards the goal. Immediately,

Alita saw how carrying the ball changed his balance and his speed; he wasn't quite as fast or as stable. She drove harder, refusing to lose her balance as she zoomed after him towards the goal.

Tanji looked surprised for half a second when she drew even with him, then tried to cover it with that smug expression. She was going to wipe every bit of smug off his face, Alita thought, looping around in front of him. He feinted left then went right, thinking he'd get around her. He brought up his arm, intending to elbow her in the face—just what she was hoping for. She took hold of his arm and twisted, spun around, then kicked him behind his knees. Tanji went down hard, skidded off the track with his arms and legs in an awkward tangle, and fetched up against a low wall. Alita scooped up the ball, took a flying leap and smashed it into the goal.

The loud *krang!* of the metal ball hitting the goal brought her out of the fury that had taken hold of her. Alita barely managed stay upright as she hit the track again and slowed to a wobbly stop while replaying the last minute in her memory, shocked. What the hell had she done?

Koyomi gave her a slap on the back, grinning like this was some kind of major accomplishment. Hugo had materialised on her other side looking impressed while poor Tanji was getting shakily to his feet, clutching his arm.

"I'm sorry, Tanji. I didn't mean—" Alita said as he glided past on one foot, unable to put his weight on the other.

He wouldn't even look at her and stopped in front of Hugo. "Your freak girlfriend's got some serious malfunctions," he said.

Hugo looked at him with a deeply worried expression. "I'm really sorry," he said, then suddenly burst out laughing, "that she humiliated you so severely!" He ruffled Tanji's hair.

"Yeah, *sure* you are." Tanji slapped at his hand and rolled away.

"Aw, come on, Tanji," Hugo called after him. "Who owns this city?"

Tanji swivelled around to face him and clapped his hands over his head. "We do!"

"Okay, see you tonight," Hugo said, resisting the urge to say he was glad Tanji's arm was better. "And she's not my girlfriend."

Tanji paused. "She's a Total Replacement cyborg. You know how we feel about those."

"She's just a kid," Hugo said, not laughing any more.

"Uh-huh."

"She's also from Zalem," Hugo told him.

"Whatever." Tanji skated off.

Alita heard them but she was too wrung out to pay close attention. It seemed to take everything she had just to get the borrowed wheels off her feet.

"You have some talent for this game," Hugo said, sitting down beside her.

Is that what they call it? she thought. *Brutalising a kid who's all flesh and blood with no cyborg parts is talent?* Guilt and confusion were bubbling around inside her; all she wanted to do was get away before she started crying like a baby or something equally stupid. "I gotta go home," she said. "Ido wants me in the house before dark."

"You wanna ride?" Hugo asked.

Suddenly she no longer felt like crying; in fact, she couldn't smile widely enough.

Hugo hadn't really believed she'd never ridden on a gyro before. But the way Alita was clutching his waist and laughing as the wind whipped her hair—she was definitely enjoying it far more than anybody else he'd ever given a ride to. It was like this was some kind of special treat. But then, from what she'd told him about herself, *everything* was a special treat.

"So you can't remember *anything*?" he asked her. "Not family, friends—not even favourite food?"

"No," she said. "Well, maybe oranges. But that's just since yesterday."

"Nope," he said. "Unacceptable."

"What do you mean?" she asked, baffled.

Hugo jumped a kerb and came to a stop in front of a market stall. This girl needed a *real* special treat. "Give me some chocolate," he said to the woman minding the stall, handing her a few credits. He passed the small brick to Alita. "Eat this. It'll change your life. Trust me."

Alita hesitated, holding the brick between finger and thumb and studying it closely like it was something from another world—which for her it was, he supposed, nodding encouragement at her. Still hesitant, she bit off a small part of one corner.

"Oh my God!" The way her face lit up, she was practically

glowing with delight. She took another, much bigger bite, then another, making ecstatic noises between each until it was all gone. "That was *soooo great!*" she said finally, licking her fingertips. "Hey, Hugo—I have a favourite food!"

Hugo laughed, enjoying her reaction. The woman behind the stall was chuckling too, though she also looked a bit puzzled. As well she might, Hugo thought. No doubt this was the only time she'd come across a kid who had never tasted chocolate before. He felt pleased with himself for being the one who had introduced Alita to her new favourite food.

Hugo turned around to fire up the gyro, then paused when he spotted a familiar figure making his way towards them on the sidewalk. The night-time crowds didn't give him much trouble—people were only too happy to get out of his way.

"Check it out," he said, giving Alita a nudge. "Hunter-Warrior."

The cyborg had stopped to take a look at the people around him, a predator in search of his prey. He was all metal and proud of it, his cyborg body an idealised version of the male form, decorated with a profusion of carved designs that everyone was supposed to think were symbols of highly significant things. They might have been, for all Hugo knew—the guy spent as much on body art as he did on plastic surgery to keep himself looking handsome and dangerous. It should have been silly, and maybe on anyone else it would have been. On him, it never failed to intimidate.

"Who *is* that?" Alita said in a low voice.

"He's a bounty hunter. Named Zapan," Hugo told her. "Scanning for his mark. I wouldn't want to be *that* guy."

Zapan was coming towards them now. As he went past, Hugo saw that he'd upgraded his face with new cheekbones and a stronger chin. He had a few more fancy carvings on his back, too, but he was still carrying his trademark weapon.

"What's with the sword?" Alita asked.

"Guns and advanced AI are outlawed in Iron City, punishable by death. Those are things that challenge Zalem."

She looked so creeped out and unsettled that he wished he'd kept his mouth shut and not put such crappy stuff in her head, especially when she couldn't remember anything about her own life. Then it occurred to him how he might be able to make up for that and he started the gyro again.

Alita stared open-mouthed at the enormous ruin of a cathedral as Hugo brought the gyro to a stop. This must have been an incredibly important place since it was so big, she thought. The windows were all empty holes now and part of the roof had fallen in; what bits were left were home to some wind turbines turning lazily in the breeze. But there was still something about it that was—she searched for the right word and came up with—*majestic*.

It really is, she decided. *Like even though it's a wreck now, it's refusing to give in.*

She looked at Hugo, who had gone a bit solemn.

"It's a harsh world," he said. "The strong prey on the weak

down here and the Factory doesn't care about anybody. Which is why you gotta stay focused on your dream."

"What's your dream, Hugo?" she asked.

"I'll show you." He motioned for her to follow him.

It didn't take very long to climb up the scarred face of the ruin—there were plenty of handholds and toeholds. Hugo led her all the way up to a platform attached to one of the towers. The sight of Iron City spread out below made Alita catch her breath.

"This is my secret place," Hugo said. "Best view in town."

"It's cool," Alita said, gazing at the lights dotting the darkening land below. "I like it."

"Uh uh, not *that* view down there," Hugo said and pointed upwards. "*This* one. Up *there*."

"Oh," she breathed, staring at the floating city. The structures near the edge were glowing a reddish gold, and here and there she saw lights shining like jewels. Or maybe stars.

"Especially this time of day," Hugo added. "The way the light is. It's the most beautiful thing in this whole ugly world."

Alita wished she could see the buildings better. The people in all those buildings glinting in the dying sunlight—what were they doing? Were they watching the sunset? Was it more beautiful from up there? Or did they have something better to look at?

"I wonder what it's like up there," Alita said wistfully.

"Better than this dump down here," Hugo said. "I mean, it's *gotta* be."

Alita wished he didn't sound so dispirited, that being

here with her could make him as happy as she was to be with him in his special place.

Suddenly he touched her shoulder and said, "Listen!"

She heard a whooshing noise above her and looked up to see the long arc of a tube stretching upwards across the sky, all the way to the floating city.

"That's the sound of stuff going from the Factory up to Zalem. But the tubes are only for supply shipments, food and other things, not people." Hugo sighed; his longing radiated from him like heat. "Y'know, if I were as strong as you, I'd climb that tube to Zalem right now."

She blinked at him. "But they don't let anybody go up."

Hugo gave a short, humourless laugh. "That's what they *want* everyone to think. You gotta know the right people. I happen to be connected." He pointed at the skyscrapers sparkling as sunset turned into night. "You have to be willing to do what it takes—*whatever* it takes. One day—and not too long from now—I'm going to be waving down at this garbage heap from right up there."

Alita couldn't take her eyes off his face. It was like he was glowing as the wind lifted his dark hair. The way he looked now—*he* was the most beautiful thing she had ever seen, not Zalem, and she wished she could tell him that.

"You're looking at me funny," Hugo said.

"No." She smiled. "I'm just… looking."

"You think I'm crazy," Hugo said, a bit accusingly.

"I don't," she told him. "I respect you for your dream."

Something fluttered around her. She put out her hand and a butterfly came to rest on her finger, its orange-and-black wings beating slowly and deliberately, almost like a heartbeat. A heart with wings. It let her study it for a few seconds before it lifted off again, flying a leisurely course down into the cathedral, where golden sunlight poured through the vacant windows onto a small area of grass that had grown up to make a wild meadow in miniature among the rubble and broken stones.

"I want to see what's up there so bad I can *taste* it," he went on. "And the funny thing is—" he turned from Zalem to her. "You've already seen it, but you can't remember."

"What do you mean?" she said, puzzled.

"Doc found you in the scrapyard. All that stuff is dumped from Zalem. So *you* must be from up there."

"Oh. Well. I guess... I dunno." She shrugged awkwardly, unsure what to say.

Hugo took her by the shoulders and looked earnestly into her face. "If you could only tell me what your eyes have seen."

"I wish I could," she said, thinking he had no idea how much she wished she could, if it would make him happy. "But to be honest, I have a feeling I couldn't have been anyone very important. Just an insignificant girl, thrown out with the rest of the garbage." She looked over at Zalem and, as if on cue, trash poured out of the torn bottom of the sky city.

They sat and watched as debris continued to fall.

CHAPTER 7

Ido caught Alita trying to sneak in undetected. He was at the top of the stairs leading from the basement, wearing an apron, which should have made him look silly with all the frills and ruffles, but it didn't, not even a little.

"I asked you to be home before dark," he told her sternly, marching her into the kitchen and sitting her down at the table.

"I'm sorry," she said. "I lost track of time."

Ido sighed. "I told you, don't trust anyone. People can do terrible things to each other here."

Her gaze fell on the bandage on his forearm. He'd changed it since she'd gone out but a little heart's-blood had seeped through. She looked up at him. "Are you okay?" she asked with a slight emphasis on "you".

"Yes, I'm fine," he snapped as he put a plate of food in front of her. "Eat this. You still need proper nourishment for your brain."

She hesitated, frowning at her dinner doubtfully. It

smelled pretty good but it didn't look terribly exciting. She looked up at him again. "Do you have any chocolate?"

They stared at each other for a long moment, then they both burst out laughing. He was still chuckling a little while he expounded on corn, potatoes, green beans and chicken, which was actually fortified chicken product, and how each food would benefit her brain and central nervous system because even Total Replacement cyborgs did not live by the nanos in cyber-blood alone. It was all pretty good, but none of it was chocolate. Not even close.

Alita went to bed as soon as Ido told her to, making a big show of yawning and looking like she could barely keep her eyes open, but a show was all it was. She was wide awake when she heard the *squeak-squeak-squeak* in the hall, and she was ready. She fully intended to count to thirty before she followed him out of the house so there would be less chance of his catching her but she barely made it to twenty; losing him, she decided, would be worse.

Fortunately, the suitcase slowed him down. It wasn't very big but it was awkward on rough pavement. It was also heavier than she'd thought. He kept having to turn around and tip it onto two wheels so he could drag it over kerbs and broken sections of pavement. Following him on the street, she had to hang back so much there was a very real chance she'd lose him.

But there *was* a way she could put more distance between them and still stay close—and she had Hugo to thank for it.

The building she scaled didn't have quite as many hand- and toe-holds as Hugo's cathedral, but it did have windowsills and pipes and it was only two storeys tall. She was able to keep pace with him, leaping the gaps between one rooftop and another with no trouble. Sometimes she could even move ahead of him and wait to see which street he would choose, whether he would go left or right or straight on.

This was how she spotted the woman. All she could really see of her was a pair of very shapely legs and a few centimetres of very short skirt; the rest of her was hidden under a hooded jacket. At first Alita thought she was merely on her way home after a night out and hadn't been able to find a cab. But while the woman was walking at a good pace—her high heels clicked so loudly on the pavement, Alita knew where she was just by listening— she was in no hurry.

She also seemed to be taking a very roundabout way home; she saw that the woman walked along streets without making much progress in any one direction. Was she lost? If so, she didn't act lost. She didn't stop to peer at building numbers, she never stopped to look around or get her bearings. She just kept walking and walking and walking, the way people did when they knew exactly where they were going.

And so did Ido. Alita saw from her elevated vantage point that the route he took was somehow connected to the woman's. Sometimes he got to within a block of her and Alita knew he must have been able to hear those high heels going *tik-tik-tik* on the pavement. But he never got within sight of her—

Ido, she realised with cold horror, was *stalking* the woman in the hood.

No, he couldn't be. Not Ido. He *wouldn't*.

The woman entered a narrow passageway and went down a flight of cement stairs, pausing for a moment to look behind her. Ido wasn't there. He had gone down a different street and stopped on a corner. Alita held her breath. The woman came down the stairs barely a block up from Ido and was now walking straight towards him.

And Ido knew it.

He opened his case and took out some metal rods, one of which had a weird head on it—one side looked like a hammer, the other came to a deadly-looking rounded point. From her vantage point above and behind him, it was hard to see exactly what the thing was. Alita leaped to the next roof, which was a little bit lower. She tried to be silent but she made a small scraping sound when she landed.

She froze, holding her breath, waiting for Ido to call out, but he didn't. Finally, she crept over the low brick wall at the edge of the roof and peeked down at him. He was apparently too absorbed in putting that hammer weapon together, he didn't hear anything—except the *click-click-click* of that woman's high heels. He fitted the pieces together and flipped a switch. The thing came alive in his hands and Alita knew he was going to use it on the hooded woman. Feeling as if her heart had shattered into a million pieces, she leaped down two storeys and landed in front of him.

"No! Stop!" She grabbed the shaft of the hammer weapon with both hands.

Ido's jaw dropped. "Alita?! What—"

"I'm *not* going to let you kill her!" she shouted, trying to pull the hammer away from him. She turned to look at the woman but she was gone. There was no one on the street except her and Ido.

In the next moment, she heard a low, rumbling laugh echoing through the labyrinth of narrow alleys around them, the alleys the woman had been walking through. The shadows around them seemed to shift as one, moving towards them and swelling into a silhouette three metres tall.

Alita heard a long, nasty scraping sound on the street behind her and Ido. They turned to see a second cyborg, a gangly metal skeleton with a tuft of purple-and-white hair and a death's-head grin, holding a blade in one hand.

"A trap," Ido said, his voice absurdly matter-of-fact.

"Looking for me, Doctor?" said the eight-foot shadow. "Or should I say *Hunter-Warrior*?"

Alita gaped at Ido. Dr Ido, the cyber-surgeon who had laboured for days to embed her core in this work-of-art body, a Hunter-Warrior? There had to be some mistake—

"Oh, no!" said the skeleton, shuddering in fake terror. "Looks like he's got us now! I'm *so scared!*"

Ido stepped in front of Alita protectively. "Alita, don't move," he told her.

"Thanks for bringing a girl," said the skeleton, and he clanged his blade against his ribs, making sparks. "That's gonna save us time."

Ido and the skeleton charged each other. Alita stepped back, hearing the hammer roar. Blue flame burst from the back of the hammer's head as it slammed into the skeleton's forearm and tore it off. It clattered loudly on the street and the skeleton staggered backwards, laughing.

"Nice shot for a meatboy!" he jeered.

Ido swung at him again, but the skeleton side-stepped and the hammer took a chunk out of a concrete wall. The skeleton laughed and swiped at Ido's shoulder with his curved blade. To Alita's horror, the hammer cartwheeled out of Ido's hands as he staggered back, bleeding.

"Nooo!" Alita screamed.

Ido dived for the hammer but a shapely leg with a spike heel slammed down on the handle, and a long black blade appeared at his throat. The woman Alita had thought Ido was going to kill crouched over him, putting her carefully made-up face close to his.

"Did you come to rescue me?" she said. "That's so *sweet*!" She used the blade to flick his glasses away. "Say, you have nice eyes."

"*He's mine!*" yelled the skeleton, clutching his mangled arm. "You can have the *girl*."

Alita took a step back and then another, moving farther down the alley behind her.

"I don't care, so long as I get his eyes," said the woman, touching the tip of her curved black blade to Ido's cheek.

The other two closed in on Ido, and the skeleton yanked him up by his hair.

Ido squeezed his eyes shut. "Alita, run!" he yelled.

Alita ran—

—flat out, hard and fast, her feet pounding the pavement as she made herself go faster, faster, *faster*, then launched herself into the air. There was a loud metal *clang!* as she slammed into the skeleton and sent him tumbling away from Ido. She stayed on him, her fists moving almost too fast to follow until there was only a pile of twisted metal junk on the street.

Ido stared at Alita and the wreckage she had created in disbelief. "My God," he breathed. "Alita…?"

The giant stepped all the way out of the shadows with a roar of anger. He had impossibly broad, muscular shoulders and thick arms that hung too low, a head the size of a barrel, and a body that looked like a tank that had been hammered into a shape that was supposed to be humanoid.

"*Rip that flea!*" he bellowed, pointing at Alita.

The other cyborg came to life, throwing off her hooded jacket, and Alita saw that her face and her shapely legs had been her only human features. From the waist up, her shiny black metal body was segmented like an insect. She extended her arms, showing off triple joints like those of a praying mantis and the nasty curved blades on the end of each one.

"You're so *beautiful*," she gushed at Alita. "I want to rip you open and see if you're ugly inside, like all the others."

Evil certainly could find its form in this city, Alita thought and then leaped at her.

Ido shook off the shocked incredulity that had frozen him in place. His little girl needed him—

Or did she?

As the insectoid's curved black blade sliced through the air, Alita jumped clear effortlessly as if she were levitating. She rebounded off one of the old causeway pillars and sprang back towards the cyborg. Ido dived for his hammer, started it up, drew back for a swing—

Only to find his hands empty. The eight-foot monster took the hammer in one hand and Ido by the neck with the other. It pinned him against a wall, turning his head, forcing him to look at Alita.

"Watch her die," the cyborg commanded him.

The insectoid's homicidal madness was in full bloom as she slashed at Alita with her nasty black blades. Alita evaded every swing, gradually moving nearer until she was close enough for a powerful kick that sent the insectoid flying backwards to slam into the wall behind her. But just before smashing into it, the insectoid twisted her body with a sudden frightening ease and hit the wall on her feet, upside down and unhurt. Grinning, she clung there for a second, then sprang at Alita.

Alita was already in motion. She met the insectoid in mid-air with a crash of metal, ramming her into the wall again. Moving with the fluid grace of a dancer, Alita turned her body, pointed her toes at the insectoid's skull, and drove it against the stone. The segmented body slid down to the ground, headless, blue cyber-blood gushing out of its ruined neck like a fountain. Alita somersaulted backwards and dropped into a crouch facing the eight-foot cyborg.

The monster dropped Ido and smiled at her, showing gleaming metal teeth like knives.

"Come here, little flea." He raised one massive hand and pressed his forefinger and thumb together: *Tick! Tick! Tick!* "Come here so I can pinch your head off."

Alita sprang at him, easily dodging his arm, which smashed into a concrete barrier hard enough to make his whole body shake. She came down behind him and immediately launched herself straight up to make her next move. But just as she rose past his head, he reached up and swatted her, sending her backwards into—

A sudden blinding flare of light.

Time stopped.

Alita found herself looking down at a stark black-and-white landscape, lifeless rock and dust under a black sky filled with unblinking stars. Time started again, but it moved at a crawl now as she drifted down towards the lifeless, dusty surface. Her body was different, much more heavily armoured. This was a body meant for danger, for combat, although she didn't know how she knew that, any more than she knew why the number 99 was printed on her shoulder. She only knew she was ready.

Her shadow was floating down in front of her. She pointed her toes and they met her shadow in a burst of ancient dust. Immediately, time shifted into normal speed and she was bounding over the dead landscape, charging towards a squad of enemy soldiers also in combat armour. She knew they were as ready as she was.

Alita exploded into action, becoming a lethal storm of blows and kicks, her movements not frenzied but disciplined, born of the martial art that she lived to follow and that now kept her alive. Each enemy soldier that advanced to kill her died at her hands instead; each death was another move forward. She had to keep moving forward, too fast and too deadly for anyone to stop her.

One after another, the enemy soldiers reached for her, lunged at her, then fell away from her as she took them out, twisting their bodies, tearing them apart. Fighting her way through them, she turned to look at the person fighting by her side with moves just as fast and deadly. The face looking back at her was one she saw every day, fierce and unafraid and unrelenting: Gelda, her squad leader.

There was a sudden brilliant flash overhead and everything went white. She heard Gelda yell, "Incoming!" The white faded out and Alita looked up to see warships soaring through the black sky, firing missiles and energy beams while the unblinking stars looked on in silence.

The enemy command centre was in sight. Alita gathered herself and leaped again. Gelda watched her trajectory with a warrior's pride.

"You're going to be the best!" Gelda called to her. "The best the world has ever seen—ours or theirs!"

She was flying through the void, saw the Earth hanging in the airless black before the blinding light flared again. The battle was gone and there was a stone wall rushing at her.

The memory of combat suffused her body with knowledge and expertise that let her move without thinking. She caught herself on the top of the wall instead of smashing into it and held on. They were at the causeway now, where the road curved out over empty space to meet connections from high ramps that no longer existed. Beyond it was a darkness unbroken even by the streetlights. Alita took a firmer grip on the wall, watching the monster cyborg advance on her. Behind him, Ido's gaze met hers; then he was running at the cyborg.

As the monster turned to knock him away, Alita bent her knees and aimed herself at the place where his arm met his shoulder, letting out a war cry that came from a place her body remembered even if her mind didn't. She rammed into the cyborg's shoulder feet first, adding a sharp twist just as she hit—another move her body remembered. There was a scream of metal, drowned out by the cyborg's bellow of anger and disbelief as his arm dropped to the ground, splashing cyber-blood on the pavement.

Alita tucked and rolled away, bouncing to her feet with the rocket hammer at the ready when he lunged for her.

"Who are you?" he roared.

In answer, she slammed the hammer into his chest.

There was the loud *crack!* of something enormous breaking apart, something that should have been invincible but had met a force that it could not stand against, a force that had shattered not just its material but the faith behind it. Alita watched as lines of breakage spread over the front of the cyborg's body and, for a moment, she thought the monster might actually fall to pieces in front of her. But he used his remaining arm to hold himself together as he staggered backwards. Ido was gaping like a man going into shock, but he was safe. Alita hefted the hammer and advanced on the cyborg, intending to finish him off.

"You'll pay for this, little flea," he rasped, backing away from her. "Grewishka does not forget! I'll be coming for you—*both* of you!"

Before she could draw back for another swing, he toppled backwards over the side of the causeway. Alita ran to the barrier and looked down but couldn't see anything in the darkness below.

"Alita, are you all right?" asked Ido, his voice high and fearful. "Alita?"

"Another second," she growled, looking down into the darkness. "Another second and he would have been mine."

She raised her head and suddenly felt cool night air blowing into her face. The frustration and disappointment of not being able to finish her enemy drained out of her, leaving her with the feel of bodily lightness that came after expending so much physical energy in an extremely forceful way. It wasn't so much a letdown as a return to a base level that, under battle conditions, didn't even exist.

"Alita? Can you *hear* me?"

She blinked up at Ido, at the blood trickling down his face—heart's-blood. "Oh my God, Ido!" she said, horrified that he was injured. "Are you all right?"

He stared down at her and she couldn't tell if he were mad or sad, scared or confused. Maybe after seeing what she had done with this body, he was sorry he'd put her in it, she thought; maybe he wished that when he'd found her core in the trash pile, he'd left it there.

Abruptly he turned away, pulling her with him.

The little killing machine that looked so much like his daughter walked quietly along the night-time streets beside him. There was no sign of aggression or belligerence, not even a little adolescent bad temper. Since Grewishka's long fall off the edge of the causeway, she had reverted to being only a young girl, worried that he was hurt, wanting nothing more than to go home.

Or more precisely, since about half a minute *after* Grewishka had fallen, when she'd glared down into the shadows and growled about how a second longer and he'd have been hers. As if *she* were the Warrior around here.

Which, he understood now, she was. He had seen it in her, and all the pretty flower designs and silver and gold inlays on her pretty body wouldn't, couldn't, change that. Perhaps he could try to keep it at bay, keep it dormant by being a good father and keeping her out of danger, something he had once again failed to do, and in an even more spectacular way than the first time.

When they got home, she insisted on bandaging his shoulder and he let her. She looked so contrite as she prepared the dressing and cleaned his wound. The fourteen-year-old girl trying to make up for disobeying him, for sneaking out, and putting herself in the middle of a bad situation—

Except if she hadn't, I'd be dead, he reminded himself unhappily. And now she was doing a superb job with his shoulder, using just enough paste to close the laceration smoothly, without lumps. He wondered if this was something she learned from Gerhad or whether it was actually battlefield first-aid that came with her Warrior nature.

But the night wasn't over yet—he still had to deliver the bounties to the Factory. While he didn't really want to take Alita with him in case something else happened that would flip her into full-on combat, he didn't want to leave her home alone, not after everything that had happened. She needed him to talk to, to be with her so she wouldn't have to think about it all by herself. And that was leaving aside the possibility of her sneaking out and following him again if he didn't. Or the possibility that friends of the two cyborgs they'd killed might come looking for payback. If some of them broke in—

He clamped down on the thought and shut it off. It wasn't very likely, given who he was to the Iron City cyborgs, but it wasn't totally out of the question.

He decided to take Alita with him to the Factory. Case closed. No agonising necessary.

He sneaked a sidelong glance at her as they headed for the Factory. She was still quiet, still looking contrite, like any other young teenage girl who had defied a parent and found herself in the middle of a situation far more serious than she'd imagined. And now she was probably wondering how much trouble she was in, how angry he was, how he was going to punish her, and would things ever be the same between them.

Are you sure about that? asked a tiny voice in his mind. *Seeing as how* she *saved* your *ass, could you be projecting? Is* she really *the only one here with something to apologise for? Yes, she thought* you *were the killer—but if she hadn't, Grewishka would have your head on a pike and the bug would be wearing your eyes as earrings.*

Alita—*this* Alita—had been in his life for a grand total of two days, not fourteen years. She wasn't really a young girl, not the way his daughter had been. His daughter had been defenceless, needing his protection. This Alita needed no protection. She might be worried about how angry he was with her, but maybe he should consider about how angry *she* was with *him*. Because he'd seen what happened when she got angry.

The killer in her was core-deep. It wasn't a bad habit she could break or a problem to handle with anger management classes; it was her nature. On the other hand, it wasn't a pure drive to kill. No matter how heated she was, she distinguished between friend and foe. But once she was in motion, she was set to go all the way. She didn't stop once the immediate danger was past.

Another second and he would have been mine.

Even just remembering the sound of her voice gave him a chill.

As they walked up the steps to the front door of the Factory, Ido felt Alita looking at him with a question on her face. When they reached the top, he hefted the sack he was carrying and turned to her.

"Listen," he said, and then his mind went blank. "Listen," he said again, taking out his Hunter-Warrior ID badge. "You—*we*—just killed two of the most notorious criminals in the city, and pissed off a third. Grewishka *will* come for us, even if friends of the other two don't."

Alita nodded. "I understand."

"Before the Fall, there were police to stop criminals and protect the innocent," said Ido. "Now the Factory pays people like me to do their dirty work and stop criminals." *And nobody protects the innocent*, he added silently. He raised his badge over his head. "Hunter-Warrior 17739."

"You're *really* a Hunter-Warrior?" Alita said, her voice quiet and tremulous.

"Can I trust you to stay right here, while I'm inside?" Ido asked her. "You don't move for any reason?"

"Yes," she said in a small voice.

"Good." He didn't really want to leave her outside, but he didn't want her to have any part of the bounty process, not even as a witness. He had no qualms about her safety—no one would start any trouble on the Factory's front steps unless they had a death wish.

The enormous front doors rumbled open. Ido started to go in, then turned back to her. "And *don't kill anybody*."

"I won't," she promised meekly.

Ido upended the sack, dumping the two heads out onto a metal plate so they could be scanned. A deckman slid into place on the other side of the counter. Exactly what deckmen were for was one of the Factory's great unanswered questions. As far as Ido could tell, their only role in the bounty process was to pop up and creep humans out, looking like trash-cans with their cartoon faces and machine voices.

"Bounty for the cyborg Nyssiana is twenty thousand credits," the deckman informed him. "Bounty for the cyborg Romo is fourteen thousand credits."

Ido had a strong urge to tell the deckman that, after all he'd gone through to deliver the heads, the Factory was getting a real bargain. And Romo would have been outraged to know that Nyssiana was worth more than he was.

Tough stuff, fella, Ido thought, watching a mechanical arm sweep the heads into a disposal chute. *She had better legs.*

He had a sudden mental image of the cyborgs' heads tumbling down the chute, falling and falling and falling until they landed on a trash pile where a sadder and even more downtrodden version of humans hunted for salvage while looking up at Iron City, believing it was a better place and wondering what it was like to live there.

His reverie broke as another mechanical arm dropped a sack of credit chips on the counter in front of him. He stuffed them into the pocket of his coat.

Alita was waiting exactly where he'd left her, despite the fact that it was now pouring and she could have taken shelter closer to the building. The killing machine that didn't know enough to come in out of the rain. What *was* he going to do with her?

"You should have told me who you really were," she said.

I could have said the same thing to you, he thought, and bit his tongue so he wouldn't say it aloud.

"Is this just something you do for the money?" she asked as they descended the stairs and headed for home.

"I take the money *for the clinic*," he said firmly, and a bit more defensively than he meant to. "Otherwise I'd have had to close up shop long ago. And there are other reasons I do this work, but I'd rather not talk about them."

"But you *have* to!" she insisted, grabbing his coat sleeve. The emotions of a fourteen-year-old girl were always so close to the surface, so ready to flare. "You're not who I thought you were—but something happened tonight, and *I'm* not who I thought I was!" She stopped, and took hold of both his hands with hers. Her pretty little hands, decorated with pretty little flowers and designs, had a grip too strong for him to pull free. "You know more about me than you're saying, I *know* you do. I need the truth."

He was helpless before her, more helpless than he would have been before the killing machine. After a bit, he heard himself say, "I had a daughter. Her name—her name was Alita…"

CHAPTER 8

Looking out over Iron City confirmed to Vector once again that the best thing about the view wasn't how, during the day, the horizon stretched without limit in all directions, or how, at night, it looked as if there were a fortune in glittering jewels spread out below him.

No, the best thing about it was that he *owned* it. It was his to enjoy, his to control, his to keep. It would always be his and his alone. It was like owning a chunk of the world. Or maybe all of it.

He heard a soft rustle of sheets on the bed behind him. Those were very expensive sheets. Not the legendary Egyptian cotton, but something even more exquisite, thanks to certain textile nanos, very special and very hard to obtain, which he also owned. The woman he shared his treasures with had said she loved the feel of those sheets. He knew Chiren loved the view as well, just by the expression on her face when he let her look at it.

Lately, though, he'd begun to think she no longer had

the proper amount of appreciation for the finer things, or gratitude for the generosity of the man who deigned to share his prized possessions with her. It wasn't like she could find anything better lying around, just waiting for her to come along and pick it up.

Vector turned to look at her. Chiren was lying with her back to both him and the view. In one of her moods again. Time to remind her of what was important. He went to the bed and rolled her over, gently but firmly, so she was looking at him.

"I only want my players losing when I tell them to," he said, "and I don't want that left to chance. You promised me champions."

Her blue-eyed gaze was icy and intense. "And you promised me the best of everything. Get those military-grade servos I asked for. Or get your street rats to jack something decent for a change."

He chucked her under her beautiful chin, mainly to push her beautiful mouth shut. "You don't have a winning attitude," he said. His voice was soft but there was no mistaking the edge in it. "Now, how do we look for tomorrow's game?"

She gave him her put-upon look, like he was making her life harder than it had to be. Like she wasn't her own worst enemy. "Claymore's a complete rebuild. Zariki's not tracking in the high-gee turns."

"That so? You know the betting will be very high on Zariki." He leaned in close, wanting her to feel his breath on her face. "How soon you go to Zalem is determined by the quality of your work. And the size of my profits."

She lifted her face as if she were going to kiss him. "I'll be ready."

He didn't have to tell her she'd better be. He got up and left, pausing to opaque the window as he went.

When Vector left a room, it was, as far as he was concerned, empty. It certainly felt that way right now to Chiren. There had been a time in her life when she would have found his attitude totally unacceptable; she'd have done something about it, railed against it, taken a stand. But that time was long gone. Everything was empty now—this room, this building, this world. Her life.

She was about to close her eyes against the outer emptiness and retreat to the emptiness within when she heard some kind of funny scraping sound coming from the window. Vector's precious view; annoyed, she threw on a shirt and got up. If some of Vector's dirty little street rats had climbed up here again, she was going to drop-kick them off the ledge and see how they liked *that* trip.

She tapped the control to clear the window and almost screamed at the twisted, blood-drenched horror looking in at her. Reflexively, she jumped back; at the same moment, the glass shattered and the thing toppled forward into the room, red blood and bright-blue fluid splashing on Vector's expensive carpeting. This room was no longer empty.

Its breath came in raspy shudders as it rolled over and fixed its tortured gaze on her. "Help… me…" it begged.

"Grewishka!" She spat the name, almost gagging. It

was hard to believe this bloody mess at her feet had ever been a Motorball star and a serious contender for Final Champion. "You're not the pampered star of the coliseum any more! Why should I waste any of my precious talent on *you*?"

Grewishka made a strangled gargling noise. "Look— *look* what she did to me! Ido's little cyber-bitch!"

All at once, the world tilted sideways and Chiren had to put a hand on the wall to steady herself. "What did you say?" she demanded. "*Who* did this?"

"A… li… ta," Grewishka said, getting the syllables out with a tremendous effort.

Alita. Chiren stared down at the cyborg, at the cracked and broken armour that barely kept his insides from spilling out, the empty socket in his shoulder where his arm had been. She had never seen a cyborg reduced to such a state, on the Motorball track, or anywhere else.

Alita.

As soon as Ido had secured Alita in the surgical frame, the doctor in him took over. He set a neural block to prevent her feeling any pain and removed her legs for scanning and diagnostics. The small cracks he found were right where he'd expected them to be. Otherwise, her pretty, flower-bedecked legs were sound. Now he was studying the solid-state organs in her thoracic cavity and checking the efficiency of circulation in both cyber- and heart's-blood in her upper body.

"I don't see any internal damage at all," he said. "Just those cracked bushings in your leg. You'll have to go easy on it until I get them replaced." For once there was something other than more servos at the top of his shopping list. Gerhad would faint.

He was running through a mental list of other parts he might upgrade or replace when he heard Alita say, "So this girl was your daughter? You built this body for her."

She was looking at the holo on the desk behind him. It was the last picture he'd taken of Alita. She was thin and frail, as she always had been throughout her too-short life. But she'd had a smile that could light up a room. She always looked so hopeful, like she was sure something good was just around the corner. That had been his fault.

"Yes," he said, "that was my daughter, Alita." Dr Dyson Ido, CMD, consummate professional, wavered slightly and had to take a steadying breath. "She was really looking forward to waking up with legs that worked—legs that would walk and run and take her anywhere she wanted to go."

In his peripheral vision, he saw tears welling up in Alita's eyes and he willed her not to cry. He wasn't sure Dr Ido could maintain control if she did, and she needed a doctor to close her chest cavity and reattach her legs, not a grieving father.

"You made her a pair of fast legs," said Alita.

"She never got to use them," Ido replied. He meant to leave it at that but he couldn't. "A patient of mine came to the clinic one night… looking for drugs. He was a Paladin, a star of the track—or he had been, before Motorball used him up and threw him away. The Game did that. It still does. A lot of Hunter-Warriors started out looking for glory on the track. The lucky ones end up looking for bounties on the street. The unlucky ones—"

In his mind's eye, he could see the crazed cyborg rampaging through the lab as clearly as if it had happened an hour ago. Once upon a time, this cyborg had been a man like any other, not perfect but reasonable, a man who had wanted something other than the Factory treadmill of producing goods for people living better lives in a better place. With no way to get up there, he'd tried to make the best of what Iron City had to offer, and like most things in Iron City, it had all gone bad on him.

"I was a Tuner for the First League," Ido went on, "and when I looked at him, all I saw was someone strong and healthy, ideal for cyborg enhancements. I gave him a body of obscene strength, and then I made him even stronger and bigger." For the cheers; because when the crowd had cheered for the Paladin Ido had made, he felt as if they were cheering for him, too, for his talent, his skills, his dedication to the Game. He hadn't been able to get enough of those cheers. Back then, he'd thought the adulation of Motorball fans was the most addictive high in the world. He'd been sadly, terribly, horribly wrong.

"I turned him into a demon—*my* demon," Ido added, "and he came back to me."

Ido had barely recognised the creature running amok in his lab, ripping the doors off cabinets, yanking out drawers, sweeping equipment off shelves and tables in search of the drugs that made him feel invincible on the track. His right arm was gone below the elbow; his left was a mish-mash of cheap tech that had been swapped out for the better hardware he had sold to buy drugs.

Ido's first thought had been to talk him down from the frenzy of his need so he could get close enough to hit him with a sedative. But his scarred and battered demon had taken one look at him and known immediately with the sharp and unerring instincts all junkies develop that there was no help for him here, that Ido only wanted to stop him, and once that happened, the days of feeling invincible would be over for good. He had picked Ido up with his one hand and heaved him through a bank of equipment, destroying delicate machinery it would take months to rebuild. His demon had made him part of the destruction.

As Ido had struggled to get to his feet, wincing at the broken glass stuck in his hands and face, the cyborg finally gave up looking for the drugs his system craved. He turned away and blasted through the double doors into the hallway, where—

"Alita—" Ido's voice trembled a little. "Alita couldn't get out of the way fast enough."

The thin little girl in a cyber-chair, always hopeful, always anticipating something good, had picked the wrong moment to follow her father to his laboratory. Ido had had a momentary glimpse of her face, pale and frightened, before the demon turned his madness on her; she hadn't even had time to scream. But the last image of her face burned forever into Ido's brain (he couldn't remember her smile without the holo), made him think it hadn't really been so quick for her, that the terror she'd felt had made the last second of her life seem like an eternity.

Not for the demon, though—he'd killed Alita without even slowing down. Ido reached the hallway just in time to see him burst out the door at the other end while Alita's wrecked wheelchair tumbled down the hallway behind him as if it were trying to catch up and remonstrate.

"Alita's mother, Chiren, couldn't deal with her death," Ido said after a pause. "Or maybe she just couldn't deal with me. Or both." He shrugged. "Probably both. She went away—she went with the winning team. But I couldn't go back to the Game. I went hunting instead."

Every good Hunter-Warrior needed a weapon—not just *a* weapon but the *right* one. He'd looked high and low for that weapon. When he hadn't found it, he'd gone home and made it himself. It was the first and only thing he had ever made for the purpose of taking life rather than saving it. As soon as he'd picked up the finished product, it had felt *right* in his hands, as if it were something he had been destined to build. And use.

"I needed to kill him," said Ido. "Or maybe I was hoping he would kill me."

But he hadn't, and somewhere deep down, Ido had known he wouldn't. He could remember every moment, every swing of every kill. Each time he had gone hunting, there had never been any doubt in his mind that he would be coming back with heads for bounties. Even tonight, when three monsters had had the drop on him, when he'd been dangling from Romo's grasp by his hair, on the verge of having his throat cut, he'd been sure that somehow he'd be going home with a bag of credits from the Factory.

"It brought me no peace," he said. Calm and steady;

apparently the doctor in him decided that confession would be good for the soul. "There were other demons like him out there, and I felt somehow I was responsible for all of them. So I registered as a Hunter-Warrior. There was nothing noble about it."

"Did you ever find peace?" Alita asked.

He smiled. "I found you."

"But I'm not your daughter," she said, sounding apologetic. "I don't know *what* I am."

"I do." He hit the switch for PROJECT on one of the screens. Immediately a life-size translucent 3D graphic of Alita appeared, showing all her internal systems. "Have a look at your original cyber-core." He gestured at the graphic to highlight her head, neck and the structural column extending into her chest.

"Here's your brain," he said, pointing. "It's a normal healthy teenage girl brain—if there is such a thing." He chuckled, then lowered his hand to the chest area. "But this is your heart, part of your original core. It's powered by an antimatter micro-reactor."

"So I've got a strong heart, right?"

She didn't understand, of course. How could she? "You have a heart that could power all of Iron City—for *years*. And your skull—it's a precision-machined carbon-nanotube composite."

Her quizzical expression made him smile. "This is *Lost technology*," he told her. "Nobody's made this stuff since… *before the Fall*."

Alita blinked at him, then laughed. "Yeah, right. Like I'm three hundred years old!"

Ido waited for her to wind down, then said, "Sweetheart… you are."

Sweetheart… you are. You are.

Ido's words echoed in Alita's mind as she sat on her bed hugging her knees and gazing out of the window at the full moon beneath Zalem. The moon; she'd been there, fought there. Killed there.

What you saw was a flash from your previous life, Ido had told her. *You were someone very special, and* very *important.*

Her gaze fell on a stuffed animal and she picked it up. This had belonged to a different teenage girl, one who didn't have memories of fighting and killing on the moon or anywhere else. How could *she* be holding it in her hands?

Abruptly she got up and went to the full-length mirror.

Who was I? she had asked Ido.

Good question. All at once, she was moving with graceful strength, her body taking itself through a martial kata, moving fluidly from one striking position to another with a precision that felt reassuringly familiar.

In time, you'll remember, Ido had told her.

She threw her fist straight at the mirror, stopping the movement with her knuckles precisely one centimetre away from the glass. She had no idea how she knew it was a centimetre but she did.

Slowly, she lowered her arm. The girl in the mirror looked lost.

CHAPTER 9

"A *space* battle?" Hugo said, standing beside Alita as she looked over the makeshift Motorball track they'd set up in the drainage canal. The girl definitely wasn't from around here, just like Ido had said, but Hugo really didn't know what to make of what she'd told him. "You really think you were remembering the War? *The* War?"

Instead of answering, Alita skated away from him. At fifty metres, she turned, and came back at full speed. Hugo grabbed a bamboo pole and held it out in front of her at knee level. She jumped it easily and landed without a wobble. He shook his head. When she'd started out yesterday, she'd barely been able to stay upright. Then she'd kicked Tanji's ass, and it was like she'd been born on wheels.

"I mean, if you're really *that* old," Hugo continued, "and you have an organic brain—"

"Ido says my biological age is somewhere between fourteen and eighteen," Alita said, in an offhand way that made Hugo grin. Closer to fourteen than eighteen, he thought. "And somewhere along the way, time must have stopped somehow."

And then, as if she'd just told him something mundane like she thought it was going to rain (always a good bet in Iron City), she skated off again. Hugo watched her whip through the obstacle course he'd set up with trash barrels, kegs, boxes, and the wooden slam-dummies he and Tanji had cobbled together for serious practice. Tanji would probably kick his ass if he knew he was letting Alita use them, Hugo thought. But even at full speed, she swerved and dodged around all the obstacles without hitting even one.

"Wait a minute,' Hugo said when she skated up to him, catching her arm to keep her from rolling away. "You were in a space battle and then time stopped? How does *that* work?"

"Suspended animation," Alita said, shrugging. "Ido thinks I entered some kind of time field." As if that explained everything—although for Ido, it probably did. It was probably some kind of genius-scientist shorthand for complicated stuff regular people couldn't possibly understand, and Alita was simply going with it.

Before Hugo could say anything else, she zipped back through the obstacle course. This time, however, she made a point of *hitting* every single thing. Kegs flew, barrels shattered, dummies cracked and splintered, wood fragments went everywhere. Hugo wasn't sure what he was going to tell Tanji. Maybe he wouldn't have to tell him anything—one look at the wreckage and Tanji would know what had happened.

"This is all baby stuff for you," he said to Alita as she rolled up to him. "I think it's going to take more if you want to trigger any of those memories. You need a bigger challenge."

Alita nodded, her face thoughtful. After a moment, she looked down at her skates. "Okay, rip out my feet."

Hugo wasn't sure he'd heard her right. "Say again, Ali?"

"The pros have onboard wheels, not skates, right? It makes a big difference in how they move. They can manoeuvre faster. That's what I need to do. You've got some wheel-feet I can try, don't you?"

She had a point about the manoeuvring but Hugo couldn't help hesitating. "It'll be a big change for you," he said slowly. "But okay, I'll swap them out for you. Hop up on that—" He pointed at an empty barrel lying on its side. "—And I'll get my tools."

She was grinning like a little kid as she watched him remove the skates. They were pretty good skates, but she'd taken them to their limit. Hugo peeled her socks off and then stared. Her feet were as beautiful as the rest of her, perfectly shaped with flowery designs and silver and gold inlays. Ido's work was always recognisable by its sheer excellence, but he had really outdone himself. These weren't merely feet, they were works of art—or rather, part of a larger, even more beautiful work of art.

Hugo looked up at her. "Are you sure?" he asked. "I love your feet. They're pretty special—you wear them well."

"Lose 'em," Alita said, waving one hand in a careless, dismissive gesture. Hugo obeyed, removing them carefully, making sure he didn't tear any connections before he set each lovely foot on the ground by the barrel. He gazed at them for a moment, then realised to his horror he was mentally calculating how much he might get for them on the black market.

Alita's feet—his friend's feet.

He got busy attaching the wheel-feet to her legs, hoping she wouldn't pick up on any of his thoughts. Also hoping she would never find out he was the kind of person who thought about how much body parts would sell for. You didn't jack a friend, and you didn't screw with anything Doc Ido made. Those feet were so obviously the doc's work, even if he had been low enough to jack them, he wouldn't have been able to give them away.

There was a name for someone who knew the price of everything and the value of nothing, wasn't there?

Yeah, he thought; in Iron City, they called that "normal".

"You know, I've never seen anyone pick up the Game so fast," he said chattily, focusing on matching up the muscle and nerve links. The doc had made her legs so adaptable, they could probably make a couple of rocks operate as feet.

"I mean it, Ali," he added, double-checking the connections before he attached the other. "You've got the kind of talent it takes to go pro and make serious cash." She smiled at him, but he could tell she was getting restless; she wanted to see what she could do with wheel-feet. As soon as he was finished, she was off the barrel and rolling around as if she'd been on wheels all her life. The girl was unstoppable.

All at once, she was shoving a two-by-four into his

hand and explaining how she wanted him to hit her with it. "Aim right at my head," she instructed him, "and don't hold back. Give it everything you've got. Okay?" Without waiting for him to answer, she glided off to set up some of the targets she had hit earlier, the few that were still usable. When she finished, she rolled farther up the track and took a moment to remind him via gestures how to swing the board at her head.

Hugo gave her a thumbs up. The girl sure had talent but she also had a control thing, which might be trouble for her down the line. Only a player with a mountain of talent could get away with bossing everyone around.

Never mind, he thought, watching her come at him full-throttle. By the time Alita hit the pros, her talent would probably be the size of an entire mountain range.

She was definitely faster on wheel-feet and more in control of every movement, changing her roll-stride and posture like a barefoot marathoner. Or like a barefoot marathoner ready for a fight. Using open-palm blows, she took out three of the four remaining wooden slam-man dummies—there'd be no setting those up again, Hugo thought, as they shattered into wood-chip confetti—and destroyed the last one with a perfect flying roundhouse kick.

Hugo frowned. When had she learned how to do *that*?

She landed and, without missing a beat, drove towards him, her legs pumping so powerfully he was afraid she would take him out along with the two-by-four. But he held his ground and when she reached him, he swung the board the way she wanted him to, as hard as he could. She raised her forearm almost casually to block it; the impact knocked it out of his hands.

Hugo wondered if she were going to make another circuit—there didn't seem to be much point since all the targets were down. Instead, she detoured to the nearest ramp, hit it without slowing down, and executed a long backwards flip, which, he realised belatedly, was aimed right at him.

The next thing he knew, he was lying on the ground with Alita straddling his chest, her face scant centimetres from his and one fist cocked for a blow she had thankfully held back.

"So." Hugo swallowed hard. "Did that shake anything loose for you? Did it work?"

Alita's face softened. She drew back and climbed off him. "No," she sighed. "So *frustrating*!"

Hugo raised himself up on his elbows and looked at the remains of the obstacle course. "Well, there's nothing left to break." *Except me*, he added silently.

But he was safe. She helped him up, pulling him to his feet as if he weighed nothing (which made him think of when they'd met), and rolled back to the barrel where her pretty feet were waiting for her. Practice was over for today. Hugo couldn't have been more relieved. As he started to disconnect the left wheel-foot, a sudden thought occurred to him.

"Hey, maybe it's gotta be the real thing. I mean, maybe only a real life-or-death situation can pop up a memory for you," Hugo said. "That's what happened before, right?"

Alita nodded, her big eyes turning thoughtful and distant while Hugo wished he'd kept his big, fat mouth shut. Because he knew damned well she was going to try it, do something crazy-dangerous, just for the sake of her memory, and he'd never be able to talk her out of it. In fact, she'd probably get mad at him for not trying hard enough to kill her.

On the other hand, he thought, looking at the wreckage of the practice track he'd set up earlier that day, *I'd be a fool to bet against her.*

# CHAPTER 10

Grewishka's groans and screams were giving Chiren a headache. But then, Grewishka had been a headache even in his Motorball glory days. He'd been a major talent and a serious contender for First Champion, but he'd also been volatile, demanding, egotistical, intransigent, selfish and belligerent. It had been like wrangling a giant armoured two-year-old who had lethal weapons.

Now he was a waste of space and resources that Chiren thought should have been parted out and flushed away long ago. But somebody very important was watching his back for reasons Chiren wasn't privy to, but was obliged to accept. They were probably very good reasons to this very important person, but to her, they were absurd, like everything else in her life.

Fortunately, she was almost done with the painstaking procedure of disconnecting his cyber-core from the wreckage of his body. Grewishka had insisted that she not give him a neural block to cancel out any pain. The idea of him suffering through the operation without relief had given Chiren a sour, spiteful pleasure but it was very short-lived. Suffering seemed to be Grewishka's new passion—he did it with gusto, and he liked it entirely too much. Having to listen to Grewishka's screaming rage had become old pretty damned quickly.

Eventually, the robotic surgical arms disconnected the last of the most minute nerves and freed his core from the ruined body. It should also have put an end to any physical pain but Grewishka had not finished suffering. Hanging in the surgical frame, he looked like an oversized contorting metal worm attached to a giant human head. That was exactly what he was, Chiren thought—a human worm. But at least she could stop and take something for her headache now.

"I want to rip her in half!" Grewishka shrieked as Chiren shook two tablets out of a bottle. She paused, then added a third and swallowed them dry.

She turned around to find Vector had come in. Her head throbbed. Vector knew how she felt about him walking in on her when she was in the middle of a procedure. But it was all part of his possessiveness—he had to keep asserting ownership. He had to keep reminding her that the lab was his, the equipment was his, and she was his.

"Grewishka," Vector said, openly contemptuous. "How the mighty have fallen. You know, I had money on you in your Final Championship game. When you lost, I *lost*." He turned to Chiren. "So, are we stripping him for parts?"

Chiren hesitated, then decided that as long as Vector was here, she might as well show him. "I need you to look at something," she said as she hit PROJECT on one of the display screens and brought up a 3D graphic of Grewishka's skull. "See this?" She pointed at something small and disc-shaped at the base of his brain. "It's a telepresence chip. He's wired," she added in response to Vector's blank expression. "Someone in Zalem is riding him."

"So what?" Vector shrugged. "There are watchers behind eyes all over this town. You know that."

Chiren had never wanted to slap him as much as she did right then but she managed not to. "I'd just as soon remove it, while I'm rebuilding him."

"Why are you wasting your talent on this—this piece of burned-out street junk?" Vector gave a short, humourless laugh. "He's nothing to anyone."

"He's something to someone," Chiren said. "An important someone. It's a personal matter."

Vector drew himself up. Chiren was just a little too tall for him to loom over, but that didn't stop him from trying. "This is *business,* and personal matters have no place in business," he said in his best lecturing tone. "Stop wasting time. Grewishka's junk. Salvage what you can, scrap the rest."

Chiren turned back to Grewishka, intending to tell Vector to go assert his dominance over something else and let her finish her work, then stopped. Grewishka had gone quiet, which was a relief, but his face was calm and composed in a way she'd never seen and didn't like. His eyes were clear and strangely, disturbingly knowing as he looked past her.

"Tell me, Vector," Grewishka said in a polite tone that made the hairs on the back of Chiren's neck stand up. "Do you like your job?"

Chiren had never seen Vector so taken aback. If any of his employees had seen him this way, she thought, he'd have lost his authority over them. "Who—" He had to swallow. "Who is speaking?"

"*You know very well who it is,*" the voice that wasn't Grewishka's replied. "And if you like your position, and all the comforts, privileges and perks that come with it—" His eyes swivelled briefly to Chiren, and she hated the way he looked at her even more. "If you don't want to lose those things, you will pay attention to Dr Chiren. Business is business, but *I* say what your business is. And if *I* say something personal to *me* is *your business*, you'd do best to listen."

Vector's dark-brown skin took on a greyish quality and Chiren wondered if he were going to pass out. "Nova. I didn't realise you were—" Vector cleared his throat. "Please accept my apologies." All the arrogance had gone out of him; he sounded practically meek now. How the mighty had fallen indeed. "What is it you'd like us to do for you?"

Us? That sounded dangerously close to a willingness to share responsibility, something she'd been sure Vector was incapable of. It might have been a joke, but Vector wasn't capable of that, either.

"Grewishka is like my own son," the Watcher, Nova, said darkly. "Who did this to him?"

Vector turned pointedly to her. So much for *us*, Chiren thought, surreptitiously leaning on the desk to support herself. The thing speaking through Grewishka was making her feel nauseated.

"It was a cyborg girl—a little cyborg girl." It seemed important to Chiren that she add that detail. "These impact points—" She gestured at several different places on Grewishka's wrecked body. "To do this sort of damage would require an extraordinary amount of power. I can't fathom how that much power could be generated by such a small body."

The presence behind Grewishka's eyes gave a harsh, menacing laugh. "It was not the power of the *body* that did this. It was the *mind*. This *little cyber-girl*—" There was pure hatred in his voice. "She knows the fighting techniques of Panzer Kunst. She must be stopped. Rebuild Grewishka—make him better, stronger, more lethal. Have him bring her to me." Pause. "*Dead.*"

Grewishka's eyes lost their focus and his ugly features twisted into a grotesque mask of pain as the lower part of his core began writhing again.

"He's gone," Chiren said, almost limp with relief. She made to get back to work, thinking if Vector didn't know enough to leave, she'd tell him to get the hell out of her operating room. But, instead, he moved around in front of her.

"No, *not* gone—re-patched."

It was Vector's voice, but it wasn't. Chiren barely managed not to back away from him. The presence of the Watcher behind Vector's eyes was so much worse, so much more monstrous. She made herself stand up as straight and tall as she could and focused her gaze on the small area between his eyebrows, so Nova would think she was looking straight into his eyes without flinching.

"You're a very clever woman, Doctor, that's never been in doubt," Nova said silkily. "So I make you this offer: if and when you have pleased me, I will grant you your fondest wish—the destiny you seek."

And there it was: the one thing, the *only* thing she wanted to hear, and in so many words. *Finally.*

"Zalem," she said. "You'll send me to Zalem."

"I'm there right now," Nova said, with the easy, insouciant grandeur that was the hallmark of the powerful. "When I close my eyes down there and I open them up here, I'll step outside, go to the west viewing deck, and watch the sunset. Do you remember the sunsets here, Chiren? What it's like to see them when you're so high up that the rest of the world is already in darkness?"

Now Chiren did look directly into Nova's eyes, staring hard into the dark holes of his pupils, wanting the Watcher to feel the force of her gaze and the power of her presence. *I am here, I am real.*

"You may consider my services engaged," she said, promising everything.

Nova suddenly reached out and grabbed her by the back of her neck, bracing her so he could jam Vector's mouth over hers, thrusting Vector's tongue into her mouth in a deep, penetrating kiss that was as brutal as it was lascivious. It felt like a striking snake, vicious, uncaring, inhuman.

Finally, Nova drew back, grinning nastily. "Sealed with a *kiss*."

Disgusted, Chiren wiped the back of her hand over her bruised lips, knowing she would never be rid of the ugly taste. At the same moment, Vector's eyes fluttered and rolled back in his head. He dropped to his knees in front of her and would have toppled over sideways had she not caught his shoulders and held him up. Seeing the mix of shock and confusion on his face as he looked up at her, she could almost have pitied him. But not quite. *Welcome to my world, you bastard—this is what it's like for me every day of my life.*

"Now that you're yourself again," she said, lifting his chin to make him look at her, "would you mind telling me who—or what—I just made a deal with?"

"The Watcher behind the eyes," said Vector. He put his hands on her hips to steady himself as he got to his feet. "Pray to whatever god you believe in that we can deliver."

We. Was that a slip of the tongue, or did he really want her to think he was in this with her?

"The bigger and more powerful I make Grewishka," Chiren said, "the harder he'll be to control."

"Control?" Vector gave a short, humourless laugh. "He only needs to kill." He straightened his clothes, brushing imaginary lint off his jacket. "Get to work."

There—*that* was the Vector she knew and didn't love, Chiren thought, staring after him as he walked out and left the room empty.

Alita ran around and around the bounty kiosk, weaving in and out of the passers-by as she tried to see every screen and all the paper notices at once. Ido sighed. She had insisted on coming out with him, despite his telling her he didn't like her being out after dark, even with him. But there was no stopping her; she insisted on seeing the posted bounties for herself. If it had been up to her, she'd have dragged him to every kiosk in town.

She hadn't said what she was looking for, but he knew. After she'd made upwards of half a dozen orbits around the kiosk, he decided to put her out of her misery.

"You can forget about finding anything on Grewishka," Ido told her. "There's no bounty on him. Not tonight, not tomorrow, not next week, or in our lifetime. Or ever."

Alita's big eyes got bigger. "But you reported him to the Factory, didn't you? You told them about how he killed all those women with the other two, right?"

Ido nodded sadly, looking down at her. "Grewishka is under someone's protection. Someone important."

"Like who?" Alita demanded. "Who could be so important they'd have that kind of power?"

"Someone far beyond our reach, or the reach of anyone else in Iron City," replied Ido. "So for now, we should stay off the streets. If we lie low, we'll live longer." He put a hand on her shoulder, intending to steer her towards home, but she dug in her heels and wouldn't budge. When Alita *would not* be moved, she *could not* be moved.

"Now, Alita—" he started.

"No, listen to me, I've got a *great* idea," she said. "I want to become a Hunter-Warrior like you."

Ido winced. The way her big eyes were shining, she might have been talking about wanting to take ballet lessons. "*No*, absolutely *not*," he said, trying to be gentle but firm. "You can forget about it right now."

"But we can be a team!" she enthused. "We're *already* a team. We were a team when we—"

"You don't know anything about this," he said, trying to control his impatience. "It's dirty, dangerous work. It doesn't just scar you physically. Ending someone's life is a strike on your soul—"

Alita glared at him, her big eyes dark with anger. "Why are you always holding me back?"

Always? Ido blinked at her. Even in the midst of carnage and catastrophe, a teenage girl was a teenage girl was a teenage girl. *Why are you always holding me back from killing crazed cyborgs?* Of course, given the fact that she'd only been in his life for three days, her claim that he was always holding her back might not be so exaggerated.

"I can't allow it, and that's that," Ido said with all the parental finality he could muster and tried to usher her away from the kiosk again. But again Alita stayed put.

"And just how is that *your* decision to make?"

And here was the typical adolescent demand that parental authority stand and deliver justification for bossing the adolescent in question around. Someone brushed past Ido roughly, knocking him off balance. The same person bounced off Alita without moving her. She noticed; Ido saw her chin jut forward and lift belligerently. He knew this bit of physical superiority proved to Alita he had no business reining her in. He also knew to surreptitiously check his pockets in case the passing stranger had off-loaded some stolen chips or circuits they planned to recover later. The criminal element in Iron City was nothing if not resourceful, and that was only one of many things his little immovable girl didn't know.

"I said it's out of the question and I mean it," he told her. "Don't you remember the cracked bushings in your leg? Your body is not built to take that kind of physical stress—"

"Then make it *stronger*!" she said, as if that were the simplest thing in the world and the solution to everything. "When I'm fighting, I don't just *remember* who I was, I can *feel* who I was. Even if just for a moment."

Ido felt himself sag. "Alita, if that's the only way you can remember anything, then you're better off leaving it all forgotten." He took both her pretty hands in his and turned them palm-up. "I don't want blood on these hands, too."

Alita yanked away from him, practically shaking with rage and frustration. As Ido reached for her again, she turned and ran.

"Alita!" he called, but she had disappeared into the night.

Hugo was hanging out in front of the CAFÉ café with Tanji and the rest of his crew, talking about the upcoming Game, when his cell vibrated on his wrist. When he saw it was Alita, he grinned; Tanji gave him a sour, knowing look. The poor guy was still smarting from the spanking Alita had given him. Perhaps because Hugo hadn't stopped laughing about it. He moved away slightly to answer.

"Where are you?" Alita asked.

"I'm about to head over to the arena for tonight's game,"

he said, smiling at the sound of her voice, which made Tanji even more sour-faced.

"Can you pick me up?"

His smile got bigger and he hopped on his gyro. "Say where and I'm there."

CHAPTER 11

"…and he just wants me to be his *perfect little girl*," Alita fumed as she followed Hugo through a narrow access tunnel that led to the Motorball track.

Ever since Hugo had picked her up, she'd been venting her frustration with Ido. She'd had no idea how much she had built up in such a short period of time. Now, however, she was finally winding down. Hugo had said she'd have other, better things to think about tonight, and the distant muffled roar of thousands of people cheering and screaming seemed to promise exactly that. Her heart beat faster in anticipation.

Hugo handed her a laminated tag on a lanyard like the one he was wearing around his neck. "Here, put this on," he told her. "It gets us in anywhere."

Alita obeyed, feeling a rush of pleasure at hearing him say *us*.

"So you gonna live by his rules or yours?" Hugo added.

The question took her completely by surprise, partly

because she hadn't really been sure he'd been listening to everything she said. "Whose rules do *you* live by?" she asked, honestly curious.

"Nobody's."

The sheer defiant independence of his answer made Alita catch her breath in admiration. *Nobody's.* That one little word contained a whole world of freedom. *Nobody* could force him to do anything. *Nobody* could hold him back. *Nobody* could touch him—except her, because she had a pass like his that would get them in anywhere, and together they were *us*.

She was still marvelling about it when they came up to a tough-looking guy wearing a black t-shirt that said SECURITY on the front in big, danger-yellow letters. Alita watched how Hugo flashed his pass at the man and flashed hers the exact same way, so the SECURITY guy would know where they could get in—anywhere—and whose rules they lived by—*nobody's*.

"I have a small crew," Hugo was saying, "and we only deal in high-end parts." He had to raise his voice to make himself heard over the crowd noise, which was getting louder and louder. "Low overhead, high profit—it's the only way."

Alita nodded, trotting happily along beside him. Low overhead, high profit, and nobody's rules—it was the only way. Easy to remember, too.

The tunnel sloped upwards and then opened out into the enormous, brightly lit stadium where a game was already in progress. There had to be tens of thousands of people, all screaming for their favourite players while an announcer who sounded as if he were in the throes of delirium called the action.

Alita turned around and around, trying to see everything at once. Hugo caught her hand and led her away from the tunnel to a passageway beside the track, which was bordered by a low concrete barrier topped with ten-foot-high plastic shields. Scratches and marks high up on the plastic showed where players had hit hard.

"It takes time to build a name for yourself in this business," Hugo said, yelling now. "Like me, for example—I built a reputation for getting the real hard-to-find stuff. Now people know if there's something they're having trouble getting hold of, I'm the guy to call." Alita could hear the pride in his voice and she felt proud, too. Low overhead, high profit, hard-to-find stuff, and nobody's rules; she'd never learn things like this from Ido.

Hugo stopped and pointed at a knot of heavily armoured cyborg Paladins far up the track, approaching at high speed. As they screamed past, a player in red-and-black armour with knife-like blades running the length of both arms suddenly leaped up and delivered a powerful spin-kick to a player covered in shiny chrome like the knights Alita had seen in one of the books in her bedroom. The shiny chrome Paladin skidded across the track and crashed into the barrier directly in front of her. Alita jerked back, startled but thrilled. A second later, a third player in bright crimson flew over both of them, landing safely out of reach. That Paladin was a woman, Alita realised, watching her zoom away. Women were Paladins! She'd already known that, but actually seeing a fully armoured woman on wheels made her heart soar. *Hello, sister!*

She felt Hugo's lips close to her ear: "Welcome to Motorball."

Alita smiled, thinking it was more like, *Welcome home.*

"And *what* a *combination!*" the announcer raved over fifteen thousand screaming fans. "A double-spin kick from Ajakutty sends Claymore into the boards while Crimson Wind leaves them both eating her dust—*and here comes Jashugan!*"

Hugo grinned as the giant screens switched briefly to Jashugan's bodycam to give the crowd a Paladin's-eye view of the track. The stadium crowd was a blur as Jashugan skated into and then out of a steeply banked turn; there was a slight, rhythmic side-to-side motion as he pushed himself to go faster, followed by a brief shot of the Motorball in his possession before the point of view returned to track-side.

Alita had her face pressed to the plastic shield, her big eyes fixed on the action. Hugo couldn't help laughing a little. The last time he'd seen that look on a girl's face, she'd been falling in love. But this girl—well, he'd already figured she wasn't like anyone else he'd ever known, especially when it came to her talent for Motorball. She was absolutely smitten with the game now.

Hugo was about to suggest they move along when something massive flew through the air above them, high enough to clear the shields but close enough for them to feel a breeze in their hair, and landed on a Paladin right in front of them. Damn, Hugo thought, the girl was some kind of action magnet. Things happened around her.

"…and Kinuba hops the pit wall and lands right on number seven, Takie, who goes down hard!" the announcer rhapsodised. "You gotta know *that* one's not in the playbook!"

Kinuba—*that* figured. Hugo watched the one-time champion—not Final, but Kinuba acted like he was— raise his arms to acknowledge the crowd while skating backwards at a hundred miles an hour. Kinuba was a good player and definitely a contender for Final Champion, but the one thing he did better than anyone else was show off.

Hugo nudged Alita and pointed at the giant screen where Ajakutty had just roared out of a banked turn and was now coming up fast on Kinuba, pumping his arms as if he were cutting through the air with the blades. Ajakutty wasn't superstar material—not yet, at least— and he had a smaller following than most of the Paladins. Hugo had never been that interested in the guy himself, but if he made Kinuba eat track, it would be a big boost for Ajakutty and one hell of a comedown for Kinuba— something Hugo would definitely enjoy seeing. From the way the fans were screaming as Ajakutty gained on Kinuba, a lot of them felt the same.

Just as Ajakutty got within metres of him, Kinuba swivelled around to skate backwards and pointed a finger at the other Paladin.

What the hell was that supposed to be, Hugo wondered. Ajakutty looked as taken aback by the gesture. A second later, Kinuba's finger flew out from his hand towards Ajakutty, trailing a long writhing metal coil.

Ajakutty reared back, trying to slow down and get out of range, but he was going too fast. The bullwhip sliced through his armour, chopping his legs out from under him, then cutting through them again below the knees. Ajakutty went down in a spray of bright-blue cyber-blood mixed with a small amount of red heart's-blood. Hugo felt like gagging. Up on the big screen, one of the crowd cams caught a few fans actually fainting. Well, it wasn't a *real* party until somebody passed out.

The steely whip whistled viciously, like it was slicing through the air itself as Kinuba's finger snapped back into place on his hand. Ajakutty's feet rolled on for a few metres and then, as if finally realising there was no point in going on without the rest of him, toppled over. The crowd reached a new level of frenzy.

"...the Champion Kinuba went through Ajakutty like a red-hot blade through a butter-ball with that newly acquired grind-cutter. And that was only one, folks, the man's got four more!" sang the announcer, transported by such innovative violence. "Somebody tell me, *is that even legal?*"

The passageway was starting to get crowded as pit crews ran to meet their Paladins or to fetch parts for quick repair. "C'mon," Hugo said, pulling Alita away from the barrier. "I know all the pit crews and Tuners. I'll introduce you around. If you're gonna play Motorball, you gotta know these guys. They can save your career, even your life. For *real*."

Hugo towed Alita farther along the pit lane while she

kept straining to look back, until they came to another SECURITY guy. Mel was big and scary-looking and he usually had only one facial expression—stone-cold killer—but he actually raised his eyebrows when he saw Alita. Hugo grinned at him but only received his stone-cold killer face. Good old Mel.

Hugo gave Alita a quick explanation of how the pits were organised and how each team had service bays facing onto the pit lane. Paladins always had the right of way on the pit lanes, so you move aside when you see one coming towards you.

Alita's big eyes got even bigger as she took in all the furious activity. She made Hugo stop briefly so she could watch Ajakutty's and Claymore's respective crews swarming over them. The din of power tools and hydraulics actually drowned out most of the crowd noise. She seemed enthralled by how quickly the crews could swap out parts and even whole limbs.

"So, who's the best player?" she asked.

"Well, the best player *ever* was Grewishka," Hugo said and was surprised by her reaction. She seemed startled when there was no reason why she should have been; she didn't know anything about Motorball, so she couldn't have heard of him. Unless Ido had told her something, and, given the doc's feelings about the game, that didn't seem too likely.

"Grewishka had a pretty wild story," Hugo said. "He spent his whole childhood underground—like, actually under the streets, in the sewers and stuff. Somebody found him—don't ask me who or how, nobody knows.

But they gave him all the best training and they built him up to be Final Champion, the best Paladin ever."

"But that's not how it went," Alita said, sounding thoughtful.

Hugo paused, remembering. He'd wanted to feel sorry for Grewishka, but he'd never been able to find any sympathy for someone who'd been given everything he needed to succeed—money, a place to live, training, opportunities—and blown it all. "Grewishka burned out and went bad. Got himself banned from the Game. They even scrapped his number."

He pulled Alita to one side so she wouldn't get trampled by Jashugan's pit crew as they ran to meet him. A moment later, the Paladin himself rolled past going the other way while his crew buzzed around him with scanners and other gadgets, checking him for damage.

"Wow," Alita breathed, staring after Jashugan with an expression of utter hero-worship that didn't make Hugo feel at all jealous. Besides, he couldn't really blame her. He'd seen Jashugan up close thousands of times and he still found the guy impressive.

"Right now, I'd say that guy—Jashugan—has the best chance of becoming First Champion," Hugo said. "You know, he runs some of my parts. A lot of my parts, in fact." He couldn't tell if she were impressed or not, but then, it was hard to impress anyone when Jashugan was in the vicinity.

Hugo and Alita followed Jashugan and his crew to their service bay and watched as they strapped him into a maintenance frame so the techies could open him up. The Paladin seemed completely at rest under their ministrations.

They removed his helmet to reveal a face composed and calm, with grey eyes fixed on some faraway place or thing that only he could see. Everyone said the best Paladins, the real contenders, were those who could find a still place among the chaos of the game, instead of letting themselves be seduced by the high life, with the booze and drugs and all the other pleasures until they woke up one day with no nerves, no reflexes and no pit crew because they'd moved on to someone without permanent damage.

"What's a Final Champion?" Alita asked.

"It's the highest, biggest, best honour a Motorball Paladin can get," said Hugo. "Every few years, when there are enough really good players to make it worth it, they have these play-offs. Last one standing is Final Champion, and they get to go to Zalem."

Hugo decided they should move on before Alita got too entranced. He took her past several other service bays, introducing her to the various techies, Tuners, and bosses who waved, called out or high-fived him as they went. Now she did look impressed, and he realised that he very much wanted to impress her, wanted her to think he was important around here and not just some dumb guy who hung out at the Motorball track pretending to be special.

He was about to remind Alita about his reputation for getting hard-to-find stuff when he saw she was staring at something with a weird look on her face. He followed her gaze to a tall, dark-haired woman in one of the bays just ahead of them. She had a fancy-looking servo in one hand and was giving somebody hell on her head-set.

"Twenty-two needs to pit *right now*!" she said angrily.

"Unless you really *like* losing? Is that what you really like—losing? No? Then get him in here *now*!"

Then she looked up and saw Hugo and Alita. To his surprise, her expression mirrored Alita's. It was almost like Chiren recognised her, but Hugo knew that couldn't be right. Abruptly, she turned away to talk to the expensively dressed dark-skinned man who was overseeing all the activity from a seat behind the service bay. Or maybe it was a throne.

"The guy over there? That's Vector," Hugo told Alita. "He pretty much runs Motorball. Everybody's supposed to think it's run by the Factory Commission, but it's really Vector calling the shots—who skates, who doesn't, which teams play which, and when, and who's a serious contender and who's washed up. Me and my crew, we do a lot of business with him and the teams he owns personally, getting all the best parts for his new Tuner."

"Chiren," Alita said, nodding. "I know her."

Hugo's jaw dropped. For once, he couldn't think of a single thing to say.

"Hey," she said, her big eyes twinkling with amusement at his reaction, "you're not the only one around here who's *connected*, you know."

Damn, he thought as they continued along the pit lane. How the hell was he supposed to impress her now?

Chiren watched the two of them move on, then turned back to what she was doing. On a nearby screen, Kinuba emerged from another messy pile-up intact and relatively unscathed, except for a few scorch marks on his armour. He was holding the Motorball high over his head, and the crowd's screams were especially loud because another Paladin's detached, smoking hand was still stuck in the finger-holes. God, the guy just never stopped showing off.

Vector gave her a tap on the shoulder that wasn't quite hard enough to be a physical blow and shoved a palm-sized display under her nose. "Look at this," he ordered her. "It's Kinuba. He's too strong with that new weapon and it's screwing up the odds. Bets are in the toilet."

As if that were *her* problem, she thought, annoyed. Betting was his turf, tech was hers. "Well, did you talk to him?"

"Of course I talked to him," he said, almost snapping at her. Almost; he made a point of never losing his cool unless he was behind closed doors. "The prick refused to take a fall, even for a twelve-game guarantee."

"Those grind-cutters *are* pretty remarkable," Chiren replied. "I'd like to have something like that for our, uh, other project."

An approving smile spread slowly across Vector's face. He really hadn't thought of that himself, Chiren realised, hiding her amazement. Vector, the big boss, in charge of everything, Mr Big. It made her wonder how he'd managed to stay on top for as long as he had.

Oh, right—he had her.

Vector grabbed a pit boss by the arm as he was going past and pointed at the kid with the big-eyed girl. "Hey, what's the name of that kid who runs the parts crew? You know, the one that gets all the hard-to-find stuff?"

The boss looked. "That's Hugo. Don't know who he's got with him but she's cute."

"Yeah, real cute," Vector said, smiling as he sat down again. "Thanks."

That magic time of the evening arrived, the golden hour when a portion of the crowd were no longer satisfied with watching violence and had to cut loose themselves. Several times Hugo pulled Alita off the pit lane so she wouldn't get caught up in any fistfights or run over by crazed fans trying to climb onto the track. But not because he was afraid she'd get hurt—he doubted even a cranked-up giant had much of a chance against her.

"So how do you like the Game?" he asked her.

Her answering grin was practically feral. Alita had heard the call of the wild and she couldn't wait to answer. "I *like* it," she said.

Before Hugo could say anything else, Tanji appeared beside him with the rest of the crew. "Call came in from a VIP," he told Hugo. "We gotta go."

That only meant one thing and it wasn't *Let's go out for a beer.* "Sorry, Alita," Hugo said. "Can you get home okay?"

"Yeah. Sure." The girl was trying not to look too disappointed, but those eyes said it all. She'd never be able to hide her feelings, Hugo thought, which wasn't a good thing in Iron City.

Behind him, Tanji made an impatient throat-clearing noise to let Hugo know he was keeping them waiting, which meant he was keeping the VIP waiting, and that was no way to do business. Still, Hugo hesitated; he had to think of something or those big sad eyes were going to be in his head all night.

"Hey, can you go out tomorrow?" he asked her. "I want to show you a place me and Tanji know." He glanced at Tanji with a smile, as if Tanji weren't trying to blow up his head with a death-ray glare. "It's out in the Badlands. I think it might even help with your memory."

Alita's face lit up and Hugo felt everything in the world glow. "I'd appreciate that. Thanks." She caught his arm as he started to leave and added, "For *everything*."

For a moment her radiant smile had him rooted to the spot, and he wished he could stay just a little bit longer. But he'd pushed it to the limit with Tanji, and now even the rest of the crew were antsy. Hugo hopped the rail between the pit lane and the front row of seats to join the crew already following Tanji to the access tunnel. But he couldn't resist taking one quick look back.

Alita had her face pressed up against one of the shields again. In profile, she looked oddly serious, like she thought Motorball might be the answer to all the questions in her mind.

CHAPTER 12

There were three main kinds of drinking establishments in Iron City: joints, dives and hell-holes. The Kansas Bar was definitely behind door number three. But it wasn't just *any* hell-hole—it was a Hunter-Warrior hell-hole.

The owner had long ago resigned himself to the fact that bounty hunters had made his place their turf; this meant, among other things, they called the shots as to who could drink with them. Usually these were either attractive companions who were partial to the company of Hunter-Warriors without insisting on commitment, breakfast or being remembered from one night to the next, or Paladins, mainly because a lot of Hunter-Warriors had been Paladins themselves. Only a few of them were like Dyson Ido, who was welcome everywhere.

In general, the Kansas Bar's core clientele preferred to drink with winners, like Paladins who had won at least half a dozen games in a year. The number wasn't an absolute cut-off but it served as a guide. Having winners on the premises raised everyone's property values; losers were ejected as quickly as possible before they stank up the joint with failure.

Kinuba had earned his way into the Kansas Bar many times over. He was not only a champion, but a Hunter-Warrior favourite. There were a lot of advantages to being a Hunter-Warrior favourite. For one thing, he couldn't remember the last time he'd bought his own drinks; in the Kansas Bar, that was really saying something. The Hunter-Warriors who drank there could afford to be generous but they weren't charitable. If one of them bought you a drink, you deserved it.

And for another thing, he could walk out with the three best-looking ladies and nobody would shoot him in the face. Well, not unless he tried poaching a lady from someone who already had her attention, and Kinuba had never been *that* drunk or crazy. Kinuba had *standards*, dammit. Sadly, not everyone did.

That was the way of the world, though, and he knew he shouldn't have been surprised whenever he met someone without standards. But somehow he always was, mostly because the slimeballs would show up in places where they shouldn't be.

Like that son of a bitch, Vector. He ran the whole damned Motorball Game *and* had a whole stable of Paladins playing on teams he owned. The guy had to have money falling out of every hole in his body, out of his friggin' *pores* even, and still he didn't think he was rich enough. Vector had actually asked him to take a dive just so he could get better odds.

Kinuba had thought it was a bad joke at first. When

he'd realised his mistake, he'd had a strong urge to use the grind-cutters on Vector and then skate around the track with his head on a pike. His pit crew had actually strapped him down, telling him he wouldn't live long enough to make it around the track once, and neither would they. The pit boss told him to channel his anger into winning and, as stupid as that sounded, it had worked. He'd won three straight games since Vector had come to him with his slimy offer, and each win was sweeter than the last. The next one would be sweeter still. He was going to keep on winning—he didn't need Vector to give him a twelve-game guarantee; he could get those twelve games all on his own. He'd win all of those, too, and each time he did, Vector could go home to his fancy Factory penthouse and cry himself to sleep. While Kinuba celebrated with the prettiest ladies on the premises.

Tonight he needed three—two just to hold him up on either side while he carried the third over his shoulder. Fortunately, these ladies were pretty *and* strong; they were doing pretty well at keeping him upright. Of course, he was in his street body now, not his game body. The street body was nowhere near as heavy, although he still had his grind-cutter hand. That stayed on twenty-four seven so he'd always know where it was. And he wouldn't have to disappoint any pretty ladies who asked him to demonstrate how it worked.

As they staggered out of the Kansas Bar into the street, Kinuba decided that the real problem wasn't all the booze he'd poured down his throat. It was the third lady over his shoulder who was throwing his balance off. He should have taken four ladies—a lady on each shoulder would have stabilised him.

But it wasn't too late. They were still right in front of the bar; he could just go back inside. Maybe he could avoid any misunderstandings if he made it clear to number four that she was strictly for ballast.

He was still thinking it over when something hit the ground in front of him with a crash and the pavement burst into flames.

"What the hell?" he roared as the ladies screamed and ran, even the one over his shoulder. Well, that was ladies for you—fire scared the spit out of them unless they were Paladins, so they'd have been no help to him anyway. Kinuba staggered around in a small circle, looking for some part of the street that wasn't on fire. When this happened on the track, it was usually because some idiot didn't know how to secure their fuel line. But he wasn't on the track and he wasn't an idiot—drunk as a punk in a trunk, but not stupid enough to roll with his fuel line exposed.

But he wasn't rolling, he was on the street and he wasn't carrying a fuel supply. Kinuba tried to think. He was—he was—

He was in deep shit, he realised as a net dropped over his head and shoulders. Two gyro riders circled him, wrapping the net around him. Their faces were covered by goggles and bandannas, making them look like cyborg bugs on wheels. *Little* cyborg bugs—these were *kids*.

"You little bastards, I'll kill you!" he yelled and gave the net a hard yank. Said little bastards went flying off their gyros. Not into the flames—those were already dying down—but they'd get a good case of road rash.

Unfortunately, the movement threw him even more off balance. He swayed and staggered, flailing his arms as he tried to fling the net off and stay upright. Then the ground rushed up on his left and he met it with a crash of metal loud enough momentarily to drown out his slurred curses.

Didn't *anyone* hear that? he wondered as he struggled to get himself up on his hands and knees. It must have sounded like a truck crashing into a building. That kind of noise should have had every Centurian in town heading straight for this very spot. What the hell was wrong with them? Why wasn't there ever a Centurian around when you really needed one?

As Kinuba pushed himself up to his knees, he caught sight of two more cyborg-bug gyro riders holding what looked like spears. He had a second to think how unfair it was for a champion like him to be so well and truly screwed before lightning struck him in the back of the neck.

Every nerve in his body exploded with pain. His arms and legs stiffened and flailed, his torso jerked and twisted, as if every part of him were trying to rip itself free. All five grind-cutters flew out from his hand to twist and turn wildly on the pavement, as if they were trying to escape. He tried to call them back, but his mind was too full of pain and lightning that went on and on and on, until he lay on the ground, breathless and dizzy and unable to feel anything below his neck.

"You bastards," he panted, staring up at the black sky. Somewhere behind him, he heard the sound of a truck pulling up. "You bastard jackers, you're dead!" he told them. "Do you hear me? You're all dead!"

He was still cursing them as they hooked him up to a cable. It dragged him backwards along the street, up a short ramp and into the back of the truck; the grind-cutters trailed after him for a few seconds before he heard them snap back into his hand. Three more little cyborg-bug bastards strapped him down.

"Who owns this city?" yelled one of them suddenly.

"We do!" the rest of them replied and shut the door.

They ignored his promises of long, painful deaths for all of them as the truck lurched forward and accelerated. Little bastards couldn't even drive a truck right, Kinuba thought. He was going to kill them all *twice*.

Separating a cyber-core from a Total Replacement cyborg body was a painstaking procedure for a cyber-surgeon; for the average jacker, however, it was just a big pain. Doing it in a hurry was hard, and the job wasn't made any easier when the person being disconnected wouldn't stop bitching about it.

Putting them to sleep, or even sedating them, would have made everything easier but it never worked. Jacking sent their adrenaline into overdrive and they just wouldn't *shut the hell up*.

A lot of jackers started out kind of squeamish. They didn't want to jack a whole cyborg body. But, really, who did? Times being what they were—i.e., desperate—

even the most well-intentioned would eventually find themselves backed into a corner. If your pockets were empty enough and your cupboard was bare enough, you'd do whatever you had to do.

One jacking was usually enough to give even the most tender-hearted first-timer a massive case of compassion fatigue. The way the person in the cyber-core yelled and hollered, anyone would have thought they were getting killed instead of jacked, when nothing could have been further from the truth. Total Replacement cyborgs were set up so their cores could survive for days without a body. They'd go into standby mode, which was sort of like a coma, until the Factory Prefects picked them up. Jackers weren't savages—they *always* called the Prefects to let them know there was a cyber-core lying around loose. The Prefects put the cores on life support until they could get a new body. And, yeah, it wasn't exactly anyone's idea of fun, but it wasn't murder. It wasn't even painful.

Besides, it wasn't like most of these Total Replacement cyborgs couldn't afford another body. Like Kinuba, for example—he was a Motorball champion and he was loaded from tonight's win. What he saved just from everyone always buying him drinks was probably enough for top-of-the-line hardware. So what if he missed a few games? He'd come back with a TR body a hundred times better than the old one. So the jackers were actually doing him a favour.

Not that *he'd* ever see it that way, of course. Even after he got all tooled up in a better body, he'd still piss and moan about big, bad jackers stripping him for parts. Kinuba had been almost too drunk to walk but it had taken four of these so-called big, bad jackers just to get him off his feet and another three to strap him down in the truck after he was paralysed.

Rich people were such big babies, and Kinuba was one of the biggest. All rough and tough on the Motorball track, but get him out on the street and he was practically crying for his mommy.

The still-masked jackers were hard at work when headlights appeared at the other end of the alley. The car rolled slowly towards them, lighting up the open back of the truck. They all stopped, waiting for a sign that would tell them whether to bail or stay. Their goggles glowed with reflected light.

The car came to a stop and two men got out. They were silhouettes in the headlights but their outlines were familiar. One was tall and neat in a bespoke suit, the other had the enhanced build and ready posture of a professional bodyguard.

One jacker straightened up and motioned for the others to keep working. He jumped down from the van and went to meet the men, raising his goggles and pulling down the bandanna covering the lower half of his face.

"Nice work, Hugo," said Vector. His tone was approving, even warm, but his expression as he watched what was going on in the van was more sneer than smile. "My compliments to your crew."

"Thank you, sir. I'll pass that on." Hugo winced, thinking he sounded like some Factory suck-up hoping to make employee of the month.

Vector seemed to find his answer amusing. His bodyguard passed him a thick package, which he handed to Hugo. Credit chips; from the weight, it felt like enough for everyone with a little bonus on top. Hugo felt awkward as he stuffed the chips in his jacket pocket and covered it by pretending he had to check on how his crew was progressing with Kinuba's chop.

"Hey." Tanji detached himself from the crew and crouched at the open door. "When you gonna tell your little hardbody you jack cyborgs for a living?"

"I'm not," Hugo growled at him. "And neither are you, if you know what's good for you."

Tanji shook his head. "What I know is, hardbodies are only good for one thing. And so do you; you're the one who told me that." He jerked his head at the bulge in Hugo's jacket. "And while I'm at it, where's *my* cut?"

Kinuba's cursing suddenly became louder. The crew had finished separating his cyber-core from his body and it took three of them to heave him out the back of the van. Kinuba roared with anger as his core hit the street and rolled. Hugo automatically pulled down his goggles and replaced his bandanna. The last thing he needed was a pissed-off Paladin coming after him for payback in a new, improved body.

"Get the body over to Chiren right now," Vector ordered. "Use the service gate."

Hugo frowned. Vector wasn't masked so he probably didn't think it mattered if he used Chiren's name. At least he hadn't used Hugo's. And Vector was so powerful, he probably figured he didn't really have to care that Kinuba could identify him. Still, Kinuba was pretty popular, enough that Motorball fans might not take it too well when they found out Vector was behind his jacking.

Unless Vector was going to pay Kinuba off to keep his mouth shut. Vector could afford it. The pay-off was Vector's speciality. Kinuba would probably give him a lot of grief but eventually Vector would find a number he liked. And Kinuba still wouldn't have to use any of it to buy his own drinks. Hugo was pretty sure that was how Vector would play this.

He realised Vector was staring at him expectantly. He nodded at Kinuba's cyber-core. "What about him?"

"Don't worry, I'll have my people tip off the Prefects," Vector replied. "He'll be fine, they'll pick him up and take care of him. Now will you get the hell out of here already?"

I don't believe you, Hugo thought, looking into Vector's face. But that was stupid—Vector wouldn't lie to him, not to *him*. Not about *this*. Vector hadn't got to where he was now by lying to people he did business with and double-crossing them. When you lived outside the law, your word had to be your bond. Everybody knew that.

It still didn't smell right to Hugo, but there was nothing he could do. It wasn't like he could take his jacked merchandise elsewhere.

He slammed the van door shut and banged on it twice. "Let's go," he yelled. The van sped off and he followed on his gyro.

As soon as they were gone, Vector strolled over to what was left of Kinuba and crouched down to make sure Kinuba got a good look at his face.

"Vector, you *prick*!" Kinuba snarled. "I should have known you were behind this."

"No," Vector said with a small laugh, "what you *should* have known, my friend, is that no one—*no one*—is greater than the Game."

He reached for something beyond Kinuba's range of vision, then held it up for him to see. It was nothing special, a plain old arc-cutting torch, the kind used by every pit crew in the Game.

For a couple of seconds, Vector let himself enjoy the expression on Kinuba's face as it dawned on him what was going to happen next.

Then he turned the torch on and showed him.

CHAPTER 13

Passage into and out of Iron City was strictly regulated. Nobody came or went without being accounted for. It was a matter of keeping track of numbers—so many in, so many out—and detecting the presence of hazardous or illegal materials. This didn't require much processing power, which made it ideal for Centurians. The single determination they had to make was a mere yes or no, and only yes required them to do anything: open fire.

Centurians didn't engage in conversations, so the law-abiding had only a minimal delay, while those attempting to smuggle in banned goods could not argue or make excuses, allowing contraband to be confiscated promptly. There was no bureaucracy, no justice system so badly backed up with pending actions that the Factory had to waste resources providing free food, clothing and shelter to criminals when the same things could be sold to people in Iron City at a profit. The savings in time and money were substantial.

Plus, the Factory handled all data so no one ever had to fill out forms. In fact, no one in Iron City had any idea what paperwork was. Iron City itself had come into existence not long after the arduous era of bureaucracy characterised by forms and paperwork.

While the Factory hadn't really set out to make life simple and uncomplicated for people at ground level, it had just worked out that way. Of course, while most of them weren't idiots, none of them understood the nature of their existence well enough to be as appreciative as they could have been. But that wasn't the Factory's problem. People could complain to the weather for all the good it would do them; they had no direct access to the Factory except in the persons of deckmen or Prefects. Or Centurians.

The only thing left over from the tail end of a less efficient, more complicated era was the Hydrowall and the Victory Gate. These were actually a single thing in two parts, originally built as a war memorial. The Victory Gate had been made to commemorate Zalem's remaining aloft after all the other sky cities had fallen. The Hydrowall was a sort of fountain, but much fancier and more ambitious than the old-fashioned devices that dribbled and spat water into the air.

The designer had intended for people to walk through a tunnel of continuously running water that would lead them to the giant, shiny metal Victory Gate, which was supposed to elicit feelings of pride and contentment. Unfortunately, assumptions of victory had been slightly premature. The gate had been badly damaged in the final attack, during the War that no one knew very much about any more. The Factory had restored it and made it into something useful, an actual gate that allowed people to enter and leave under supervision.

The Hydrowall was left as it was. People liked it, and the white noise of rushing water kept people calm while they waited in line to be approved for either entry or egress without any additional action on the Factory's part. Very handy.

Hugo had definitely been right about the Hydrowall, Alita thought. It really was amazing, and the noise was kind of pleasant and soothing. But after you'd been stuck in a long line waiting to get out of Iron City, it wasn't so much amazing as it was boring. And noisy.

Although she couldn't say she really minded sitting next to Hugo in the front seat while he drove.

In the backseat, Koyomi seemed to have dozed off while Tanji was wide awake and as sour-faced as ever. He was still mad at Alita for what she'd done to him playing Motorball. Well, he should have expected payback. Anyway, the boy sure could hold a grudge.

Alita shifted position, while trying not to appear impatient or restless. It really was great being with Hugo and she was so happy they were going to spend the whole day together. But they weren't even inching forward—it was more like millimetring. At this rate, it might take them half the day just to get out of the gate. She'd really been hoping they'd be doing something a lot more fun with their time than waiting in a queue for Centurians to decide not to shoot them.

"Oh, look," Tanji said. "It's the iron fist of Iron City. Everybody tremble before your masters."

Hugo shushed him as a Centurian plodded towards them. Alita could feel him tense up, which made her tense, too. He'd said there wouldn't be any problem and she'd been sure he was telling the truth, so why was he nervous? She had been surprised when he picked her up in the van; she'd thought they'd be going on gyro-wheels. And the van was big—*really* big. Where had Hugo got it, she wondered, and why would he ever need anything so enormous?

But she'd kept all her questions to herself, figuring she could ask him about it later. But what if the Centurian thought it was strange that they had such a big truck for only four people? What if it decided they must be up to something illegal? Would it confiscate the truck and then shoot them? Or would it shoot them first?

By the time the Centurian reached them, Alita barely dared to breathe. It stuck its brutal machine head through Hugo's window and scanned them.

A hundred years later, it pulled its head back. "MOVE ALONG," it ordered them in an expressionless, mechanical voice and stomped away to investigate the vehicle behind them.

Alita felt everyone relax a little as Hugo shifted the van into drive. But it wasn't until they were in the shadowy tunnel of the Hydrowall with water thundering on either side that everyone really calmed down.

"They always make me nervous," Hugo said, giving

her a smile. "Even though getting out is really pretty easy. They don't give a crap what people do in the Badlands."

Hugo steered the van up an entrance ramp and onto the open highway, where unlike Iron City, the traffic was non-existent.

"Welcome to the land of the free," Hugo said cheerfully.

"'Land of the free'—that's a good one," said Tanji. But his tone wasn't so much sarcastic as it was wistful.

Alita couldn't help goggling at the acres and acres of cultivated land on either side of the highway. It stretched for as far as she could see in all directions and there were no people anywhere, only an occasional spidery machine raising clouds of dirt and dust as it harvested crops or planted more in long furrows in the soil. The dust clouds made her think of the impact of her boots on the lunar surface.

"So," she said, turning away from the passenger side window she'd been leaning over for almost half an hour. "Who started the War anyway?"

Tanji did a sort of double take, so surprised he forgot to look disgusted, but Koyomi took the question in her stride.

"I don't think anyone remembers what the fight was about, or even who won," she told Alita. "But Factory schools don't teach you *squat*."

"'Cause they don't want us knowing anything," Hugo added.

Alita frowned. This didn't sound quite right. Someone

had to remember everything. Although Hugo was probably right about the Factory not wanting people to know much. If the Factory would protect a murderer like Grewishka, there was no telling what else they were hiding, or how far they'd go to keep their secrets.

For the next hour, they talked about the War on and off. Cultivated land had given way to fields of tall grass and weeds. Here and there along the roadside were remnants of things Koyomi said were "guard rails". Alita thought they must not have been very good guards—all that was left of them were stubs of damaged concrete, some with bits of wire sticking out of the side. Had the guards covered them, Alita wondered? And what did they do with the rails? The road and the land were more or less even, without any sharp drops.

Koyomi told her about how the road they were on had been part of a system that started at the shore of the eastern sea and spread out over the land like an enormous spider web, all the way to the western ocean.

"If there *is* a western ocean," Tanji put in. "Personally, I don't think there is."

"Oh, here we go," Koyomi said, rolling her eyes.

"Why don't you think there's a western ocean?" Alita asked Tanji.

"Because there's land and there's water—one of each. The land's in one place and the water's in the other. The so-called 'western ocean'"—Tanji made air quotes—"is just the other side of the eastern ocean."

Alita frowned, remembering how the Earth had looked in her memory of battle. "That's not how it works."

Tanji gave a short laugh as Koyomi launched into a lecture about continents and oceans, speaking so quickly that Alita had trouble keeping up with her.

"Don't mind them," Hugo said to her as Tanji began to argue. "Tanji only says that stuff because he knows it makes her crazy. The schools in Iron City suck but I never heard anything *that* stupid."

Alita thought again of the Earth as she had seen it. "I hope not."

The fields began to alternate with wooded areas before finally giving way to them altogether. The air took on an aroma that Alita could only describe as *greeny.*

"Everything out here is wild and overgrown," Koyomi said when she remarked on it. "No one takes care of these places, although the Factory sends people out every so often to take samples and readings."

"What for?" Alita asked.

"So they can measure how contaminated the soil and the trees and plants are," Koyomi said. "They can't reclaim the land till all the poisons have broken down. It's because of the War. Nobody lives out here—"

"That's not true," Tanji said. "A few people do. But they aren't anyone you'd want to meet. They lived off the land, hunted and planted crops, and now they're all deformed and mutated. Biological warfare ruined the world."

"The *whole* world?" Alita asked, appalled.

Tanji and Koyomi nodded in unison. "You think people

would stay in Iron City if there was anywhere else to go?" Tanji asked.

"Truth," Koyomi assured Alita.

They had been driving for almost two hours when Hugo turned off the highway and onto a narrow dirt road that took them deeper into the forest.

"It's gonna get bumpy," Hugo told Alita unnecessarily as the truck bounced and swayed.

"It's easier on gyros," said Tanji. "But somebody seems to think we might find something big that's worth bringing back."

"You never know," Koyomi said with a slightly sassy tone in her voice.

"Oh, here we go," Tanji said and rolled his eyes as Koyomi winked at Alita. "But then, what can you expect from someone who believes there's a western ocean? Someday they'll announce the Earth is flat and her head'll blow up."

"If the Earth were flat, you'd have already tripped and fallen over the edge," Koyomi said, sassier now.

"This is it," Hugo announced, bringing the truck to a stop and killing the motor. "This is as far as we can drive. Gotta walk the rest of the way."

They all got out and Alita stretched, glad to be out of the confines of the truck. She heard a cry and looked up to see a hawk circling above the trees.

"It's *free* out here," she said with a happy sigh.

"Yeah," Hugo said.

"It can be dangerous, too," said Tanji. Alita saw he had something in his sleeve like a metal rod; it had slipped down so he was holding the end in his hand. "Stay alert."

Koyomi rolled her eyes as Hugo motioned for them to follow him into the woods.

"All we know for sure," Hugo said as they made their way up a steep incline in the rainforest, "is the Enemy launched one last attack with every ship they had and it caused all the sky cities to fall in one night. All except Zalem."

For the last hour, conversation had been made a bit more difficult by the sheer effort of getting through the densely overgrown forest. Well, it was more difficult for Hugo, Koyomi and Tanji. Alita tried to be considerate, but she was dying to know what they knew, even if it wasn't very much. She wanted to compare it to what Ido had told her. He seemed to have left out or glossed over some things.

"Who was this Enemy anyway?" Alita asked as she held a clutch of branches back for Koyomi.

"The *Urm*," Tanji said in a spooky voice, as if he were saying *the bogeyman.*

"United Republics of Mars," Koyomi said, giving Tanji a look. She paused to catch her breath. "You know—U-R-M, Urm."

"Yeah, I get it," Alita said. Why hadn't Ido mentioned Urm, she wondered. He had to know about them.

"On the last night of the War," Hugo continued,

grabbing at branches to pull himself the last few feet up to the top of the slope, "they say the earth shook and the sky itself caught fire. They *say*." He glanced over his shoulder to smile at Alita. "But the next morning, the sun rose and Zalem was still there, still flying." Standing at the top of the incline, he pointed. "What I want to show you is just up ahead."

Alita took giant climbing steps, like when she went upstairs three at a time, and made it to the top beside Hugo. And then she caught her breath sharply, staring at the sight laid out before her.

The lake was at least half a mile across, fed by a turbulent waterfall on the right-hand edge. But it wasn't a naturally occurring lake—it was actually a crater that had been gouged out of the earth by an unbelievably massive object. The land had reclaimed itself; overgrowth and weather erosion had hidden or smoothed over a lot of the old scars, though some of the blasted and broken rock was still visible.

But it was the unbelievably massive object itself that dominated the scene. The spacecraft sat partially submerged in the centre of the lake, its hull badly damaged. Chunks had been blown out, showing a skeletal framework within. Now it was succumbing to Nature's final insults of rust and corrosion. But it hadn't fallen completely into ruin—here and there Alita saw a few shiny spots.

"This ship is from the Battle of Zalem, the last battle," Hugo told her. "I thought if you saw something actually from the War, maybe it would help trigger your memory.

And it would be safer than—well, you know, the other way."

Alita barely heard him; she was already making her way down the slope towards the lake.

Hugo showed Alita how part of the ship was close enough to the shore that they could walk on it all the way out to the main part of the wreck. Before he could show her the best route, though, she was halfway to the centre, more sure-footed than any of them on the wet metal.

"Salvagers have picked plenty off the bones over the years," Hugo said when he finally caught up with her. "Mostly metal." He pointed at the numerous small gaps and holes. "But because it's all Urm tech, they left most of it alone. People don't wanna mess with stuff when they don't know what'll happen."

"This is really an Urm ship?" Alita asked, wide-eyed.

Tanji gave a sarcastic laugh. "Pretty hard to sell crap when nobody knows if it's gonna blow up in their faces or—"

Alita shushed him. In her peripheral vision, she saw him roll his eyes and make a face at Hugo, but she didn't care. She could hear something, or rather, she could *almost* hear something—it faded in and out at the very edge of audible. It was special and rare and so much more important than how condescending Tanji looked right now.

But it was no good. No matter how hard she tried, the sound eluded her.

Alita looked the wreck over carefully, measuring with her eyes, trying to estimate its true dimensions. "We need to get to the command deck," she said after a bit and pointed at the section in the middle of the lake. "It's forward. There."

"How does she know?" Koyomi asked just as Tanji said, "What does she mean, *we*?"

Alita saw Hugo motion for both of them to be quiet, and she smiled to herself. She moved farther along the hull, all the way to the point at which it sank below the water.

"Aw, can't get there because it's underwater," Tanji said. "What a shame. Oh well. So what should we do next? I vote no to swimming."

Still smiling, Alita stepped off the hull, plunging feet first into the dark water. She dropped in slow motion, though not as slowly as she had on the moon. Ribbony aquatic plants below her leaned back, rippling, disturbed by the water she had displaced.

Alita looked down at her pointed toes. As she touched bottom, swirls of mud blossomed and swirled around her feet. She took a moment to orient herself in the murky water. Looking up, she could just make out the edge of the hull and a vague shadow that was probably Hugo looking for her.

Don't worry, Hugo—I'll be back.

She lowered her gaze. The part of the spacecraft that was underwater was festooned with patches of moss, mostly green, but some with gold overtones, others with bits of red. Or maybe that was rust.

Alita took a few long, slogging steps, stirring up more muddy clouds, until she reached the hull. The spacecraft was stuck deeply into the earth—getting it out wouldn't be easy. That was probably why the Factory hadn't already dug it out for their own purposes. And like Hugo had said, nobody wanted to fool with something when they didn't know if it would blow up in their face. Which meant the Factory didn't have a clue either. Good to know, she thought, as she put her hand on the hull just above an irregular green patch of moss.

The sound she hadn't quite been able to hear jumped into her hand and ran all through her like an electric current. It was talking to her, telling her it had been waiting such a long time for her to find it and there was so much to tell her.

Keeping her hand on the hull, Alita began plodding towards the command centre, every step raising billows of mud from the soft lake bottom. Not quite like on the moon—there was no one to fight here and this place was anything but lifeless. Still, she had a feeling of déjà-vu. Maybe that was the ship.

Hugo looked from the time on his wrist cell to the spot where Alita had vanished into the water and back again, aware he'd done almost nothing else for so long that the sun had moved and the shadows had begun to stretch. The girl was practically invincible on land, but there was nothing about her that suggested she could breathe underwater.

"How long do you think she can hold her breath?" Hugo asked Koyomi and Tanji.

Koyomi was pacing back and forth looking worried. Tanji only shrugged, looking bored.

Hugo looked at the time again. If anything happened to Alita, Ido would kill him. But that wasn't really what he was so worried about.

The sound-sensation led her into a place of complete darkness but she kept moving, trusting the feeling under her hand. After a while, the sound-sensation changed and somehow she knew she had to swim upward. Barely a minute later, she broke the surface somewhere inside the spacecraft. The call was much clearer now but everything was still pitch black.

Alita felt around until she found a surface that seemed solid and stable enough to take her weight. The moment she boosted herself up out of the water, her surroundings lit up with a soft violet glow. She was in some kind of antechamber. Pushing her wet hair back from her face, she stood up; the surface remained stable under her without buckling or moving. She looked around until she spotted an open doorway and moved towards it.

The light grew brighter as she went, still trailing one hand along a curved, rust-covered wall. She was curious but at the same time oddly comfortable. This strange place didn't *feel* like a strange place, but she had no idea why.

As she stepped through the doorway, the hum that had been calling to her intensified into a deep, choral thrumming. This was the flight control room, which meant the skeletal remains in the half-dozen seats had been the flight crew. Their uniforms had rotted away and their bones were covered with various kinds of moulds that flourished in the tropical humidity.

The crew had been mostly biological with only a few cyborg enhancements, rather than TRs like herself. Alita found that a bit surprising—she'd have thought everyone on a warship would be a Total Replacement cyborg as a matter of course. Maybe there hadn't been time to give them new bodies, she thought as she stood over the lead pilot's chair. The eye sockets in the skull lying on the rotted cushion had been enlarged to accommodate sight enhancements. Whatever they had been, however, were gone. With one finger, she rolled the skull over; a neat, egg-shaped hole at the back of the skull showed where something had been added to the visual cortex. It, too, was missing. Had someone come in and helped themselves to some tech they later discovered they couldn't understand? Or had the crew somehow destroyed all of it themselves when they'd realised they weren't going to make it?

Alita let go of the skull; it rolled back to its original position, staring up at her with its too-big eye sockets. *Have we met?* she asked it silently. *Were you in the black sky above me on the moon?*

The thrumming wanted her to keep moving. But to where, she wondered, looking around. There was no other open doorway. The purplish light grew a little brighter and she spotted a large, sealed metal blast door.

With a last glance at the flight crew, she went to the door and felt the thrumming intensify even more. While she stood in front of it, wondering what to do, she saw her hand move of its own accord and slide open a cover plate at chest height, revealing a thick handle. Maybe it was the humming that guided her hand, Alita thought as she twisted the handle a hundred and eighty degrees. A motor somewhere in the door came to life with a long, drawn-out noise that went from rumble to whine, as if it were dragging itself out of standby to activation.

Rusty metal made shrill complaints as the door slid open to her left. This was it, she thought as a brighter, purple glow spilled out and flowed over her. Whatever was calling her was right here.

As soon as she stepped inside, however, her eager anticipation turned to bafflement. Most of the space was taken up by an enormous mirrored sphere, leaving very little room for anything else, including herself. The sphere was actually too big for the room—the top passed through the ceiling and the bottom penetrated the floor. Weird, but also incredibly beautiful. The surface sparkled with flashes of purple light as some kind of energy danced on it. Or within it?

After a second or two, she realised the light was sparkling in rhythm with the thrumming. So were her nerves—every part of her, in fact, was vibrating in time with whatever was inside that sphere. Careful but unafraid, she pressed her hand to the surface. Light danced around her hand and sent long flickering threads out from each point of contact. It tingled in a lovely way, as if it welcomed her touch, but she could get no sense of what the sphere was made of, whether it was cloth or plastic or metal or even if it might be alive.

Alita closed her eyes and immediately had a sense of

the sparkling brightness flowing around her and through her. After a moment, she reached out and put her other hand on the wall. Her eyes were still closed but she felt the keypad take form under her fingers, which knew what to do. They danced over the keys in a precise, perfect pattern that felt sensible, agreeable, irrevocably correct.

Because sense memory stays in the core and moves with it from body to body. Thus there is no need to relearn motions from one incarnation to the next. The cyborg embodies an answer and a challenge to what was once referred to as "The Hard Problem". Consciousness is, in fact, always embodied in the cyber-core and easily adapts to inhabit any corporeal—

Oh, not now, *professor. I've got my hands full with—*

The words evaporated from Alita's mind as she opened her eyes. At the same moment, the sphere flickered, then collapsed in on itself.

She jumped, startled but unafraid as she looked around. The part of the room that had been contained in the sphere was shiny, polished, completely untouched by damp, rust, or corrosion. It was as if no time had passed here at all, she marvelled.

No, not *as if*—it *was* the case that no time had passed here. Was this the same kind of time field Ido said she had entered when time had stopped for her? The difference between the parts of the room that had been outside the wall and the parts that had been inside was dramatic—the rust and dirt ended sharply at a curved line of demarcation.

Urm technology. She wished with all her heart that Ido could have been there with her so he could see it, too. Except she was pretty sure he'd have tried to stop her from going inside in the first place. Still, she wished he could have seen it all, especially the thing in the centre of the room, the thing that had been calling and calling and calling until it had finally brought her here.

The cyborg body hanging on the rack was a work of art, but not in the same way as the body Ido had given her. That body had come directly out of Ido's heart, a labour of love and now a memorial to the daughter he had lost. But as lovely and loving a gift as it was, it would always be a body meant for someone else, for Ido's perfect little girl.

This body in front of her was a magnificent instrument: strong, steadfast, resolute, made to withstand, to defend and protect. It wasn't pretty with flowers and leaves. Its beauty was fierce and powerful.

Its perfect fluid lines were androgynous; it could adapt as male or female or non-binary. This alone was tech far ahead of anything in Iron City.

Alita moved closer and reached out to touch it.

A blue-white arc of energy leaped from the body to her fingers, not a shock but a connection, a link. In the next moment, she heard the body exhale long and slow, and somehow understood it was acknowledging they were now bonded. It had waited patiently for such a long time and at last she had come. Now they would belong to each other for as long as they both existed.

Hugo had insisted they all go back to wait on the shore so Koyomi could pace without risk of falling into the water.

Now, as the sun was getting lower in the sky, Hugo was becoming less certain that Alita was all right. She had just jumped into the water, taking it for granted that she wouldn't drown. How could she possibly know that? He didn't think she'd ever been in water before. Hell, he didn't even know if she'd been out in the rain. What if she shorted out? Or mud got inside and gummed up her works. Or—

Tanji suddenly elbowed him hard in the ribs and pointed. Hugo jumped up from the rock he'd been sitting on with Tanji and stared open-mouthed as Alita walked out of the lake, carrying what looked like a headless body in her arms.

"That can*not* be good," Tanji said to Koyomi. She ignored him and ran to meet Alita with Hugo. After a moment, Tanji followed, although he was certain anything that came out of a wrecked Urm spaceship had to be bad, especially if it looked like a headless corpse.

"You heard me: no. I won't do it," Ido said without taking his eyes off the complicated figures on the screen in front of him. "Should I spell it out for you? N-O. No. So you might as well forget it."

"But you *have* to!" Alita insisted with the desperation that a fourteen-year-old is especially adept at. "This would help us fight Grewishka and anyone else that comes after us!"

Ido looked over his shoulder at the cyborg body on the operating table. Alita had been fluttering around it like a butterfly since she'd brought it in. Now she had the right arm raised and was flexing it at the elbow, checking the range of motion. It didn't take a cyber-surgeon to sense the power contained in the body. He turned back to the screen before Alita caught him looking.

"This body has the strength I need," Alita declared. "Also the speed, the flexibility and the endurance. And I'm *connected* to it—it's *mine.* We're bonded for life. This could be who I am, who I've always been."

Ido sighed and swivelled around in his chair to face her. "Alita, you've been given a chance to start over with a clean slate," he said heavily. "Do you know how many people get that chance? Almost none. None that I've ever heard of, certainly."

"I don't want to start over when I can't remember how I started out in the first place," she said. "And the slate can't be all *that* clean if I could wake up an Urm warship. You got any thoughts on why that would happen?"

Ido got up, intending to leave the room, but Alita swung a gurney in front of him to block his way.

"I *knew* that ship." She looked into his eyes as if she were trying to hold him there by sheer force of will. "I've been in ships like that before, haven't I? *Haven't I?*"

Ido leaned on the gurney, suddenly overwhelmed by fatigue. He felt as if every day of his life had been a little heavier than the one before it, and now he was barely able to stand up under the accumulated weight.

"Whatever you *were*," he said, "it's not who you are *now.*"

Alita moved back to the cyborg body on the table. The body was breathing slowly and deeply. She laid both her hands on it. Ido had a sudden absurd mental image of her making it levitate like a magician. *Presenting the flying cyborg body of Iron City. Like the flying city of Zalem, but in humanoid form.*

He wished he'd been there with her in the Urm spacecraft when she had reached out her hand, just so he could have pulled it away or even knocked her down before the arc of connecting energy could jump from it to her. He wasn't sure what would have happened if the body had sent out a connecting arc of energy and there'd been nothing to receive it. Probably it would have just hung there and gone on waiting, taking shallow little breaths, unbonded, permanently out of action.

Or maybe the arc would have found her. It might have gone right to her, homed in on her, and she'd be even angrier at him.

"Alita," Ido started.

"This is an Urm warrior body," she said, talking over him, "and I activated it when I touched it. Which must mean *I'm* a warrior. And *you knew*. You've *always* known."

Ido dropped his gaze to the floor. Why couldn't Hugo have taken her anywhere else? Fourteen-year-old girls were supposed to come home from a day out with a bouquet of wild flowers or a handful of shiny stones, not a lethal cyborg body.

A loud crash of metal made him jump. Alita had smashed both fists down on the edge of the table, leaving deep dents. Those weren't going to buff out.

"It's a Berserker," he heard himself say. "A Berserker is a humanoid weapon system created by the Urm

Technarchy. Your cortex was designed to interface with this type of body." Ido moved to her and touched her temple gently. "Your identity code activated it."

Alita's face lit up as if this were the best thing she'd ever heard.

"The instinctive fighting technique you use is called Panzer Kunst," he continued. "It's a lost combat art specifically for machine bodies, and used almost exclusively by Berserkers. This is why you're drawn to conflict without hesitation and without fear. It's how you were trained."

She was flexing her hands as she listened. Ido wasn't sure if she knew she was doing it or if it was a training reflex.

"You're not just a Berserker, Alita," Ido told her, wishing he could shut himself up. "You're an *Urm* Berserker—the most advanced cyborg weapon ever created."

This bit of information seemed to startle her a little. Perhaps finding out she was someone else's weapon would give her reason for pause.

"And *that*," he added, "is why I will *never* unite you with that body."

They stood facing each other in the lab for some unmeasured amount of time. He tried to will her to understand he had made this decision because no human being should be weaponised and made into a killing machine, especially not a fourteen-year-old girl. Even if she was, in fact, over three hundred years old.

Alita set her jaw. "Fine."

Ido's heart sank as she whirled around and fled into the night.

CHAPTER 14

The enormous Factory doors rumbled open the same way they had the first time Alita had come here with Ido. That night, he'd been mad at her. He'd made her stay outside while he went in, despite the fact that if it hadn't been for her, he wouldn't have been able to collect any bounties. In fact, if it hadn't been for her, he wouldn't have been able to do *anything*—he'd have been a splattered mess on the street with three homicidal cyborgs picking over his bones. With one of them making earrings out of his eyeballs.

But did he appreciate it? Hell, no! She'd saved his life and he'd showed his gratitude by forcing her to live a lie, to be someone she wasn't, refusing to let her discover her identity.

Well, tonight *she* was absolutely furious with *him*, and she was taking charge of her life—*her* life. She was calling the shots now, and if Ido tried to make her be his perfect little flower-covered darling, she'd tell him whose rules she lived by: *nobody's.*

Alita strode between the gargantuan doors. (If they tried to close on her, she would shatter them with *one blow* from her open hand.) Her footsteps echoed in the cavernous entry hall; she liked the sound.

Centurians were lined up along the walls on either side of her, and she could sense they were tracking her as she went. Ready to open fire if she did something against the rules. Alita gave them a sidelong glower. *You know whose rules I live by?* Nobody's. *What are you gonna do about it, you walking junk-piles?*

She stared hard at the platform ahead of her. Maybe she'd find out there was a rule against what she wanted to do. Well, too bad—if the Centurians even *tried* to get in her way, she was going to send them all to walking-junk-pile heaven. Her footsteps were even louder when she reached the platform and stomped up the few steps to the counter. She rested her elbows on it, pretending it wasn't just a little too high for her to do so easily. A couple of seconds went by. What the hell, she thought, was the night shift asleep on the job? There wasn't even a switch or a button to press for service, just a trashcan behind the counter.

Abruptly the trashcan spun around, and Alita found herself looking at a weird cartoony cat face. "State your business," the trashcan ordered her in a voice that was somehow both cartoony and mechanical. The Factory used *trashcans* for receptionists? Was this place for real?

"I'm here to register as a Hunter-Warrior," she told it. "Any questions?"

"Name?" asked the trashcan.

She came out and found Hugo sitting right where she'd left him, at the top of the steps. Just like she'd done with Ido, she remembered, and then pushed the memory away; it wasn't the same at all, not even slightly.

"Well? How did it go?" he asked. "Did they give you any crap?"

Alita scowled for a second, then broke into a broad, triumphant grin as she held up her new ID badge. She let Hugo take a close look at her photo and ID number before she put it away.

"Congratulations," Hugo said. "You're an official Hunter-Warrior. But man, is the doc gonna be pissed. He's gonna lose it bad."

Just like that, she was scowling again. "He can be pissed and lose it all he wants," she said. "Whose rules do I live by?" She gave him a look, one eyebrow raised, then she stumped down the steps and Hugo followed.

In Hugo's experience, Hunter-Warriors came in two varieties: a) big; and b) big and drunk. The two who came staggering out of the Kansas Bar were definitely the latter. They stumbled around in a small circle, which made Hugo think uncomfortably of Kinuba, before they finally zigzagged up the street, barely managing to keep each other upright. Hugo hoped that might make Alita think twice about her current life plans, but no such luck. She reached for the door handle like she was a Kansas Bar regular.

"Hold up a minute!" Hugo caught her arm. "Are you sure about this? This is a bounty-hunter joint—"

Alita shoved her new ID in his face. "What do you think this is, a shopping list? Besides, everybody in there must *hate* Grewishka. I just know it!"

Hugo felt something brush his leg and looked down. The little stray dog Alita had saved from the Centurians in the marketplace was dancing around their feet, tongue lolling and tail wagging in doggy delight.

"Hey, I know you!" Alita stopped to pet him and scratch behind his ears while he licked her face. Hugo shook his head slightly. Ali was about to go into the toughest Hunter-Warrior bar in town, but first she had to let a dog wash her face. Could the night get any more surreal?

When the stray had been thoroughly petted and scratched, Alita stood up. "Okay, just watch my back in there," she said and went inside. Hugo was about to follow when the dog cut in front of him.

"Oh, boy. She was talking to *me*," he told the dog, and then wondered if that was true.

The fun was already in full swing, Hugo saw. They entered just as Zapan slammed another hunter down onto a table, which collapsed into splinters. Somehow Zapan still managed to look like he was posing, in case someone was taking pictures or making a video.

"Dammit, Zapan," yelled the barkeep, his sweaty round face red and irate. "You know the rules: you gotta break something, break each other—*not* my furniture!"

Zapan turned to look at the man. Behind him, the hunter he'd just body-slammed got to his feet. Without looking at him, Zapan drove his elbow into the guy's face; he dropped like a stone.

"And we're done," Zapan announced cheerfully. He was posing in the centre of the room like he was waiting for applause, Hugo thought. The guy was a hell of a hunter but entirely too in love with himself. He wondered why Zapan hunted at all, given the enormous risk of getting hit in the face; plastic surgery wasn't cheap. Zapan could obviously afford it, though. It looked like he'd upgraded his cheekbones *again* in the last couple of days.

Abruptly, he realised that Zapan's gaze had fallen on Alita. The hunter dusted himself off and ran a hand through the narrow strip of hair on the top of his head, and swaggered over to her. He actually thought he was oozing charm when, in fact, he was just oozing. Hugo leaned against a column, waiting to see how this portion of the Zapan Show would play out.

"And what brings such a pretty lady like yourself to this fine establishment?" Zapan smarmed. "Did you come to see some real live Hunter-Warriors up close and in the flesh? Close enough that you can actually touch them?" He offered her his arm. "Go ahead, feel free. And freely."

Instead Alita showed him her ID badge. Zapan stared at it incredulously for a couple of seconds, then snatched it out of her grasp and held it up high, laughing. "You guys ain't gonna believe this," he said, "but Cupcake here? She's a *bounty-hunter*!"

The whole room, including the barkeep, stared at him in silence. A young girl claiming to be a Hunter-Warrior was something none of them had ever seen before. Hugo could feel in his bones that this was going to end badly; he just didn't know how badly or who would get the worst of it.

Zapan turned back to Alita and bent down, putting his hands on his knees as if he were talking to a child. "So you took that cute little behind of yours down to the Factory and told a deckman what you wanted. Say, did you get the one that looks like a kitty-cat or the sad clown?"

"I thought it was a trashcan," Alita murmured.

Zapan didn't hear her. "And now you've got your very own official ID, which means *you're* just like *us*!"

Hugo's glower deepened as he gave his right arm a little shake. The compact paralyser bolt he kept up his sleeve for emergencies slid down into his cupped hand. *Give me a reason*, he told Zapan silently as the Hunter-Warrior made a big deal of presenting Alita to the room, talking in the exaggerated voice of a game-show host. *Just* one *reason.*

"Allow me to introduce some of your professional colleagues!" Zapan was saying as he made an expansive gesture at a very wide, very grim-faced Asian man sitting alone at a table. He was completely organic, dressed like a Samurai, and busy emptying the bottle in front of him shot by shot, his dark eyes and scarred face inviting the rest of the world to go to hell.

"Here we have Master Clive Lee, he of the White-Hot Palm!" Zapan enthused. "With over two hundred confirmed kills—"

"Two hundred and seven," Master Clive Lee said in a low, dangerous voice.

"Two hundred *and seven*! I stand *corrected*!" Zapan made a deep, apologetic bow and turned Alita towards a different table.

"Over here, we have the one and only McTeague, Dogmaster Supreme, with his infamous yet notorious Hellhounds!"

McTeague was grizzled and even more fierce-looking, not a Total Replacement cyborg but definitely more metal than flesh. The dogs lying on the floor around him were about half and half; they were the size of mastiffs, and they all got to their feet with a warning growl as soon as Zapan took a step in their direction.

Zapan immediately moved back, putting his hands up. "McTeague's only problem is having enough left of his prey so he can collect the bounty." He laughed as if this were hilarious.

Hugo had forgotten about the little stray organic dog until it ran over to the Hellhounds and started bouncing around like it wanted to play. Horrified, Hugo closed his eyes, not wanting to see what came next. But instead of the ghastly sounds of a canine massacre, he heard slurping noises. He opened his eyes; one of the Hellhounds was running its enormous tongue all over the little stray while the dog wriggled in ecstasy.

Then McTeague reached down, picked the little guy up, and put him on his lap. "Who wants to be a Hellhound?"

McTeague asked him, his gravelly voice full of tenderness. "*You* wanna be a Hellhound, dontcha? Yeah, you do."

Hugo blinked, wondering if he were about to wake up.

Zapan seemed to be just as nonplussed at the sight of McTeague ruffling the stray's fur affectionately. He turned Alita around to face him. "And of course, there's *me*!" He struck a pose that was supposed to be heroic. "I am Zapan, the ultimate Hunter-Warrior, chosen as the keeper of—" He drew his sword with a sweeping gesture. "—the Damascus Blade!"

Zapan whipped the sword through the air in a series of complex patterns before holding the cutting edge up in front of Alita at eye level, so she could marvel at the full effect of its otherworldly iridescence. Despite everything, Hugo couldn't help being impressed himself. The blade looked like a supernatural blend of diamonds and steel.

"Honed to a monomolecular edge, it slices armour like butter," Zapan said in a melodramatic tone. "Forged before the Fall by the lost arts of Urm metallurgy—"

"Oh, really?" Alita sounded bored, but Hugo knew her ears had pricked up as soon as Zapan mentioned Urm. "So who'd you kill for it?"

Zapan peered over the top of the blade at her and didn't like what he saw. He sheathed the sword and put his arm around her shoulders in sham camaraderie. Hugo started calculating how many seconds he'd need to get behind Zapan and plant the paralyser in the back of his neck.

"Cupcake, you're a cutie," Zapan said. "But a Hunter-Warrior is a solitary predator—a lone wolf, if you will. No offence!" he added as the Hellhounds growled again.

"What this means for you is, every time you go out for a kill, you're competing with us—*all* of us. Do you see what you're up against here?"

Much to Hugo's delight, Alita shrugged his arm off as if it were nothing and stepped away from him.

"Listen to me," she said to the room at large. "I came here because I want your help. We have a common enemy. You know who I mean: Grewishka. Once he was a Paladin, a champion, even a contender to be Final Champion. Even now, everyone says he's the best there ever was. But he blew every chance he was given. He's not a champion any more—now he's a thief and a murderer. He murders women and he steals from Hunter-Warriors—from *you*. He takes your weapons and he uses them to kill people!"

She turned back to Zapan. "Do you want to lose your sword to him? Or you—" she looked at McTeague. "Do you want him to take your Hellhounds?"

McTeague looked uncomfortable but he didn't say anything. No one did. The place had never been so quiet while it was still open, Hugo thought. Most of them were actually *listening* to her.

"Grewishka's being protected by the system," Alita went on, her expression serious. "He can go on rampaging, killing, doing anything he wants, and nobody's even trying to stop him. Now he's after Ido—and me." She turned in a slow circle, looking at all of them, and Hugo noticed more than one had trouble meeting her gaze. "So I've come to you, my Hunter-Warrior brothers, to ask you to help me. If we band together, we can take him down and get rid of him once and for all."

Zapan gave it two seconds before he stepped up beside her. "No takers? What a surprise. A shock, even! Too bad, Cupcake." He put his arm around her shoulders again and Hugo felt another surge of white-hot rage.

"Look, sweetheart, I wouldn't normally take a rookie under my wing and give them the benefit of my vast knowledge and experience and wisdom. But your story is so touching that for you, I'll make an exception." Zapan gave Alita's shoulders a little squeeze. "All you have to do is cut meat-boy over there loose—" He jerked his over-chiselled chin at Hugo, who had begun to vibrate with fury. "And let me buy you a drink or two and we'll see where the night takes us? How does that sound?"

Hugo thought it sounded like someone really needed a paralyser in the back of the neck.

"Hey, watch it," he said in a warning tone and took a step forward, intending to stick the slime ball like a pig and see where the night took him then. But Alita made a small gesture at him with one hand—*back off*—and he stayed put. But only for now, he told himself. The paralyser's charge was good for another eighteen hours; he could wait.

Alita turned to Zapan and gave him a long look of appraisal, up and down, that took in the various designs carved into his steel body. "That's really some offer," she said finally. "But what could *I* possibly learn from some jumped-up, loudmouth pretty-boy who obviously spends all of his money on his *face*?"

There was a moment of shocked silence. Then everyone in the bar burst out laughing. Even McTeague's

Hellhounds were laughing. Guys Hugo had never seen crack a smile, hunters he'd thought were too scarred to change expression, were pounding their fists on tables or stamping their feet. Cyborgs were bent double, holding their middles and howling. Hugo was laughing pretty hard himself until he caught sight of Zapan's face. His jumped-up, loudmouth, pretty boy features were twisted with rage. He was so angry he actually forgot to pose.

Hugo's heart started to pound. Alita had really done it now. A guy like Zapan didn't let anyone get away with humiliating him, not even a cupcake. *Especially* not a cupcake.

When the room finally quieted down enough so Zapan could make himself heard, he loomed over Alita and said, "Maybe I oughta rip out your pretty little arms and legs and kick your head around the block a few times. Teach you some manners."

"Better not. You might mess up your hair," Alita retorted, and stuck out her tongue at him.

And there went Zapan's last nerve, Hugo thought as the Hunter-Warrior lunged. Alita sidestepped him effortlessly. Moving in a manner that appeared casual, she grabbed his arm, twisted it up behind him, and struck him hard in the middle of his back with her open palm. Zapan crashed into the pillar Hugo had been leaning against. Hugo stepped away just in time, sneaking a look at Master Clive White-Hot Palm Lee to see if he was taking notes; he should have been.

Zapan whirled, heart's-blood dripping from a gash in his no-longer-perfect forehead, and whipped out his sword. Alita ducked his wild swing and popped up close enough to give Zapan two more hard blows with her open palm. The first knocked the sword out of his hand, the second landed squarely on his nose. Before Zapan could holler with pain, Alita leaped into the air with a dancer's grace and thrust one leg out in a kick that sent Zapan flying across the room to land on the floor like a pile of dirty laundry.

Alita used her toe to flip the Damascus Blade up into her hand and hurled it at the far wall, where it stuck. "You don't deserve such a magnificent weapon," she told Zapan, marching across the room and looking down on him as if from a great height before she turned her attention back to the rest of the bar.

"I heard you guys were supposed to be the 'heroes of Iron City'. *Heroes.*" She spat the word. "That's not what *I'd* call you—*any* of you."

Oh, God, no, Hugo thought and was on her in two giant steps. "Okay, I think that's enough excitement for tonight," he said, trying to pull Alita towards the door. "We'll just be going now—"

Alita shook him off. "*Real* life and death, remember?" she said in a low voice. "I need you to stand way back."

Hugo gave ground until he felt a wall behind him. He had a feeling that wasn't going to be far enough.

"Listen up!" Alita shouted, openly angry. "I'll take on anyone in this room—*anyone*! If I win, you agree to fight alongside me. Deal?" She waited a beat. "Okay, who's first?"

On the floor, Zapan sat up with one hand cupped over his face. "Bitch broke my nose," he whined.

"Buy a new one," Alita said without bothering to look

at him. She took a running leap and landed on top of a table where half a dozen Hunter-Warriors were nursing beers. "*Heroes*," she jeered, looking down at them. "There aren't any heroes in this dump. All I see are junkyard punks, assorted cyber-trash, and Motorball burnouts too slow to cut it against *real* Paladins."

And there went everyone else's last nerve, Hugo thought, watching the room explode as a lot of very pissed-off Hunter-Warriors decided to let their inner homicidal maniac come out and kick her ass. Two of the guys at the table lunged for Alita; she stepped back and stomped hard on the edge, flipping the tabletop up like a coin. Beer mugs went flying; a few well-aimed kicks and punches sent them into the faces of Alita's nearest attackers.

Hunters at the edge of the room were getting up now, Hugo saw. Guys who never let themselves get drawn into anybody else's drama were leaving drinks unfinished, wanting to get a piece of the upstart who had dared to impugn what few shreds of honour they had left. Or thought they had left.

But they weren't going to do any better than Zapan, Hugo thought, watching them lumber towards the centre of the room where all comers were getting their asses handed to them. Because in this fight, size *wasn't* an advantage, something none of these guys were used to. They were powerful but not agile, tough but not fast, set in their ways instead of adaptable, while Alita was all those things and more, not to mention sober. It was easy for her to evade their wild swings and clumsy lunges, knocking them down before they even knew where she was. Two hulking Hunters thought they had her trapped between them; she did one of her dancer-style leaps, as strong as it was graceful, and they smashed into each other, knocking themselves out.

Hugo looked over at the barkeep, who was also the owner. He was watching the free-for-all with a look of sad resignation on his saggy face. There probably wouldn't be much furniture left after this. Hugo felt a sudden rush of pity for the man, then frowned. That wasn't much like him at all.

A chair suddenly flew towards the bar. The barkeep ducked in time but the chair hit the liquor shelf, breaking every bottle. The barkeep popped up again, drenched in booze and decorated with bits of broken glass in his hair.

"Aw, son of a *bitch*!" the barkeep said miserably and disappeared behind the bar again.

Ido ran all the way from the clinic, Rocket Hammer in hand, hoping what he'd heard about the fight in the Kansas Bar had been exaggerated. People always exaggerated bar fights, blowing everything out of proportion.

Like saying a pretty young girl had started it. Ido was sure that pretty young girls had been the catalyst for lots of bar fights. But in all the bar fight stories he'd heard over the years, none of them had involved a pretty young girl offering to beat up every guy in the place and then throwing the first punch. That had to be totally made up—maybe some muscle-head's fantasy of being a slave to a pretty young dominatrix.

And for all he knew, the whole thing might be over by the time he got there. The Kansas Bar's owner, fed up with having to buy new furniture all the time, had said anyone who started trouble would be thrown out.

Ido made himself stay hopeful all the way from the clinic. But just as he reached the bar, the front window exploded outwards and two cyborgs landed on the sidewalk. Probably not what the owner had meant by "thrown out", Ido thought. Stepping around one of the cyborgs, he edged up to the broken window to have a look, then ducked as a third cyborg came hurtling out, flying all the way across the street to land on the opposite sidewalk.

"Oh, dear God, no," Ido moaned and rushed inside.

The whole place was in chaos. The first thing he saw clearly was Hugo using a paralyser bolt on a Hunter who'd been about to swing a chair at Alita. Alita herself was oblivious; she was busy giving two Hunters the kind of beating that would have scarred normal people for life.

Ido shoved Hugo aside and waded in, prying fighters apart with the shaft of the Rocket Hammer and yelling for them to stop. Several turned to him with raised fists but backed down immediately when they saw who he was. Ido struggled through the room until he reached the bar and climbed on top of it.

"Knock it off *right now*," he bellowed, "or *no more free repairs*!"

Everything stopped as if someone had flipped a switch. For a second, the only thing Ido could hear was Alita breathing just a bit heavily from all the exertion.

She stood in the centre of the room in a fighter's stance: knees slightly bent, arms up with her hands ready to protect her face and her shoulders down. Her shiny black hair was slightly mussed but otherwise she seemed none the worse for wear. Ido glared at her, then at everyone else. When he was sure they all understood the party was over, he climbed down off the bar.

Hugo sidled up to him, holding the paralyser bolt. "I'm with her," he said to a nearby cyborg with a chair-leg in one hand. "And him, too," he added, nodding at Ido.

There was a discordant chorus of grunts and groans as hunters began pulling themselves together, getting up to look around for lost weapons, armour, clothing and anything else that had gone missing during the period of temporary insanity that had swept over them. "Hey, anybody seen my arm?" a battered cyborg asked plaintively as he plodded past Ido. "It's a long metal thing with a hinge in the middle and a hand on one end."

"Try retracing your steps, Cronie," someone called to him.

"Where'd you last see it?" asked someone else.

"Someone was hittin' me with it," the cyborg muttered and plodded away to keep looking.

Ido turned to Alita. She was no longer looking for a fight but, to Ido's dismay, she didn't seem even faintly sorry about all the trouble she'd caused, not to mention all the damage. Ido turned to look at the owner, who was now leaning on the bar and watching the night limp to an abysmally unprofitable conclusion.

"I'm so sorry," Ido told him.

The owner wasn't impressed. Ido looked around and

found a chair lying on its side but miraculously intact. He righted it and pushed it up to a table. The owner was still underwhelmed. Ido couldn't blame him.

"You and I are going to have a little talk," Ido said to Alita, taking her arm.

Alita shrugged him off. "We *had* our talk. You left me no choice."

Before Ido could argue, there was a deafening *clang!* of something announcing itself with metal striking metal, followed by an explosion that blew the front door to fragments.

"Why, God? Why?" moaned the barkeep softly.

The creature that came through the ragged hole of the entrance was bigger than any cyborg in the place. Every part of its metal body was deliberately exaggerated, overdone, intentionally monstrous. The metal itself had a brutal look, as if the body were made of parts taken from weapons by someone who had wanted to build something that would be the antithesis of humanity.

The face, however, was very familiar, and not just to him. Every Motorball fan in Iron City would have recognised that face. It was older, a lot more scarred, and quite a bit uglier than the last time Ido had seen it, which was somewhat remarkable, considering that had only been a few days ago.

"Grewishka!" said a Hunter in a shocked tone. "Damn, that's *Grewishka*!"

"Yeah, but what the hell happened to him?" the Hunter beside him said.

Grewishka pointed at the second Hunter-Warrior. "To

answer your question—" His finger zoomed out from his hand, trailing a long metal coil. It whistled through the air, flying around the Hunter too quickly for the eye to follow, then snapped back to Grewishka's hand.

The second Hunter-Warrior's face went from amazed to confused. A moment later, his body came apart, the pieces making nauseating wet sounds as they slid away from each other and fell to the floor.

"I've had a little upgrade," Grewishka said conversationally.

Ido was lost for words. Out of the corner of his eye, he saw all the blood had drained out of Hugo's face; the kid seemed to be on the verge of passing out. Poor little bad boy, Ido thought; he'd probably told himself he was a black-market badass, unaware of how black things could get or how evil people could be.

And, as if fate or karma needed to remind him of the same thing, Chiren stepped out from behind the monster, looking antiseptically and frostily beautiful, and quite proud of her upgraded toy.

"Impressive, isn't he?" she said, giving the monster an admiring, practically worshipful, look.

"My God, Chiren," Ido breathed. "What have you done?"

"Let's find out, shall we?" she said brightly, as if this were just a funny little game, no more innocuous than Motorball.

Grewishka took a step forward, and then another, his angry eyes fixed on Alita. "I only want the girl," he said in a gravelly purr.

"'S far as I'm concerned, she's yours," said a very nasal voice. Everyone turned to look at Zapan, still holding his ruined nose.

Ido switched on the Rocket Hammer. Hugo produced a fire-bottle. He stood beside Ido with his head up and his shoulders back, but he was still extraordinarily pale. Poor kid was obviously scared out of his mind. Ido looked around at the rest of the Hunter-Warriors, or at least those who hadn't sneaked out of the ragged hole Grewishka had made coming in.

His gaze came to Clive Lee, who shook his head. "No bounty on Grewishka," he said to Ido. "If there's no bounty, he's not our problem."

A surge of anger sent heat rushing into Ido's face. "This—this *beast* has been killing women. Not just killing them, vivisecting them. And he's acquired weapons he has no right to. Or don't any of you remember whom you last saw using grind-cutters? Kinuba won that night— he was in here celebrating and you were all buying him drinks. Have any of you seen him since? *Anybody?*" Ido looked around, his anger intensifying. "And any one of you could be next. But here he is, on your home turf, laughing in your faces because he knows no one here will do a thing about it. Because *he's not your problem.*"

Ido looked around again, but the room seemed to have somehow stretched out in every direction so that all the other hunters seemed to be far away.

"Sorry, Doc," Clive Lee said from his now-distant table. "You're on your own."

Ido turned to Alita. She *wasn't* far away. She was very close—very, *very* close—and her wide-eyed face had a calm composure that Ido found utterly frightening.

Then, because things still weren't bizarre enough on

this planet, a small dog barked.

Ido turned to give McTeague a baffled look and saw a little mongrel that wasn't even remotely hellish or houndish spring out of the man's lap. He landed on the floor in front of Grewishka and bared his teeth in a snarl.

"The only one with courage," Grewishka sneered. "An innocent." He pointed at the dog.

Ido turned his face away. Metal whistled through the air. There was one startled yelp, followed by terrible slicing noises, and then the sound of the grind-cutter snapping back into place.

"There's no place in Iron City for innocence," Grewishka said smugly.

Ido forced himself to turn his head and look at Grewishka, trying not to see the mess on the floor, and failing.

A chair scraped back from a table as McTeague got to his feet. The Hellhounds rose with him, growling low and dangerous; they'd caught the scent of heart's-blood in the air. Beside Ido, Alita was watching the pool of blood spread out from the little stray's body. When it reached the toe of her boot, she knelt and dipped one finger into it.

Grewishka laughed at her. "Time for us to play, little flea."

The sensation spreading through Alita now was not unlike what she'd felt a few minutes earlier when she'd been kicking asses and taking names and generally showing a bar full of Hunter-Warriors that they weren't as big and bad as they thought they were. But this time the feeling was intensifying far more quickly. It was a power and intent that came from a deeper place, from her true *self*, from the very stuff of which she, Alita, had been made.

Words suddenly flitted through her mind, a memory that had come loose from its moorings, something from long ago in her life:

De profundis clamavi ad te. Out of the depths I cry to you…

What cry did she make out of her depths?

It came to her immediately: "I do not stand by in the presence of evil."

Alita dragged her blood-covered fingertip in a straight line across her right cheek under her eye, and then did the same on the left. The blood was still warm. Heart's-blood from a heart braver than a roomful of men who called themselves heroes.

She raised her head. Grewishka loomed over her, his ugly face made even uglier by his certainty that there was nothing in the world stronger than cruelty.

Alita got to her feet, aware of all the eyes on her, aware of who they all were and their locations in the room, aware of Ido and Hugo and Chiren.

"*I do not stand by in the presence of evil,*" she said again, louder this time, to make sure they could all hear this cry from her depths, this promise from her soul.

The grind-cutter flew out from Grewishka's hand and everyone dived for cover.

Go ahead and hide, you junkyard punks, Alita thought as she sprang into the air, *but keep watching, you don't want to miss what's coming up next*. At the top of her leap, she twisted to dodge the grind-cutter blade, then segued into a backflip that put her squarely on her feet again, out of reach of the grind-cutter as it chopped up the last unbroken table and the chair Ido had righted earlier. Bounty hunters scrambled away, trying to find safer hiding places, some of them diving behind the bar with the owner.

As if there really were any safe places in this world, Alita thought. Ido's Rocket Hammer roared into high gear; she turned to see him rear back to take a swing at Grewishka. Grewishka whirled and fired another grind-cutter at him. Only Ido wasn't there any more because Hugo had tackled him, sending the two of them tumbling across the dirty, splintered floor.

Hugo was big on tackling, Alita thought, feeling a surge of affection she had no time to indulge.

"Hey, ugly!" she yelled at Grewishka and cartwheeled across the floor, took a flying leap over the ruins of a table and made a three-point landing on the bar. The sight of the Hunter-Warriors cowering behind it sent a wave of pity through her and made her want to destroy Chiren's monster more than ever. "Over here, you pile of pig iron!"

Grewishka smiled nastily and fired another grind-cutter at her. She leaped away as it made kindling of the bar and scattered everyone who had been hiding behind it—everyone, that was, except the owner. He stayed where he was, looking at the wreckage.

"Last call," he said glumly. "You don't have to go home but you can't stay here. Because there's nothing here any more. Why am I talking? Nobody's listening."

Alita didn't tell him she was listening, although she

heard everything. She took another leap and aimed a kick at Grewishka's wretched face. He swatted her away and sent her crashing into a post and then the floor.

Grewishka laughed at her and mocked her with a flying leap of his own. Alita rolled away as he fired his grind-cutters at the place where she had just been. Deliberately, she realised; he had deliberately missed her. She rolled to her feet and assumed her usual fighter's crouch, watching the grind-cutters throwing up clouds of dust and splinters as they savaged the floor. Grewishka laughed and jumped again, landing on the spot his grind-cutters had just been working on—and then kept on going *through* the floor, leaving a gaping hole.

Alita scurried over to it and peered down into the darkness. It was too dark to see anything, but she heard Grewishka's voice, mocking and evil. "What are you waiting for, little flea? Come and get me!"

She raised her head for a quick look around, assessing the situation in the bar. Everyone was still alive. But where were Ido and Hugo? It took a couple of seconds for her to spot them extricating themselves from a pile of plaster and broken furniture. They had a few bruises and cuts but neither of them were seriously injured. They were all right for now.

Alita had a brief glimpse of their horrified faces, and heard them both yell, "*Noooooo!*" in unison as she jumped into the hole.

CHAPTER 15

Alita fell through the darkness and kept falling. *Out of the depths I cry, and into the depths I fall*, she thought with the wind buffeting her face and blowing her hair back. The earth was swallowing her, and it was a very long way to the belly of the beast, a long way to fall and fall and fall and fall and fall—

A heap of refuse rushed up to meet her. Landing in trash piles was getting to be a habit, she thought as she slid down from the top and assumed her usual fighter's crouch. *Yeah, pretty long fall. What else you got?* she said silently.

Laughter boomed through the darkness, seeming to come from everywhere around her. There was a metallic reverberation, as though she had landed in a tank. Alita blinked, willing her eyes to adjust more quickly to the dark as she searched the shadows for her enemy.

"Welcome to the underworld—*my* world." Grewishka's rumbling laughter was louder and even more aggressive down here. Now Alita could make out damp, cracked walls with enormous patches of mould growing on them and on the rusty pipes running in rows of four and five. Sometimes the pipes curved upwards and vanished into the shadows; others ran away into murky tunnels through openings that were vaulted, like the empty windows in Hugo's cathedral.

But this was no cathedral, or any other kind of holy place. If Grewishka were here, this place was the very opposite of sacred.

"From here, there are worlds above worlds above worlds," Grewishka said, melting out of the darkness in front of her. "They go further up than a little flea like you can imagine." His rumbling voice had become a jeer. The way it echoed made it even more repellant, every word a physical blow. "And the trash and refuse of each world falls down on the one below, and so on and so forth, until it all ends up here. This is the land of the unacceptable, the unwanted, the rejected." Grewishka had moved closer so she could see him grinning at her like a cyborg gargoyle. "This is where I used to live—"

"And it's where you're going to die," Alita promised.

She leaped at him and, dodging his fist, flew over his ugly head, rebounded from a wall, and drove herself feet first into his shoulder, intending to take his arm off again. Instead, she bounced off and fell to the filthy concrete without hurting him. Chiren had fixed that flaw in his joint, made him stronger and tougher. But he probably couldn't get any nastier, she thought as he thrust out his right hand, fingers splayed.

All five grind-cutters shot out, the pointed ends stabbing

at the concrete, throwing up damp, greasy fragments. Alita flipped to her feet and did a series of somersaults as the grind-cutter blades flashed in the gloom, whistling as they sought her out.

"That's it—dance, little flea, dance!" Grewishka laughed, as if her every move really were made at his command, for his amusement. She flipped from side to side, gradually getting closer to him, then launched herself straight at him. She hit him with her whole body, slapping him hard with both hands.

Grewishka hurtled backwards into a mouldering wall. It crumbled on top of him, burying him in boulder-sized fragments of damp concrete. Alita flipped backwards into a series of tumbles, and bounced up to assume her ready stance, only to have her right leg buckle under her. She looked down to see bright-blue cyber-blood dripping from her knee while sparks of energy flickered and buzzed around the joint. Glitching servo—damn, wasn't *that* just perfect.

Abruptly, she felt a change in the foul air and snapped her head to the right. Grewishka was charging at her, grind-cutters writhing and twisting. Alita somersaulted away, intending to build up momentum for a double airborne tumble. If she moved fast enough, her bad leg wouldn't have a chance to give. Instead, she touched down and staggered to one side. Her knee had lost too much cyber-blood. A grind-cutter blade flew at her, overshooting by several feet, but twisted and sliced a deep gash in her hip on its way back to Grewishka. *Damn!* She was going to have a hard time compensating for both that and her knee.

Hard time? More like, *no chance.* She ducked behind a thick concrete column standing between the openings to two diverging passageways to give herself a chance to breathe and think.

If she was going down, she was taking that son of a bitch with her. She just had to figure out how.

"This is all *your* fault!" Ido said angrily as he climbed down a ladder.

Below him, Hugo snatched his hand away from a rung just before Ido stepped on it. "Hey, *you're* the one who drove her to this, not *me*," he said. They had come down half a dozen filthy levels so far, and Ido had spent the whole time blaming Hugo for every bad thing that had happened. It reminded Hugo of how Alita had complained about Ido the night he'd taken her to her first Motorball game. Like sort-of father, like sort-of daughter, he thought. He smiled at the memory, but only for a second. That same night, his crew had jacked Kinuba for Vector, leading directly to their current state of deep shit. Dammit, maybe this really *was* his fault, Hugo thought miserably. The only way it could get worse would be if Ido found out about the jacking.

Hugo shook the thought away and kept going down the ladder to the bottom. Ido had said the ladders were access for maintenance workers, but Hugo was pretty sure the last time a maintenance worker had accessed anything here was before he was born. The ladders were crusted with years of greasy dirt and who knew what else. And just to make the experience really special, the garbage smell became stronger at every level. If it went on till they reached the bottom, they'd puke themselves to death before they could even look for Alita.

Ido climbed down and brushed past him roughly. He'd twisted his shirt into a makeshift back carrier for the Rocket Hammer so he could have both hands free, but it was clumsy to walk with. He'd be lucky not to trip and fall before they got to the bottom.

The doc had already found the next ladder down— they were staggered in what seemed to be a random way. "Hey, *you*! Mr Black-Market Badass!" Ido snapped. "Wake up and let's go!"

Alita stood with her back to the column. The gash in her hip was still bleeding heavily and her knee was about to short out and die any moment, while Grewishka was too in love with the sound of his own voice to shut up for even a second. What the hell was *that* about?

"I was forgotten," the ugly beast was saying in a solemn rumble, like this was the most important origin story ever told. "I was unwanted, left to rot with the rest of the garbage. I thought it was my fate to rot, to disappear into decay and putrescence, unmourned by the uncaring world that produced the very garbage I had been consigned to."

Can we speed this up? Alita thought. *I'd like to kill you before I die myself.* She peeked around the column, saw

Grewishka grinning at her, and drew back quickly.

"But then, someone saw me—saw *me*, just as I was, and embraced me. And so I was saved, remade by the same hand that shapes *your* destiny even now at this very moment!"

Alita felt the world tilt as if the monster had kicked it off its axis. And then kicked her in her stomach, so she couldn't catch her breath.

No. She kicked the world back where it belonged, straightened up, and stepped out from behind the column.

"*Whose hand?*" she demanded. "You wanna talk? Answer me right now—*whose hand*?"

Grewishka's gargoyle grin widened. "My master." He raised his fist. "My master, Nova."

"What do you know about me?" Alita shouted.

Grewishka splayed his fingers and the grind-cutters flew out from them. Alita leaped into the air, twisting and flipping, but the grind-cutters seemed to anticipate her moves now. The long blades converged on her and she felt something sharp pass through her torso, severing one arm. Another blade sliced her in half at the waist while a third cut off her legs at mid-thigh.

She was falling again, not as far as before but somehow it seemed to take a long time before she and the filthy concrete rushing towards her finally met. The smell of dirty water and damp stone fought the clean, bright fragrance of cyber-blood splashing out of her limbs as they fell around her. Somewhere in the darkness a voice very like Ido's cried out in horror. Alita supposed everyone made their own cry from the depths and the darkness.

Raising her head, she flexed her remaining arm and

began to drag herself away. She could only manage a few centimetres at a time. It was like when they were in the van waiting to get out of Iron City the day Hugo took her to the Badlands; what a wonderful day that had been. She was going even more slowly now, but she refused to lie down. She wasn't dead, not yet—

A silent explosion of white light obliterated the damp, grimy darkness and she was—

Flying. She was flying, weightless in the zero-g training sphere, completely free, nothing resisting her movements, nothing to stop her twisting and turning and tumbling.

And she was young, very young—ten years old. She was a ten-year-old cyborg and she already knew how to use the fighting stick in her hand. The stick was more than familiar in her grip; it was perfect. She knew the mass, the length, how to counterbalance, and she knew how to defend herself against the woman coming at her with her own fighting stick.

Gelda. The woman was Gelda, and one day they would fight side by side on the moon, but now Gelda was her *sensei*.

"They're telling me you're too young, too small," Gelda said, her face alive and glowing with physical exertion and fierce warrior pride. "But they're wrong!"

Alita met her attack with a flurry of kicks and strikes, parrying Gelda's stick and scoring a few blows of her own—but only a few.

"I saw what you lived through," Gelda said. "You have the soul of a warrior!"

Alita's heart swelled with joy as she struck at Gelda,

wanting to be worthy of her *sensei*'s praise.

"You'll never give up," Gelda told her, only slightly winded as she countered Alita's move. "You'll never stop. Never. Stop."

Gelda made a move to one side and Alita started to make the proper defensive parry. Gelda's arm shot out and pulled her close. Their faces were only centimetres apart and Alita felt the cold flat blade of Gelda's knife against her throat.

"Know what is hidden," Alita's *sensei* said sternly.

Gelda watched Alita closely as she let her go. Alita met her gaze steadily, composing her face into a stony, expressionless mask that wouldn't show her defeat. You never showed defeat to an opponent, never let them see you felt conquered, never let them into your head, not even if you were dying.

"Always ask: what is it that you are not seeing?" Gelda said.

Alita saw him then, the man in the observation gallery. He had been watching, but he had no eyes. Instead, he had chrome surgical optics. Chrome was the highest grade, reserved for the most elite of the elite, a social class so rarefied they were never actually seen by any of lesser stature, including people like her.

Only she *did* see him, and she saw him seeing her. As exalted as his chrome optics were supposed to be, they looked like they had been pushed into his head by a careless surgeon who had left too much sticking out of his face.

The man was smiling, but not at her. It was more like he was enjoying a private joke no one else would understand.

"Only when you see what is hidden can you win!" said Gelda. "Again!"

Alita twisted in the air—

And she was back on the filthy concrete floor, trying to drag herself away with her one arm while Grewishka knelt beside her and laughed. He dug his fingers into her hair and lifted her up so she dangled like a broken doll.

"Aw, my little toy doesn't want to play any more?" His face was so close she could feel his fetid breath as he spoke.

Alita stared back, letting him see her refusal to give out, give in or give up. Ever.

"I'm going to turn you into a living pendant to adorn my chest," Grewishka said in a demented croon. "I'll wear you all the time so that every moment of every day, I can hear you screaming and pleading for mercy."

Alita drew back from him, and he pushed his face forward—just as she'd hoped he would. She thrust her open palm into his face and tore herself out of his grasp as he fell back. With her decreased mass, one arm was all she needed. She guided herself into a perfect landing on her open hand, then lowered herself slowly to the cement. Bright-blue cyber-blood was still pouring out of her, although it was starting to slow. She was in a pool of it now but she knew there was enough left for what she wanted to do.

Grewishka struggled to his feet, roaring with rage. Good; anger made him stupid. As he came thundering at her, she raised her body up, flexed her elbow and launched herself into the air. Sending herself into a spin, she aimed herself at Grewishka. Keeping her arm straight out, she flattened her hand like a blade and plunged it into his eye.

Now his scream was high and shrill, full of pain and terror. Alita smiled as she steadied herself so she could look directly into his other eye.

"*Fuck* your mercy," she told him.

She tried to yank her hand free but it was caught on something inside, probably one of his enhancements. In a way, that was even better, she thought. She twisted hard until her forearm cracked and broke just above her wrist and she dropped away from him.

Enjoy the souvenir. It's better than a pendant. There's a flower on it. I left a flower in your eye, a beautiful flower. You're welcome.

Grewishka's scream deepened with outrage, but not a lot—there was still more pain than anything else in his voice. Alita watched him lumber towards her, his hand over the eye with the flower in it. The flower would always be there, she thought; even after they took it out and gave him a new and better eye, he'd still feel the pain of her pretty little flower for as long as he lived.

She smiled up at him as he raised his foot to stomp her.

The next thing she knew, Grewishka was staggering sideways. Joy surged through her as she heard the unmistakable sound of the Rocket Hammer. In the next moment, a fire-bottle broke over Grewishka, engulfing his upper body in flames, making him scream again.

Alita caught a glimpse of Hugo before something fast and vicious slammed into Grewishka, snarling and growling as it drove him back. Then the rest of hellhounds were on him, ripping his armour, going for his exposed innards, biting and snapping.

Still screaming, Grewishka tore the Hellhounds away from himself and fled into a passageway. The Hellhounds went after him, barking furiously until McTeague appeared and hollered, "Break off! Come! Now!"

The Hellhounds came galloping back to him and formed a protective circle around him, Ido and Hugo. Alita remembered her friend, the little stray, and felt her eyes well with tears. McTeague met her gaze with eyes shiny with empathy.

"He wasn't a dog-lover," McTeague explained grimly. "I hate that."

Ido barely heard McTeague's pronouncement. He fell to his knees beside Alita's torn and shattered form and brushed her hair back from her face. She looked up at him; and he discovered his heart could still break after all.

His little girl. She was his little girl, and it had happened again. A demon he was responsible for had gone on a rampage and his little girl had been caught in its path. That Chiren had actually made this monster was only a technicality—he had set all the things in motion that had led to this, and he had done nothing to stop this horror from getting loose.

His little Alita. She hadn't been helpless; she had fought the creature with everything she had—literally everything—and she had damaged it badly and driven it off. But the demon had been too strong, too crazed and too evil. For all that she'd hurt him, she'd never really had a chance against Grewishka. Ido had failed to protect her—even though he could have.

His little girl. The very thing that could have protected her was lying on a table in his lab, but he'd refused to give it to her. Instead he'd been a self-righteous, moralising fool, convinced that *not* giving her the power of the Berserker body was the best way to protect her from evil.

It might have been—in any other world but this one.

His little Alita. After everything that had happened, he'd managed to remain in denial about the nature of this world and the dangers around her. Worst of all, he'd been in denial as to who *she* really was, trying to make her—*remake* her—into a sweet, beautiful young girl adorned with flowers. As a result, he had failed her completely.

Ido gathered her up in his arms.

Once they were on the street, Ido had Hugo run ahead, sweeping the Rocket Hammer back and forth to clear the way for him and the precious burden in his arms. He held Alita to his chest protectively, feeling his breath coming in great, ragged sobs, not caring about anyone or anything except getting his little girl back to the lab.

Then Chiren stepped out of the shadows near the boarded-up Kansas Bar.

If Hugo hit her with the Rocket Hammer, Ido thought, he would pretend not to notice.

"You think it'll be that easy?" Chiren called to him. "Bring her back all you want, but we can do this indefinitely—forever if we have to! Can you? Can you, Dyson?"

Ido pushed past her like she wasn't there. He felt her staring after him and imagined her wilting, shrivelling, collapsing in on herself because there was nothing inside, nothing at all.

Ido was running but Chiren didn't try to kid herself—he wasn't running from her. Now he had something to run *to.* She'd lost that a long time ago—they both had—and nothing would ever change that.

But there he went.

And here she stayed.

CHAPTER 16

The operation was a marathon procedure that took twice as long as the first one, although much of that time was spent disconnecting Alita's cyber-core from the wreckage that had been Ido's work of art.

When Gerhad had seen what Grewishka had done to Alita, it had been all she could do not to break down, not just for Alita, but also for Ido. He'd been here before and, although Chiren had made the monster that had destroyed his little girl, Gerhad knew Ido was blaming himself. She hadn't thought anything could happen that would make Ido punish himself any more than he already had, and still did. But apparently she'd had no idea what Chiren was capable of. That woman had to be the coldest, most heartless person in Iron City—and that was saying something. It was hard to believe she had ever been a mother—of a human being, anyway.

Gerhad looked at the girl on the operating table. After almost two days, most of the re-embodiment procedure was finished; all the nerves were physically connected, and both circulatory systems—cyber-blood and heart's-blood—were functioning. In fact, Gerhad had never seen a face pink up so quickly. It was as if this was the body Alita should have had all along.

And yet Ido had been so dead set against uniting her with it. Gerhad had been afraid this would drive a permanent wedge between him and Alita, pushing them so far apart that they'd never find their way back to each other. Worse, Gerhad suspected Ido didn't realise what he doing. After Chiren had left, alienation had become his default setting. Gerhad was close to him only in a professional capacity, as his nurse. Given the nature of his practice, the relationship involved a certain amount of intimacy—the wellbeing of their patients depended on their understanding each other. But it wasn't the personal intimacy shared by good friends.

For a while, Gerhad had thought it was. A surgical team was a well-oiled machine, and its members were the moving parts, all working for the same goal. It was easy to feel closer to your team than anyone else, including your family, which was a quick way to lose your family. Neither she nor Ido had families to lose; the only problem would have been if Ido had shown a romantic interest in her. Fortunately, he hadn't. Before long, she realised he wasn't interested in anything beyond their professional relationship. He tolerated her personal disclosures without impatience but didn't volunteer any of his own.

Ido would always be the man who had given her back her life, and she would always love him for that. Even if it was solely pragmatism on his part, his complete acceptance of her, no questions asked, was more than she'd ever had in any other relationship, professional or personal. And so she continued her nursing career in circumstances that were less than perfect but more fortunate than most.

Gerhad had never considered doing anything that might disturb the equilibrium between her and Ido. But then he had brought Alita's cyber-core home, and Gerhad had wondered what it would do to him. He had seemed happy to be a father again, but Alita was not his daughter. Supposedly he knew that. But as time passed, Gerhad realised this Alita was going to become less and less like his daughter. How would that play out?

Then Alita had brought the Berserker body home and turned Ido's world upside down. The argument between them had started while Gerhad was still cleaning up after the usual long day. Gerhad knew Ido expected her to make an inconspicuous exit as soon as things got heated, but instead she had gone down to the basement and pretended to sort laundry, not coming back upstairs until Alita had run out.

Ido had retreated to the kitchen to sulk over a cup of tea. Gerhad knew he wouldn't want company so she'd taken a close look at the Berserker body. It was a magnificent thing—Gerhad had never even imagined anything like it. Under different circumstances—if, say, she had been a former nurse with one arm and no prospects—she might have been strongly tempted to roll it up in a carpet and try her luck on the black market.

She had tried to imagine wide-eyed, angel-faced Alita

embodied in it and couldn't. This wasn't a young girl's body.

And maybe that was the *real* problem, Gerhad thought. Ido could go on about not wanting blood on Alita's pretty flowered hands, and advanced weapons, and how lucky she was to start over with a clean slate. But Gerhad suspected that, in truth, he didn't want to let his little girl go. He'd given her the lovely young-girl body his little girl should have had, with the beautiful flowers and the silver and gold inlays, and he wanted her to stay that way.

When he'd lost his daughter, he had lost the chance to see her grow up. His Alita was fourteen, now and forever.

Gerhad had come very close to going into the kitchen that day, sitting down at the table with him, and telling him this. But it would have been the last thing she ever told him. Ido wouldn't have argued or yelled at her or told her to mind her own business; he simply would have fired her, effective immediately, and even if he regretted it later— even if he decided she'd been right—she would never be welcome in his clinic again.

Well, if this had been a more typical argument between a father and daughter—something less drastic that didn't involve having her entire body replaced, maybe just an enhancement, or even contraception—would she have hustled her bustle in there to have a word with him?

Hell, no. She wasn't a parent. For all the insight she might have, the only advice she was actually qualified to give anyone about their kids was first aid, good nutrition, and how to take their temperature. Suggesting they might be having a problem with the idea of a kid growing up was not her business, even if she was right.

But now circumstances had forced Ido to unite Alita with the Berserker. To his credit, he hadn't hesitated, hadn't substituted one of the other TRs in cold storage. He'd given her what she'd wanted and he hadn't seemed a bit reluctant about it. He had leaned over and whispered, "No one will dare harm you again."

Gerhad moved closer to the table and saw that Alita's eyes were moving back and forth below her closed lids. What could the girl be dreaming about? she wondered. Not Grewishka, certainly—her face was far too peaceful.

She appeared to be engrossed in whatever dreams her mind had conjured up. Maybe her lost memories were playing like movies in her head. But when she awoke, she'd forget them all, because nothing was that easy for anyone, not even a girl in a Berserker body.

And it would be even harder for Ido, Gerhad thought. At the moment, he was all cyber-surgeon, surrounded by display screens and swivelling on his chair from one to another, then rolling over to the table to check on the patient. But soon he would be Ido the grieving father again.

Gerhad frowned and moved closer to the table. Was she seeing things or were Alita's fingers longer than the last time she'd looked? Yes, they *were*, and they gained another millimetre as she watched. That was a relief. Going crazy was pointless in Iron City, which was itself the most insane place in an insane world.

Of course, she didn't have to be crazy to start seeing things, just tired. Two major cyber-surgeries in such a short period of time—that was pushing the limits of human stamina and technology both. Gerhad decided to run a quick diagnostic on her cyborg arm. It would flag any problems with the human operator.

Her arm checked out fine. In fact, it was more than fine. Ido had built it to perform more complex tasks and procedures than those they usually had to deal with in the clinic. Re-embodying Alita had made full use of its capabilities. Gerhad also seemed to be fine, although the diagnostic flagged her fatigue as something that needed her immediate attention. It recommended a minimum of eight hours of uninterrupted sleep. Gerhad thought twenty hours was more like it.

Fatigue was one of the reasons cited most often by people opting for a cyber enhancement. In many cases, one enhancement led to another—improvements in one area tended to make people dissatisfied with their unenhanced parts. Gerhad had never suffered from new-part fever herself but that was probably because her cyber-arm hadn't been an optional upgrade. Or maybe she just wasn't tired enough yet.

Now she could see that Alita's shoulders were measurably broader and her chest was becoming less androgynous by the second. Gerhad found this unsettling enough that she had to look away. In her time as a nurse, she had seen all kinds of things—gory, weird, eerie, scary, absurd, even miraculous—but nothing as trippy as advanced Urm technology.

Gerhad gave it a minute before looking back at Alita. Yeah, those were breasts. Alita's waist had narrowed and her hips were now quite womanly. No delicate flowers on creamy pink skin, no gold and silver inlays etched with lovely scrollwork. The biomechanoid body was beautiful, but it was a strong and formidable beauty that also happened to be anatomically correct.

"It's the adaptive technology of the Berserker body," Ido said. Gerhad jumped; she had all but forgotten that he was in the room. "The corporeal shell is reconfiguring to match her image of herself—her *new* image, that is. Her brain knows there's been a change in her embodiment. This body registered as more mature biologically, with increased capabilities, and the brain reacts accordingly. It's mutual feedback between her core and her corpus as they progress towards a state of unity."

Gerhad nodded. Re-embodiment could be tricky. If the cyber-core held onto anything from its previous incarnation, it would have trouble adjusting to a new form. Sometimes all it took was a couple of faulty pH readings and a patient would wake up with a bad case of dysmorphia or even outright rejection.

"I've never seen anything like this," Ido went on. "The body's doing most of the work, making micro-adjustments to all the systems on every level." He tilted his head at the displays. The sheer volume of data on them would have overwhelmed anyone else—and it wasn't a tea party for Ido's big brain, either, Gerhad realised, taking in his puffy, bloodshot eyes and overall haggard look. This had pushed him to the limit of his capability, and he was probably so busy relishing the challenge that he didn't know how tired he really was.

"Well, however this works, I'd say Alita isn't your little girl any more," Gerhad told him cheerfully. "She's all grown up. Officially a woman."

Ido's face went bright red and he averted his gaze. "Indeed she is. And in that spirit, we should respect her, uh, privacy. Would you mind, uh—"

Gerhad had already taken a surgical sheet from the shelf under the table. She shook it out and draped it over Ido's erstwhile little girl.

"Thank you, Nurse," Ido said in a stiff, professional tone and went back to the displays.

Gerhad put a hand over her mouth to keep from laughing. The poor guy had no idea what he was in for. Alita really *wasn't* a little girl any more. Kids here grew up too fast anyway. Iron City was that kind of place. But the social and psychological forces that acted on the average kid didn't include being maimed to within a millimetre of their lives by a monster in a sewer.

Even when Alita had been down to one arm with her hand broken off and jammed into Grewishka's eye, she had defied him, refusing to be defeated even when the monster was about to kill her. After something like that, the standard Iron City resident would probably spend the next few years curled up in the foetal position, crippled with PTSD. But not Alita—she'd have been back on her feet and looking for payback *without* a Berserker body.

But *with* one—

Urm's advanced science may have strained Ido, but he was about to discover that when it came to his little girl— who was *not* a little girl any more—he was completely out of his depth.

Welcome to the next phase of fatherhood, Gerhad thought. *You poor bastard.*

Someone kissed his forehead.

Ido woke to find himself stretched out on the sofa. He should have given it to Gerhad, he thought guiltily as he sat up blinking, trying to make his eyes open wider. He had to check on his little girl. Alita was—she was—

She was not his little girl any more, he remembered, looking at the lovely young woman standing in front of him. He looked at her sleekly muscled arms and legs and her easy, graceful stance. At least she's got good posture, his mind babbled. Without taking his eyes off her, he reached over and shook Gerhad, who was asleep in the chair beside the sofa. She slapped his hand away, started to say something, and then saw why he'd roused her.

"Well," Ido said after a bit, when he was sure he wasn't going to cry. "Look at you."

Alita gave him a warm smile. She bent casually to one side as if to pick something up off the floor and just as casually went into a one-armed handstand. Ido watched her draw her fingers together; the handstand became a one-fingerstand. Slowly, with no visible effort, and remaining perfectly balanced, she lowered her legs into a split.

Ido was still giving thanks that Gerhad had thought to put underwear on her when Alita flexed her elbow and flipped herself back up on her feet.

"You were right, Alita," he said humbly. "A warrior's spirit needs a warrior's body."

She held up her right hand, showing him the small vents on her forearm; they were breathing while a small blue flame danced over her fingertips.

"The vents draw in air to generate arc plasma," Ido said. "But don't ask me what's controlling it. I mean, you are, of course, but the exact mechanism involved—" He shrugged. "You didn't come with a manual, I'm afraid." He pointed to intake ports higher up, on her bicep. "That's part of some kind of weapon, probably also arc plasma. And that's pretty much all I can tell you. Now you know as much about who you are as I do."

Alita sat down beside him on the sofa. She was still smiling but there was a hint of uncertainty in her face.

"You know, all this—" Ido gestured at her body. "All this beauty and strength and ability—this is the shell. It's not bad and it's not good. That part's up to you."

She surprised him by resting her head on his shoulder. *Not my little girl any more, except when she is*, Ido thought, putting his arm around her shoulders. For some unmeasured period of time, they stayed that way, watching the late afternoon rain running down the windows in rivulets. He and Gerhad had slept most of the day, but Ido felt like he could sleep a few more hours. He'd almost dozed off again when Alita suddenly spoke up.

"Grewishka told me someone from up above saved him and turned him into who he is." Pause. "He said it was his master, Nova."

Ido sighed. "Grewishka is a crazed monster, spawned to play a corrupt game by an even more corrupt system. Actually, he's just the latest in a series. They've made a lot of monsters like him that roam the streets until people like me take them out."

"It's not the game or the streets that are the problem," Alita said. "The problem is up above. Up there."

"But we're all down here, in this world. Our world," Ido replied. He drew back a little to smile at her. "You know, I told Hugo I'd call him when you were awake."

Alita bounced to her feet with a thousand-watt smile. "I'll go find him!"

"Not dressed like that, you're not," Gerhad told her firmly. "Let me find you some clothes that aren't quite so—" She hesitated. "—in-patient."

Walking—the simple act of putting one foot in front of the other—was so much better now, Alita thought as she strode along the crowded night-time streets. The rain had stopped, although rain seldom had much effect on Iron City's nightlife. The Berserker body made it a lot easier to make her way through the crowds, although that may have been due simply to her being taller. It helped to be on eye-level; people gave way for a woman more readily than for a kid. Being more substantial helped, too. Not that she'd ever been easily moved, but now she looked like someone you couldn't push around.

Part of her felt a little bad about what had happened to her old body—Ido's labour of love. Maybe it was the relief of finally being who she was that gave her a deeper understanding of what that pretty little cyborg body had meant to Ido. It had deserved better—much, *much* better.

On the other hand, if *Ido* had understood what the

Berserker body had meant to *her* and done what she had asked, his work of art wouldn't have been sliced up by a monster in a sewer. So they each had some responsibility, and if she understood that, Ido probably did, too, even if he didn't say anything. Some grown-ups were like that—as Gerhad had pointed out to her once: some people wouldn't say *shit* if they were standing neck-deep in it.

Ido wasn't really like that, though. As soon as he had realised what the Berkserker body meant for her, he hadn't hesitated or tried to palm a different TR off on her. Nobody was perfect, but Ido tried to be; she had to give him that. It was a lot more than she could say for most people, especially the ice queen who had sicked Grewishka on them. Her heart had to be a frozen lump, Alita thought; maybe she'd freeze over completely and be nothing but a bunch of parts on ice. Which might be pretty soon, if those cold blue eyes were any indication.

Alita pushed the thought away, unsure how her mind could have turned to Chiren when she simply wanted to enjoy her new physicality. She couldn't remember what it had been like to be completely organic, but she thought that it must have been a lot like this—well, if the organic body in question happened to be in peak condition.

But it was more than just physical. The power she felt in her arms, her legs, her shoulders, her torso and back, seemed like something that had always been within her, waiting for her to find it. Or to wake it? Maybe she just had to realise she had it at all. Strength and endurance were things of the body but something in her core—in the core of her core—gave them life. Her memory of what had happened to her hadn't come back completely yet, but this was her muscle memory of being alive, conscious and embodied. She was a warrior spirit in a warrior body.

Alita paused, looking around. The traffic on the sidewalks as well as the streets was increasing. The crowds wouldn't start thinning out till sometime after one A.M. As convenient as it was to get around in her new, grown-up form, it might take her almost that long to find Hugo, especially in the busier parts of town. But there was a better way.

She stepped off the sidewalk into a narrow passageway between two buildings. For a minute, she studied each structure's outer surface, looking at the various protrusions—windowsills, narrow wrought-iron balconies, drain pipes, old bits of fire escapes half stripped away by scavengers. Then she launched herself upwards.

The sheer physical pleasure of the leap seemed to give her extra momentum. As she rebounded between the two buildings, from drain pipes to windowsills to wrought-iron bars, it crossed her mind that what she was doing had been known at one time in the dim, distant past as *parkour*, although she had no idea how she knew that. It didn't worry her—a tidbit of information shaken loose from some obscure nook or cranny. There was plenty she *couldn't* remember and she didn't know why that was, either, but she kept on keepin' on anyway, so what the hell.

On the roof, Alita stopped to breathe deeply, not because she was winded but because she liked the smell of rain in the air. She looked up at the overcast sky and saw something twinkle brightly. Not a star, but a light from one of the tall buildings at the edge of Zalem. The city was a slightly darker shadow in the night-time rain clouds. It was almost as if Zalem had caught something of what she'd been feeling and wanted to remind her that there was always a ceiling, always something out of reach, even for her.

We'll see, she told the shadow silently.

The bodysuit Gerhad had found for her was really a good piece of clothing, Alita thought as she bounded from rooftop to rooftop, pausing to scan the streets below. The plain black fabric was light but tough, and it breathed so she didn't get overheated when she exerted herself. (Which was a good thing, as Ido had insisted she wear a raincoat over it.) It was a lot like skin, minus the pain receptors.

Not that she knew much about human skin or pain receptors. A warrior spirit didn't give two craps about pain. She'd conquered pain so long ago, she couldn't even remember what it felt like. How she could know that, when she hardly knew anything at all, was another one of those little mysteries, along with why she could shake a memory loose only by spitting in death's face. Or poking it in the eye.

She had so many questions; she even had questions about questions. But she'd worry about that later. Right now, all she really wanted to do was find Hugo. Was he ever going to be surprised!

Alita finally spotted Hugo hanging around in front of the CAFÉ café with Koyomi and Tanji and a few other members of his crew. Seeing him made her feel like the sun had come out inside her, filling her up with light. And warmth. She had to take a steadying breath before she made her way back down to street level, going from window ledges to drain pipes to bare centimetres of uneven brick. Finally, she dropped from an old-fashioned faux-neon sign to make a three-point landing on the sidewalk, startling a couple who had been looking dreamily into each other's eyes. She gave them a thumbs up and headed towards Hugo.

Tanji was talking to him about something. His gaze passed over her without recognition—she could tell because his face didn't immediately curdle. A couple of seconds later, he looked at her again, frowning a little, and started to say something else to Hugo. Koyomi had recognised her; she gave Hugo a hard nudge and pointed.

Hugo's double take was faster. Recognition didn't come right away, but she watched it dawn on him as she approached, until finally his face lit up with joyful relief and he ran to meet her. He swept her up in his arms—with an effort—and swung her around—with even more of an effort.

"Alita! You're all right! You're—" Hugo put her down as he discovered there had been some changes since he'd last seen her. Standing back, he gave her a long look from head to toe.

"Wow," he said, noticing what she had on under the raincoat. "You're all—"

"Back together?" she suggested, making them both laugh.

"Yeah, you're *way* back together," he said. "You look real, uh—"

Alita could practically see the little gears and wheels turning in his head as he tried to find the right word.

"Different," he said finally.

Behind Hugo, Koyomi was grinning broadly as she gave Alita two thumbs up. Tanji looked unimpressed, but it took so much effort that he couldn't manage his usual sour face. Alita almost felt sorry for him. She winked at Koyomi and took Hugo's arm. He put his hand over hers and they walked off together.

"It's all nanotech this and nanotech that," Alita told Hugo. She wasn't sure how long they'd been walking or where they were and she didn't care. "I don't understand it and Ido says there's a lot about it even he hasn't been able to figure out yet."

"So you're stronger now?" Hugo asked.

She nodded. "And faster. And I feel so much more— well, *me*."

Hugo gave her a thoughtful, sideways look. "You know, some guys would be intimidated by a girl like you."

"Really?" Alita blinked at him. "Why?"

"Oh, probably because you could rip out my arm and beat me to death with the wet end," he deadpanned.

"Well, there's an easy solution to that," she said, smiling. "Don't piss me off."

Hugo threw back his head and roared with laughter and she laughed with him, delighted (and a bit relieved) he thought it was funny.

"I always knew there was a warrior in you, Alita," he said when he wound down. "And now the rest of the world gets to see that, too."

Alita. He said my name.

It wasn't the first time, not even the first time that evening. But it was the first time he'd called her Alita and meant Alita the warrior. She had never thought she would be this happy, about anything.

When they came to the bridge, Alita realised they must have walked in a large circle and they were now back near the CAFÉ café. But she had no sense of time passing or distance travelled. For all she knew, time had stopped altogether. If so, she had no problem with that.

When they were halfway across the bridge, they stopped to look down at the river. It had risen quite a lot and was flowing more energetically than usual. It must have rained practically non-stop while she'd been down for repairs, Alita thought. She was about to ask Hugo about it when he took her hand and twined his fingers with hers.

Did he miss the flowers, she wondered, or the silver and gold inlays with the pretty patterns etched on them? Or the swirling lines on her fingertips?

"I'm more sensitive now, too," she told him. "Ido says

it's due to the much higher density of force feedback and texture sensors. What that means is—" She took her hand away and slipped her arm out of her coat, then held her hand out to him again. "Well, try it."

Hugo turned her hand over and ran his fingers over the back, past her wrist and all the way up to her shoulder. "Can you feel that?" he asked.

She nodded, wondering if he could feel how she was loving his touch.

"Close your eyes," he said and she obeyed. A moment later, she smiled as his fingertip moved gently along the side of her neck. "Where am I now?" he said.

Eyes still closed, she put her fingers over his. He stroked her cheek with his other hand and she sensed his face moving closer to hers, so close she could feel the warmth radiating from his skin.

"And where am I now?" he asked and kissed her. His lips were surprisingly soft and tender and she kissed him back, hoping he could tell how much she loved this, the feel of him. The young girl covered with flowers had stood up to a monster, but she had not been ready for this; the woman she had become.

"You're with me," Alita whispered when they moved apart. All at once, she felt self-conscious and dropped her gaze. "As you can see, I can do anything a regular girl can do."

"Anything?" Hugo said.

"Anything," she promised, smiling as his finger traced a line from her temple down to her chin. "Does it bother you that I'm not—well, you know—completely human?"

He used the finger under her chin to lift her head so he

could look into her eyes. "You're the most human person I've ever met."

They went on kissing and then it was raining again, coming down hard and straight so they were both drenched within a minute, Hugo in his light jacket and Alita with her raincoat half on and half off, and no night had ever been so utterly, wonderfully perfect.

Sitting by the window in CAFÉ café, Tanji made a contemptuous noise. Koyomi looked up from her wrist-cell screen and followed his gaze. The sight of Hugo and Alita kissing made her grin from ear to ear. Tanji shook his head.

"God, what's your damage?" Koyomi asked him, annoyed. "Why don't you like her?"

"I just never got that whole hardbody thing," he said, making his usual disapproving face. "And that Urm body she's wearing fits her like it was made for her. Which probably means she was the enemy."

Koyomi rolled her eyes. "Oh, sure—three hundred years ago. Get over it already, why dontcha?"

CHAPTER 17

Her body was stretched out on Vector's desk, but Chiren's eyes were fixed on Zalem.

She had a good view of it through the tall windows behind the desk. A few lights from the skyscrapers near the edge of the disc showed through the rain clouds. Eventually, the clouds would blow away and she'd be able to see Zalem unobscured. She needed to see it; she had to keep her eyes on the prize, no matter what happened, either to the world in general or to her in particular.

Like this business on the desk—some kind of masculine power thing, she supposed. It was uncomfortable as hell but she put up with it. At least Vector didn't play rough. And it was easy to see Zalem.

Abruptly, Vector took his hands off her. Annoyed, she was about to tell him to scratch on his own time. Then she saw his eyes.

"You." Her stomach turned over, and for a moment she thought she was going to throw up on the spot. She scrambled off the desk in revulsion, buttoning her blouse and tucking it back into her skirt.

"Why aren't you rebuilding Grewishka?" the Watcher behind Vector's eyes, Nova, wanted to know. The sound of his voice made Chiren sure Vector's throat was going to hurt when the Watcher was through with him.

"He won't let me touch him," Chiren said. "I can't even get near him. That's a problem."

"Well, then, why don't we go see him?" Nova said, and Chiren knew it wasn't a request.

She also knew he wasn't going to like what he saw.

Chiren stood in the doorway of the laboratory with Nova. The lab was fairly large, three times the size of the sad, shabby place Ido called a clinic. The equipment was also superior—everything from scanners to test tubes to surgical tech was high quality, not jerry-rigged and held together with duct tape and spit.

Or rather, it had been, before Grewishka had crashed his way in through the bedroom window again, with iridescent-blue cyber-blood leaking from cyborg-dog bites and a hand sticking out of his eye. By the look and smell of him, he'd spent the previous couple of days hiding in the sewers and doing unspeakable things to vermin.

Having finally found his way home, he had proceeded to express his existential displeasure by demolishing the entire laboratory. When Chiren and Vector realised he would also demolish anyone who got near him, they had used the blast doors to shut him up in the place and waited for him to run down and pass out. Or die.

A day later, Grewishka was still rampaging around the room, even though there was nothing left to break. Although he had managed to do more damage to himself; the grind-cutter hand was in pieces, more of his armour had been torn off, and his internal organs were starting to spill out of his chest. And the damned hand was *still* sticking out of his eye.

Nova turned to Chiren and raised one eyebrow. It was something Vector himself did from time to time but the Watcher made it freakish.

"I told you. I can't get near him," Chiren said, hating the defensive note in her voice. "He won't even let me fix his eye. Says he *wants* the pain."

Grewishka whirled at the sound of her voice. What the hell *was* keeping Alita's hand there, Chiren wondered— Grewishka's desire for pain or Alita's fury? Chiren wouldn't have been surprised if it were the latter. The girl should have been like an ant trying to take on a Centurian. She shouldn't have had a chance against Grewishka, and yet she had hurt him badly. Worse, she had incited others to help her. All of that should have told Nova to write Grewishka off as a lost cause and get a new hobby—something that didn't involve him riding Vector like a gyro-wheel.

"*Enough!*" Nova bellowed suddenly, making Chiren jump. But no, he hadn't read her thoughts. He was speaking to Grewishka. The cyborg roared in outrage and stumbled towards him, his one good hand raised in a fist. Chiren drew back, trying to pull Nova with her.

Grewishka might be mostly wreckage but there was still enough power left in him to cripple them or worse. Nova didn't have to care what happened to the body he rode, he could just re-patch himself into another. But if she lost Vector, she lost her best chance of going home to Zalem.

The bastard refused to move, just stood there while Grewishka rushed at him. Before the monster had closed half the distance, however, he suddenly fell to his knees and bent forward until his head touched the floor. He was actually whimpering, Chiren realised. Somehow Grewishka in submission was more disturbing than Grewishka in full homicidal frenzy.

Nova shook Chiren's hand off his arm and went to stand over the cyborg, who was now weeping. "Grewishka, my poor, tortured child," Nova said tenderly.

Chiren's stomach did a slow forward roll. She bit her lip, commanding herself not to be sick or even to make a sound. Nova was still convinced he needed her, but that could change if she made him angry. She straightened up and composed her face into the expressionless mask of a disinterested party merely observing events as they transpired. Right now, she was observing blue cyber-blood and oil ruining Vector's trousers and shoes. Vector would be furious, until she told him how it happened. Or maybe he'd already know.

"When your mother abandoned you to die in the sewers," Nova said in a bizarre silky purr, "who reached out to take your hand?"

"You did, master," Grewishka replied in a small voice.

"Because I saw rage burning in your eyes, like a flame

defying the darkness," Nova went on. "Your rage cried out for a body of equal power. And who gave you that body?"

"You did, master," said the cyborg even more meekly.

"And in return, you have *failed* me!" Nova suddenly shouted. "Stand up!"

Grewishka obeyed, head still bowed, tubes and internal organs dangling from his open chest.

"You will *never* triumph until you understand *what she is*!" Nova thundered at him. Chiren saw Grewishka flinch. "There hasn't been anything like her in three hundred years—*three hundred*! She's the last of her kind and the finest weapon ever produced by the Urm Technarchy!"

As if Grewishka had any idea what a "technarchy" was, Chiren thought, still queasy. If this went on for much longer, she really would throw up. She told herself to wait till she could do it on Vector's expensive shoes.

"She's dangerous by her mere existence!" Nova was saying. "She's a variable that threatens the very order of the world!"

"Then why not just send some Centurians to hose her down with some twenty-mill shells?" Chiren blurted, unable to help herself. "Case closed."

Nova turned to her with a twisted expression she had never seen on Vector's face and hoped she'd never see again. "Because I want her *dead*, not *obliterated*," he said, over-enunciating as if he were talking to a child. "Her core contains technologies that have been lost to us for *centuries*."

He turned back to Grewishka and his tone softened. "Doctor Chiren is going to make you faster and stronger

than ever. And *you* are going to *let her do her work.*
Aren't you?"

"Yes, master," Grewishka said, utterly chastened.

"I need you to *destroy* Alita," Nova said. "I need you to
bring me *her heart.*"

Grewishka knelt again, a grotesque knight pledging
himself to an even more grotesque king. "Master, I live
only for her death."

They stayed like that for a long moment. Then Vector—
only Vector now—turned on his heel and rushed past her
into the bathroom. Chiren heard the water running and let
him have a few seconds by himself before she followed.

"Damn, I *hate* it when he does that," Vector said, still
splashing cold water on his face. He spoke softly and left
the tap running so Grewishka couldn't hear.

"Well, on the upside—" She gave a weak laugh as she
handed Vector a towel. "He's a better kisser than you are."

Vector finished drying his face and tossed the towel on
the floor. "Joke all you want. Just keep in mind this isn't
someone who tolerates failure."

Except for creatures he finds in sewers, Chiren added
silently.

"I'm not inclined to bet my entire future on a piece of
iron that won't even let you pull a spear out of his eye,"
Vector said.

"Actually, it's a hand," Chiren said, remembering her
composure, "with the wrist and part of the forearm. Do
you have something better in mind?"

Vector looked thoughtful for a few seconds, then smiled.
Chiren went into one of two stalls, knowing that would make

Vector leave immediately, and just sat, listening to the water still running in the sink. Her stomach had already settled but she stayed a while longer, thinking about Vector and his future—that he'd said *my future* and not *our future* wasn't lost on her. She thought about how to rebuild Grewishka and wondered how long it would take to replace everything he'd wrecked in the lab. Why did Nova have an intense desire to have *Grewishka* bring Alita's heart to him, after the girl had already kicked Grewishka's ass twice, and when there were any number of other ways he might get to her through Ido? What was Nova trying to prove? And why was he trying to do it with a blunt instrument like Grewishka when there was a precision instrument like herself available?

Maybe he was crazy. Not a normal-for-Iron-City whack job, but clinically psychotic, of the variety that were a danger to others, especially since he had the power to indulge any obsessions or delusions he might have.

The safest thing to do, she decided, was to get to work on rebuilding Grewishka. At the very least, it would keep her out of Vector's office. And off his desk.

But it was another five minutes before she could persuade herself to leave the empty bathroom.

"To dreams," Vector said, raising a glass containing a generous shot of dark-gold whisky. The glass was one of a set of six genuine pre-Fall antiques he had found stashed in a forgotten corner of the Factory. The glasses were thick and curved in a way that made them a pleasure to hold in the hand. Vector only brought them out on occasions that demanded conspicuous consumption, and tonight he needed only two of them.

"To dreams," agreed Hugo, raising the other glass, which held an even more generous shot. He was ensconced in the biggest, cushiest chair in Vector's palatial office, gaping at his marble floor, his sensational view and his polished desk that was probably bigger than the sad rathole the kid called home.

Hugo looked a lot more comfortable now than he had earlier when Vector had picked him up in the limo for an impromptu private meeting. They had arrived at the Factory at shift change, just in time to see one long line of workers going into the Entrance and another long one coming out of the Exit.

It wasn't the most heartening sight in the world—the people coming out were so tired and lifeless, they might have been robots rather than cyborgs. The ones going in were a bit livelier, but only a bit. You could tell they weren't looking forward to the next eight hours.

Most of them were TRs, and the rest were almost there. But they weren't sporting flashy, shiny Paladin bodies—these people were all walking toolkits, tailored for a particular purpose, whatever that might be. No one in this group had any conspicuous adornments like a custom paint-job or a fancy etched design. The Factory frowned on customisation not required for the job as a possible safety hazard; it could distract other employees, and a distracted employee was an accident waiting to happen. It might also confuse sensors monitoring employees on duty, which might cause mistakes in attendance records. As a result, an employee might not be paid, and nobody wanted that. Payroll mistakes were notoriously difficult to straighten out, sometimes taking as long as six months, which was a very long time to go without a pay cheque.

The expression on Hugo's face at the sight of these two sorry groups gave Vector the idea that this could be what they called an object lesson or a teachable moment.

"If you're not the lead ant," Vector said, "the view never changes."

Hugo had turned to him with wide eyes and Vector knew instinctively the kid had been thinking something very similar. He might as well drive the point home, Vector thought, and decided to take a little detour on his way up to the office.

When they reached the executive elevators, Vector had made a business of waving the Centurians aside just before they read his internal ID. He knew how it would look to Hugo, like he had more power in his fingertips than regular people could even imagine.

Then they made a stop at the control booth high above the Factory floor so Hugo could see what it was like to look down on operations through the floor-to-ceiling windows.

Seen this way, it was actually quite amazing. Cyborgs worked among much larger robot arms, their machine attachments performing tasks in perfect rhythm. The human workers were so integrated into the mode of production that it was actually hard to tell where they left off and the machines began, even when you saw their faces, which sort of bobbed around near the assembly line like balloons with unhappy, careworn faces painted on them.

While the unhappy expression on Hugo's face suggested he might throw up, Vector decided he'd suffered enough and took him up to his office.

Vector wasn't especially fond of letting street trash sit on his expensive furniture—he'd have to have everything shampooed and maybe fumigated to get rid of the stink of poverty and failure. But if you wanted something from one of these little weasels, you had to give them the idea that if they pleased you, they actually had a hope in hell of climbing out of the hole they'd been born in.

"Smooth, isn't it?" Vector said, as if he thought Hugo would know. "This is the stuff they send up to Zalem, not the watered-down rat piss they serve locally."

"So it's like tasting Zalem," Hugo said happily. As if he really believed it.

"You know, Hugo, I was born in a poor village on the outskirts of the Badlands," Vector said chattily, pumping sincerity into each word. No one could do honest like he did. "I came to Iron City when I was nine, and I was surrounded by scum. Everywhere I looked, it was all scum, all the time. But I survived. I worked hard, and pretty soon I gained a reputation. People knew me, knew who I was." He paused to look out of one of the windows and the kid looked too. *His* view, although the kid probably didn't understand that yet. But he would, unless he was stupider than he looked.

"The poor in this world, they suffer and work, work and suffer," Vector went on. "That's how it's always been and how it always will be. Insects never know they're insects." He turned to the kid, looking wise. "But we know the truth, don't we?" As if "we" would ever mean him and Hugo.

"Well—" Hugo frowned a little. "*I'm* no worker ant, I know that."

No, you're a worm. "I like your drive," Vector told him, enthusing a little, as if he didn't usually but Hugo was so special he couldn't hide his admiration. "You have the determination not to fail. You could have a pretty solid future with my organisation."

Hugo took another sip of the whisky Vector was wasting on him. "*My* future's in Zalem," he said confidently. "I remember your promise every day."

Vector's smile never faltered. His policy was to forget promises as soon as he made them, sometimes even *while* he was making them. Whenever some fool came around expecting him to cough up a reward, he always found a way to show them they'd failed to hold up their part of the bargain and were therefore entitled to nothing except an ass-kicking for trying to con him.

But somehow the kid picked up on the fact that he'd drawn a blank. "You know, to send me up?" Hugo prodded. "You said when I bring you a million credits, you'll send me straight to Zalem."

Vector covered his surprise by taking a hefty swig from his glass. "Of *course* I remember," he lied amiably. "And you have that many? A million credits?"

"Almost," Hugo said, beaming with pride. "Just a couple more months and—" He looked through the window and pointed up at Zalem. "I'm there."

"*Really.*" Vector refilled Hugo's glass more generously. "Hugo, I do believe I'm *impressed.* You don't see that kind of spirit in kids these days. Not in too many adults, either." He gave himself a refill. "Let's drink to Zalem."

They clinked glasses and Vector watched him throw back a healthy gulp. The little shit-bag had to be living on next to nothing, Vector thought, careful not to show his amazement. He could have been living high in a nice apartment—well, nice for Iron City—dressing like royalty and taking pricey companions to restaurants and bars where fights *didn't* break out every night. Instead, he was living like a beggar while he saved up for his big dream. It was almost enough to make him *like* the kid. He could use someone like that on his payroll.

On the other hand, guys like Hugo could suddenly grow a conscience at the worst possible time. Although, Vector reminded himself, the kid jacked cyborgs for a living; he knew damned well he wasn't an angel. But he was smart; he was more likely to start second-guessing every order he was given. Either way, Vector would end up having to get rid of him, because you couldn't buy someone like that off.

Still, he wouldn't have minded having someone with a real work ethic to do the heavy lifting; it would be good while it lasted. Maybe he could talk the kid into reconsidering his plans.

"I agree that Zalem's great," Vector said before Hugo could say anything else about his real dream, "but personally, I'd rather rule in hell than serve in heaven. If you see what I mean." The kid nodded but he was starting to look a little bleary. Vector gestured at the tiny lights in the night sky. "If we went up there right now, we'd have to start all over again, at the bottom of the food chain. Down here, though—" He gestured at their surroundings with both hands. "Down here, we can live like kings. We can make our own rules—they look the other way because they need me to keep the wheels turning at the Factory and keep the Games running. Someone's gotta keep the masses distracted; bread and circuses, you know the drill." Hugo didn't; Vector gave him a thousand-megawatt smile as if he did. "Might as well be me. And you, if you're up for it."

He gave the kid another unnecessary refill, then brought over one of the other, slightly smaller and less cushy chairs and sat down so they were eye to eye.

"So, tell me about this girl of yours," Vector said, his voice low and confidential. "The one you brought to the track the other night."

"You mean Alita?" Hugo looked a bit surprised at the sudden change of subject.

"Oh, is that her name?" Vector said innocently. "Word on the street is she's a pretty good Motorball player. Left a lot of guys eating her dust." As if she were the talk of the town.

"Oh, she's the *best*!" Hugo's face was flushed with good booze and impossible dreams. And, if Vector wasn't mistaken, puppy love, too. "She's got more natural talent than anybody I ever saw. I swear, she could play for the Second League right now. Tonight!"

Vector made an impressed face. "Well, if she's *that* good, bring her to Second League tryouts and I'll see to it she gets a shot."

"You mean—you mean at the *stadium*?" If the kid's eyes got any bigger, they'd pop out of his head and drop into his whisky. "Are you *serious*?"

"Hugo, you and I have a common trait," Vector assured him, his tone even more confidential. "We can both spot talent in its natural habitat."

"You won't regret this," Hugo promised him.

"Oh, I know I won't," Vector replied. The kid was so boggled that the compliment had gone right by him. That was some bad case of puppy love he had. He raised the level in Hugo's glass to make sure he was too drunk to think of running off to give Alita the good news right this minute. The tryouts were weeks away; she could use the time to train. Vector wanted both him and the girl all pumped up on faith, hope and puppy love so that when she went down in flames, Hugo would be too destroyed to say the word *Zalem* ever again.

CHAPTER 18

Eventually, Hugo realised the warmth on the side of his face was sunlight. He guessed it must be morning. Furthermore, judging by the angle of the light and by how sweaty he felt, he realised he had belly-flopped onto his mattress fully clothed last night.

The sun was getting brighter, like it was nagging him to get up and do something to justify his existence, when all he wanted to do was go back to sleep. The only way he could avoid the monumental hangover waiting to strike him down was by not moving. Ever.

All at once, a shadow fell over him, and he felt himself smile at the blessed relief. A second later, it was gone and he winced as the sun threatened to cook him where he lay. The hangover decided it could wait no longer; his brain turned into a big bass drum and started beating itself.

The shadow returned and this time it stayed where it was. The relief from the sun was welcome but it did nothing to alleviate the pain in his head. It occurred to him that the shadow expected something from him. Hugo hoped it was the Angel of Death, come to put him out of his misery. He opened one eye.

Not the Angel of Death, but his head hurt too much to let him smile. "Hey," he croaked.

"What *happened* to you?" Alita asked with real concern. Like she'd never seen a guy with a hangover before. Then he remembered she probably hadn't.

Moving slowly, he sat up, holding his head so the big bass drum wouldn't pound it off his neck and send it rolling across the floor.

"Oh, nothing." He tried to sound casual. "I wound up hanging with Vector last night. Alcohol was involved. Apparently. He said it was the good stuff." Everybody claimed the good stuff wouldn't give you a hangover. Obviously everybody was a big fat liar. So what else was new?

"Vector?" Alita squatted down to peer into his face. "Is he your connection for getting up to Zalem?"

"Yeah."

"Oh," she said, and Hugo watched her wilt like she'd just lost the last thing she'd ever had to be happy about. "I was hoping you'd want to stay."

God, sometimes he could be such a boob. "Well, it's not right away," he added quickly. "I've still got—"

"No, it's okay," she said and he saw her forcing herself to perk up. "It's your dream. What you've always wanted."

"Used to be." Hugo got to his feet and kicked through the clothes lying around on the floor, searching for a shirt that might be even just marginally cleaner than the one he had on. "I was always so sure about that. Then you come along and nothing's clear to me any more." He paused to look out the window at the Factory complex. Alita followed his gaze, then looked quizzically at him.

"All I know is, I'm not gonna end up like my dad," Hugo told her. "A Factory drone who had to replace himself piece by piece."

The night his father had come home with the extendable arm, Hugo had been frightened by all the metal and rubber, and when his father had hugged him with his real arm, the smell of oil and plastic cement had made him gag. He'd just been a little kid but he still felt ashamed of the way he'd run away crying.

"And for what?" Hugo gave a harsh, humourless laugh. "So he could drop dead on the assembly line one day making things he could never have. He never even *tried* for anything better. But I'm getting the hell out of here before it's too late." He paused. "My dad always used to joke about Management having a rule that if you felt yourself passing out, you had to fall *away* from the machines. Otherwise it made a mess and it took longer to replace you. Some joke, huh? Or maybe the joke is, he didn't have time."

Alita was silent for a long moment. Then she said, "How much more do you need before you can go?"

"Ninety K." Although the way he felt now, he'd have had trouble making nine credits.

"But I can earn that in bounties!" Alita said, perking up again. "I'll just see who's got the highest bounties on their heads and take 'em out!"

Hugo stared at her incredulously. Even his head was

too surprised to throb. "I'd *never* ask you to do that for me," he said.

"I'd do *anything* for you," she told him cheerfully, like it was no big deal. She pulled up her shirt and pressed a spot at the base of her throat, which opened her chest cavity.

Hugo was horrified. "What are you *doing*?"

Alita reached into her ribcage with one hand, removed her heart, and held it out to him, like she was offering him a sandwich. Or a bar of chocolate. For the first time in his life, Hugo couldn't speak, couldn't move, couldn't do anything except stare at the exquisite white ceramic heart beating away in her hand, pumping heart's-blood and cyber-blood through the vessels attached to it.

"I'd give you my heart," Alita said, and Hugo knew it was a promise. He had never fainted but he was starting to feel like he might. Unless he woke up first.

"I mean it," she went on. "And it's a good one. It's got an Urm micro-reactor for a power supply. It's worth *millions*."

Tanji appeared suddenly in Hugo mind's eye, looking as grim-faced as ever. *Don't just stand there, dumbass—jack that shit and run! We'd get enough to live on for the rest of our lives.*

"With your connections, you could find a buyer easy," Alita was saying. "You could get enough so w e could *both* go to Zalem. Then you could find me a cheap replacement."

The memory of the crew heaving Kinuba's cyber-core replayed in his head. But when it hit the street, in his mind's eye it was Alita, looking up at him with those big eyes. *I told you I'd do anything.*

"No!" Hugo snapped.

Alita gave him a nudge. "Oh, come on. You buy and sell pieces all the time."

When you gonna tell your hardbody you jack cyborgs?

"No," he said again, more quietly but just as firmly. "Look—don't just *do* things for people, no matter how good you think they are or how deserving or—or anything else. Especially not things like this."

"It's all or nothing with me, Hugo," she said, her big eyes serious. "That's just who I am."

Hugo pushed her hand gently back towards her chest cavity. For a moment, his fingertip touched her heart and he *felt* it beating. "Please put it back," he begged her. "*Please.*"

Alita did so without further argument. Hugo watched her close up her chest and pull down her shirt, knowing the sensation of her heart beating was going to haunt him for a very long time, possibly forever.

"Okay, see?" she said brightly. "All gone. That was pretty intense, though, wasn't it?" she added.

"Yeah, *very* intense," he agreed and went back to hunting for a shirt so she wouldn't see how freaked he still was. But at least it seemed to have scared off his hangover.

Outside, Hugo was about to start his gyro when he paused to look up at Zalem. "Maybe there's another way to get there," he said. "I meant to tell you, Vector wants you to try out for Second League."

"*What?*" Alita wasn't sure she'd heard him right. "What did you say?"

"Hey, if you become a big-deal Motorball star, you'll make a fortune and we can go up together."

Alita burst into hearty giggles. "What are you talking about? I can't be a pro Motorball player!"

Hugo twisted around and took her head in both his hands. "Alita, you *could* be a champion. For real. No kidding. You win the Second League tryout and scouts'll be killing each other to get to you. We'll be home free—home in Zalem."

Alita frowned. "Well, let's ride while I think it over."

Shrugging, Hugo turned around to start the gyro and Alita burst out laughing again. She grabbed him around the waist and squeezed.

"Okay, I'll do it!" she said. "But *only* if *you'll* be my coach!"

"If that's what it takes—" He gave her a quick kiss. "I'm your man!"

She was leaning back as she rode behind the kid, stretching out, letting the wind blow her hair around like she didn't have anything to worry about. Like nothing bad could ever happen to her. Like this wasn't Iron City, where all good things came to a bad end, often before they even had a chance to begin.

"You gonna kill her?" asked the cyborg in a whiny voice.

"Worse," said Zapan, keeping his gaze on the happy couple as they sped away. He rubbed the bridge of his nose, which would never be the same again. "I'm gonna break her heart."

"Come again?" the cyborg said.

Zapan had to force himself not to take the cyborg's head off and drop-kick it into traffic. He had, after all, tracked the kid down for him. But Zapan was damned if he was going to call the guy Cronie, even if that was his name. People could get the wrong idea.

"Okay, let me break it down for you," Zapan said. "Shut. Up."

Cronie nodded. "That's what I thought."

CHAPTER 19

The weeks Alita had been sure would never pass finally went by. The day of the tryout seemed to last as long as the previous month. Several times, Gerhad made a point of assuring Alita that the sun would set and night would fall. Ido promised he would go with her to the track and help her with her armour and her wheel-feet and everything else. And Hugo, to her immense disappointment, promised to meet her there because he had an errand to run. But he would definitely be there. After all the time he'd spent coaching her, he wasn't going to stand her up. Gerhad promised her the same thing, saying that Hugo would miss it only if he were dead.

"I didn't rebuild you just so you could end up as wreckage on the Motorball track," Ido complained as Alita led him along the access tunnel.

"You're right," Alita said. "Let's just go bag ourselves a couple of heads. Easy money."

"All right, all *right*," Ido said grumpily.

"Thought you'd see it my way," Alita replied, smug and happy as they walked up to the SECURITY guy. The pride she had felt at giving Ido a pass on a lanyard was completely undercut when the SECURITY guy waved them both through without even looking. Well, it was only a tiny letdown, she told herself. Hugo would be waiting for them on the pit lane.

But he wasn't.

Hugo's phone rang as he whipped through traffic on his gyro. He didn't have to look at the display to know who was calling. "What's up, Alita?"

"'What's up?' What do you think? Where *are* you?" she demanded.

"On my way," he assured her cheerfully. "Just gotta make this one stop and—"

"If you miss this, I'll *kill* you."

"Hey, I'll be there, trust me! I just gotta—" There was a hard click as she hung up on him. "Do one thing," he finished lamely and pushed the gyro faster, dodging in and out of traffic on both street and sidewalk.

Trust him? Of course she trusted him, Alita fumed, feeling more dangerous than usual. She'd spent all that time training with him; he should know that she trusted him absolutely. And that he could trust her unconditionally—to *kill* his ass if he didn't get there on time.

A moment later, she forgot all about Hugo as Jashugan appeared before her, a vision of Motorball royalty with his black-and-gold armour, while his pit crew scrambled and flitted around him with scanners and sonar wands and thermo-readers, calling out to each other.

"The camber's still off in the right bogey," Jashugan said, serene with authority and wisdom, while the crew went into a frenzy of note-taking, one guy writing on his own arm in marker.

Jashugan was about to say something else when his gaze fell on Alita and time stopped.

Then it started again as his noble, godlike features broke into a broad, sunny smile that made his grey eyes twinkle. *Jashugan was glad to see her.*

It only took a fraction of a second for the story to unfold in her head. Hugo had told Jashugan about her tryout and about what a tremendous talent she was, and Jashugan wanted to meet her. And to befriend her! Mutual respect of competitors. Brotherhood of the Paladins. Heroes of the Game. She could see it all in his face as he came towards her and reached out to shake her hand.

And then his hand went past her to Ido.

"Doc!" said Jashugan, his dignified tones warm and delighted. "I haven't seen you in ages! Really glad you're here!"

"Hi, champ," Ido said, shaking hands with him, all casual. "And here." Ido put his arm around her shoulders. "I'd like you to meet Alita."

"Hello," Jashugan said politely, absolutely and definitely offering his hand to her now. "I'm Jashugan."

"Oh, I know who you are!" Alita bubbled, grabbing his hand with both of hers and pumping it up and down. "I'm a *big* fan, *really* big—the *biggest*! I'm trying out for Second League tonight!"

He looked down at her with benign curiosity and she suddenly felt a lot more like pretty young Alita covered in flowers, not the fierce warrior who had been training with Hugo to be the next Motorball badass.

"I see," Jashugan said. "So you intend to play the greatest game that ever was?"

"Yes, sir," Alita said, pride in her voice.

"And what do you want from my game?" Jashugan asked. "Fame? Wealth? Glory?"

Alita met his gaze with confidence and certainty. "I follow the path of the warrior."

She must have said the right thing, Alita thought; he was smiling and there was a twinkle in his eye, but he seemed genuinely pleased by her response.

"Then perhaps the next time we meet," Jashugan said, "it will be on the track."

"Okay, yeah, good!" Alita enthused, waiting for him to go off with his crew. Why was he still standing there? Maybe he was waiting for her to say something more intelligent than *Okay, yeah, good*?

No, she realised, he was just waiting for her to let go of his hand.

Mortified, she released him and he inclined his head

towards her. (He *bowed* to me! she thought ecstatically. Jashugan *bowed to* me!) He gave Ido another big smile and then rolled off towards the locker room area with his pit crew scurrying after him.

"*Wow*," Alita breathed, staring after him in star-struck wonder. Did his crew have any idea how privileged they were to be in the service of such a magnificent Paladin? She turned back to the pit lane and bumped into a stout man in greasy mechanic's overalls. The top of his head came to just under her nose.

"So you're Hugo's hot prospect," he said in a flat, almost bored voice. "I'm Ed, how ya doin'?" Before she could answer, he shoved a large, lumpy duffel bag at her. "Here's some loaner gear I scraped together for ya. You're welcome." He stumped away, leaving her and Ido nonplussed.

Vector looked around at the rough, scarred men in the locker room who were currently cursing and speculating on each other's parentage. His bodyguard was stationed just inside the door, although Vector wasn't concerned about anyone walking in on them. Any Paladin would take one look at who was in there and find somewhere else to be. Real Paladins didn't mix with street thugs who couldn't get even one sponsor to sticker them. Several of them were banned from every bar in town, on the grounds that their presence could decrease property values.

But this was nothing Vector had to worry about. Owning the Game afforded him a lot of privileges. Final

Champion was the best a Paladin could hope for, but Vector was the king. And it was good to be the king, better than anything.

Vector cleared his throat and they quieted down. "I'd like to thank you all for coming in at such short notice," he said. "You—well, I hesitate to use the term 'players' because, frankly, you're the scum of the Game."

They let him know they didn't like that a whole lot. There were catcalls and jeers. But no one threw even a towel at him, and not only because his bodyguard would make garbage out of them with the automatic under his jacket. You didn't have to be the sharpest knife in the drawer to know that life could get very bad for everyone when you disrespected the king.

Grinning, Vector held up both hands and they all shut up. "Tonight, however, you're *hand-picked* scum—*my* scum. Because tonight, it's not a game, and it's not a tryout. It's a hunt. And I'll pay five hundred K to whomever kills the girl called Alita."

Now he had their attention.

Alita stopped fumbling with the connections on her leg armour and looked up at Ido so plaintively, it was all he could do not to take her in his arms, stroke her hair, and tell her everything was going to be all right. But that was no way to treat a Motorball badass.

"Can a human love a cyborg?" she asked, her voice wistful.

"Why do you ask?" Ido asked with a gentle smile. "Does this cyborg love a human?"

She sighed. "I love Hugo."

It wasn't exactly news to Ido, given all the time they'd spent together. The way she talked about him, the way she looked when she came back after training sessions, not to mention the mornings she'd pretended she'd got up very early when she had really just come home—he might have no experience with a grown daughter, but he wasn't stupid. Gerhad had advised him to stand back, give her room to move, and let her come to him, if and when she wanted to talk. And now here she was, confiding in him. If only her timing had been better.

"Well, that's wonderful," he told her. "But right now you have to keep your head in the Game. It can get crazy-rough out there on the track, even when it's just a tryout." Ido took a pair of wheel-feet out of his own bag and swapped them for the loaner wheels she'd been about to put on. "Here, use these."

Alita's face lit up with surprised delight. "Did you make these for me?"

Ido nodded as he put the loaner wheels back in the duffle bag. "They won't give you super-speed—regulations—but they'll be a lot more reliable."

Ed had actually put together some pretty good gear for her but borrowed wheels could be iffy for anyone, especially for Alita with her technologically advanced body. Ido had done his best to make this pair more compatible with the Urm connectivity. They weren't Urm-level, but there wouldn't be even a microsecond of lag between her nerves firing and the action of her wheels. Ido had watched Hugo's videos of their practice sessions so he could match the shape and wheel placement to her rolling gait and style of movement. And they were durable—they'd hold up for tonight. He could see about making an even better pair later.

Watching Alita put them on, Ido had a sudden, powerful urge to sweep her up in his arms and run for home. Gerhad had reminded him more than once that Alita wasn't his little girl any more—except she *was*, dammit, and she had no idea how brutal it could get out there. She *thought* she did, just because she'd seen a few games and she'd been training hard for weeks. But the Paladin-bodycam view they showed on the big stadium screens didn't convey what it was really like to be in the thick of things.

"What is it?" Alita asked, looking up at him curiously.

"Nothing," Ido said and forced himself to smile as if he didn't think this was a terrible idea. "Now, look—here's our deal: you go out there, you win, and then you skate right back to this locker room. And you wear *all* the protection—*all* the pads, *all* the armour. And this." He pushed the helmet down on her head and adjusted the sizing.

Alita's smile turned to a grimace as she looked from him to the padding and body armour piled on the floor. "I don't *really* need all that crap, do I? It'll slow me down."

"You *do* need every bit of it," Ido told her firmly. "Remember, if you wreck *this* body, you're outta luck. It's Urm technology; I can't fix it."

Alita immediately began padding up, and Ido helped

her while congratulating himself on finally saying exactly the right thing. She didn't even mind him double- and triple-checking everything to make sure nothing would come loose or fall off. He took a few extra minutes to give her wheels one last pre-game check. They really were good wheels; in a previous lifetime, he would have been proud of this work. Now his only concern was that it was the best he could do for his little girl. His little girl, the Motorball badass.

As soon as they were finished checking everything, Alita surprised him by asking him to leave.

"I need a little time to myself," she told him, her voice gentle. "You know, to think about what I'm gonna do, compose myself."

Ido stood back and looked her over, his little girl, the warrior spirit in the warrior body. Even in borrowed padding and armour, she looked formidable.

"Good luck, honey," he said.

"Thanks," she said absently. She had found a marker in the duffel bag and was too busy scrawling "99" on each shoulder to see him leave.

Alita plumped down on the bench with relief as the door closed behind Ido. It wasn't really that he'd been making her nervous, although his checking and rechecking had started to feel more than a little obsessive-compulsive. She wanted him in the stadium so he could watch as she made her entrance onto the track. Then he'd see she was ready for anything and there was nothing to worry about.

She gave herself a few quiet seconds before rolling out of the locker room into the hall where she almost collided with Ed, as stout as ever but even shorter when she was wearing wheel-feet. He didn't look at all impressed; maybe because she didn't have her game face on yet, she thought.

"Have you seen Hugo?" she asked him.

"I've seen everyone," Ed assured her. "Track's this way." He started down the hallway without looking back to see if she was coming. "Unless you changed your mind and you wanna go out for ice cream."

She'd show him ice cream, Alita thought as she rolled after him. She'd show them all.

CHAPTER 20

Hugo heard them even before he turned the corner into the alley.

"Please, just stop!" the cyborg begged Tanji and Dif. They had him on the ground tangled up in a net. "I haven't done anything to you, I just wanna go home and catch the game highlights!"

That was pretty much what all the cyborgs said when they got jacked. In the past, it hadn't meant a thing to Hugo, just the noise an unlucky cyborg made while he and the crew made a living.

"Hey, this is *just business*," Tanji was telling him in an exasperated tone of voice while he pried off the cyborg's actuator mount from the back of his neck. It came away with a loud wrenching pop that made Hugo feel sick, even though he'd done the same thing himself more times than he could count. "It's nothin' personal. *Really.*"

Hugo skidded to a stop and hurriedly leaned his gyro against a wall. He was barely aware of hearing the gyro topple over as he ran to Tanji.

"Tanji, *stop!*" Hugo yelled, pulling him off the cyborg on the ground.

Tanji's astonishment was plain even though his face was completely hidden behind his goggles and bandanna. He dropped the actuator, turned back to the cyborg and bopped him on the head with the pry bar, knocking him out. Dif seemed to be frozen in place with a bundle of wires in one hand; cheap stuff they'd probably have to give away.

"You said my *name*, you idiot!" Tanji said angrily. "What the hell's wrong with you?"

"Nothing's wrong with *me*," Hugo replied. "I can't do this any more. I *won't*."

Tanji gave him a hard shove. "So *that's* your damage now?" He shoved Hugo again, making him stagger backwards so he almost tripped over his fallen gyro. "You been gone for weeks and now you show up with this line of crap? It's your little hardbody, isn't it?"

Hugo grabbed him by the front of his jacket, whirled him around, and slammed him against the wall. "It's over for me, got that? *I'm out*—done, finito, thank you and good night! And if you had half a brain, you'd get out, too!"

Tanji batted Hugo's hands away. He raised his goggles and pulled down his bandanna. "You shoulda jacked that bitch. You'd be on your way to Zalem right now!" As Tanji made a move towards the still-unconscious cyborg, Hugo punched him.

The blow surprised Tanji more than it hurt him. He hit the wall behind and bounced back swinging. Hugo knew

Tanji had the advantage just by virtue of experience—Tanji had been in lots of fights and won most of them. By contrast, Hugo always tried talking his way out of a tight spot, and if that didn't work, he ran like hell. Right now, however, he didn't want to talk *or* run, he wanted to pound Tanji into the pavement, and the feeling was mutual.

Tanji had him in a headlock and Hugo was trying to bite him through his jacket when someone burst out laughing. It wasn't Dif, who was still standing by, uselessly clutching the wires. Hugo and Tanji let go of each other to see a familiar pampered face grinning at them.

"Bravo!" Zapan said, clapping his hands as he stood over the cyborg on the ground. "A magnificent display! *Very* professional!"

Breathing heavily, Tanji wiped his bloody mouth with his sleeve. "Hey, we don't want no trouble with you." He gestured at the cyborg. "If this is your mark, we're sorry. He's all yours."

Zapan ignored him. "Really, Hugo—jacking cyborgs? Your little girlfriend might take this kinda personally, don't you think?"

Hugo took an unsteady breath. He didn't want to imagine Alita's face if she were here. His whole life had been a waste until she had come into it. He'd sworn he would never be a drone on a Factory assembly line like his father. But there were all kinds of assembly lines, and they weren't only in the Factory. He'd told himself it was all just so he could get to Zalem, but jacking cyborgs had really been just another kind of assembly line, and he'd been a dedicated drone. It hadn't been pieces of his body he'd been replacing, but bits of his soul, swapping them for empty modules labelled *Zalem*. All this came to him as a single, fully formed thought, and then Zapan was running his mouth again.

"You know how girls are," the hunter said in an exaggerated, blasé tone. "First, she'll go all weepy and oh-Hugo-how-*could*-you. But in the end she'll forgive you—" The Damascus Blade flashed as Zapan drew it from its sheath. "When I show her your head!"

"There's no marker out for me." Hugo kept his eyes on the sword.

"Don't worry, there will be." Zapan's over-done face made his smile even nastier. "Murder pulls a pretty good bounty, even on gutter trash like you."

"I never killed *anybody*!" Hugo said hotly.

The Damascus Blade swept a gleaming path through the air, dipping downwards and then rising. On the ground, the cyborg's head rolled away from his body, trailing a mix of heart's-blood and cyber-blood.

"You just did," Zapan informed him.

In the next moment, Hugo found himself against the wall with the edge of the Damascus Blade under his chin and Zapan's face centimetres from his own. Up close, he could see how badly Alita had ruined the perfection of his nose. It really *wouldn't* ever be the same.

"She thinks she can punk *me* and get away with it?" the Hunter snarled, digging his metal fingers into Hugo's shoulder.

Oh my God, this is all about Alita! Hugo thought as the cyborg's fingers pushed through his clothing to break his skin. Blood welled up and spilled down his jacket, and he couldn't help crying out in pain, just as Zapan let go of him and fell sideways.

"Run, Hugo!" Tanji turned to Zapan with the pry bar in one hand but Zapan was faster and kicked him against the wall where Hugo had been. The Damascus Blade flashed again and there were two distinct thuds as Tanji hit the ground.

Hugo had one fire-bottle left on his belt; he flicked the fuse with his thumb and hurled it straight at Zapan. The Hunter-Warrior turned away but Hugo's aim was too good, even with a wounded shoulder. Zapan screamed and cursed as flames enveloped his entire body. He tore his clothes off, and Hugo wondered briefly if all the cyborgs in Iron City were really too stupid to drop and roll when they were on fire. Hugo pelted out of the alley and into the street.

Tears spilled down his face as he ran and he smeared them away roughly, telling himself he could cry for Tanji later, when Ido collected the bounty on Zapan. But not now, not while Zapan's screams and curses were echoing in his head.

He glanced back and discovered he wasn't hearing Zapan in his head—the son of a bitch was chasing him, even though he was still on fire! People gave ground quickly to a madman holding a sword with his arms in flames—Zapan was actually *gaining* on him.

Hugo sprinted off the sidewalk and into the middle of the road, dodging traffic. He narrowly missed losing the top of his head to the side-view mirror of a lorry going the other way, just before a pedal-car driver tossed a cup of something cold, brown and sticky at him. Everyone on the road was cursing him, but he could still hear Zapan coming after him.

His chest was starting to feel tight now and he was vaguely aware of pain in his shoulder. If he could get down to the old highway interchange, he'd have a better chance of losing the Hunter. It was only a few more blocks. He doubted Zapan knew his way around the shadowy area under the remnants of flyovers that now stood broken and disconnected.

Hugo began zigzagging his way towards the opposite side of the street, infuriating more drivers until he ran up onto the sidewalk to earn the wrath of pedestrians, as well as the people in the outdoor seating area of a café. They were all watching a big screen feed from the stadium, which reminded Hugo that Alita was going to kill him.

But only if Zapan didn't kill him first. The hunter was pacing him on the other side of the street, bellowing curses in between descriptions of what he was going to do to Hugo's head. God, didn't he *ever* shut up?

Hugo reached the edge of the interchange area; all he had to do was find the right place to jump. Zapan was coming across the street and there wasn't time to be choosy or careful. He went another half-block and hoped he remembered the layout below correctly as he vaulted over the guard rail.

The fall was longer than he expected but a lot more trash had piled up on the slope below. The landing knocked the wind out of him but no bones snapped and no joints twisted. He scrambled to get out of sight and tumbled down the incline into a dead-end lower-level street where the homeless found shelter from the rain.

As Hugo got to his feet, he saw a few of them look up from sorting through the stuff they'd collected that day, but only briefly and without interest. People down here had their own problems and they didn't need any more, especially not the kind on Hugo's tail.

Gerhad had found a spot for them with a good view of the pits as well as the track. It proved once again what an excellent friend she was, Ido thought as he sat down beside her.

The stadium was still emptying out. Most people didn't hang around after a game to watch tryouts. Usually, the spectators were mostly friends and family of the prospects and some of the Factory team jobbers, a few trainers and scouts looking for someone with potential, and a small group of hardcore fans who felt it was their sacred duty to jeer at aspiring players in an attempt to break their spirits and crush their dreams.

Ido was more concerned about who would be on the track attempting to break and crush more substantial things. He looked around, listening to the roar of motors and the higher, whining sound of cheap turbines. For some people, players as well as fans, motors were the best thing about Motorball. He could remember building in a sound-effects attachment for—

Abruptly, he felt Gerhad's hand on his knee, pressing down hard until his leg stopped jiggling.

"Thanks," Ido said. "You know, I haven't been to the track since…" His voice trailed off. Still couldn't say it.

"I know," Gerhad said kindly. She studied his face for a moment. "You gonna be okay tonight?"

Ido was about to tell her yes, of course he would. Instead, he heard himself say, "I *hate* this game." Pause. "Almost as much as I love it."

Gerhad patted his arm. "You think our girl has a chance?"

Ido sighed mournfully. "I'm afraid so."

"Next up this evening!" the announcer boomed over the PA, making Ido jump a little. "Tryouts for the Second League! *Anything* can happen—we might witness the birth of *the next champion*! Will the Factory practice team please assemble at the starting line and show us what you've got!"

Ido frowned at the players streaming onto the track in the distance. The big screen directly in front of him and Gerhad showed only clouds of dust and smoke, arty camera angles of spinning wheels that looked suspiciously like stock footage put in to sweeten the video come-on, and a few glimpses of some very scarred armour seen mostly through heat shimmers.

This was a lot of camera-tease for a tryout, Ido thought as he adjusted his glasses for long-range. The players were still throwing up a lot of smoke and dust, but now he could see their battered armour and their even more disfigured faces and they told him everything.

"That's no Factory team!" Ido said angrily.

"What?" Gerhad pulled a small pair of binoculars out of her coat pocket.

"See for yourself. Those two punks on the far right in red and blue? There are bounty markers on them."

"Damn," Gerhad said.

"And the rest of them—they used to be players but now they're bounty hunters or worse. This is nothing but a gang of street iron!"

"What the hell are hunters doing lining up with marks?" said Gerhad, appalled.

"Because it's rigged." Ido hopped over the rail and ran for the pits.

"And here come our new prospects!" sang the announcer, as if he could barely contain his excitement. Then: "Oh, wait a minute. It seems we have only one prospect trying out tonight. I guess the rest of them went out for ice cream. Well, okay then, everybody, give it up for *Alita*!"

The pessimists in the stadium gave her the traditional greeting for newcomers—i.e., thumbs down and a chorus of boos, interspersed with calls of "Go home, punk!" and "Die in flames!"

Ido saw he was too late. Alita was already on the feeder lane. Her face appeared on the big screen; she looked tough, focused, determined. It crossed Ido's mind that he wouldn't bet against her, even in borrowed armour. He pushed his way through the crews milling around on the pit lane, hoping he could get her attention before they started. He saw her scanning the stadium. Looking for Hugo, of course. Where the hell was he, anyway? This was *not* the night to play Disappearing Boyfriend. If he didn't show up, Ido was going to kill him twice before Alita got her hands on him.

"Since we have only one prospect," the announcer enthused, "there will be *no teams*! I repeat: *one* prospect, *no* teams! The name of the game is Cut-Throat! Ten laps. All players to the starting line now."

Ido climbed onto the pit-lane railing. "Alita!" he yelled, waving his arms frantically. "Alita, wait!"

Vector was enjoying some Zalem-restricted whisky along with the elevated view of the track from his glassed-in box. Part of the back wall was an enormous screen that showed feeds from any of a number of cameras Chiren controlled remotely. The picture slewed back and forth until Chiren finally found the right subject. She kept the camera on Alita as she skated onto the track. Vector had to admit the bitch actually looked a little scary.

"Hugo brought her right to us," he said, momentarily pleased with the state of the world and anticipating its imminent further improvement.

"And what did you promise him?" Chiren asked.

Vector had another sip, savouring the taste. "I'm sending him to Zalem, of course," he said and laughed, because it really was funny. No, not just funny—hilarious. Strangely, though, he was the only one laughing. He turned to Chiren and saw she was giving him her trademark Ice-Queen-Death-Ray glare.

"You're sending *me* to Zalem," she said.

"Yeah, yeah, of course I am," he said breezily, wishing she'd just shut up and have some whisky. Whisky always put her in the mood to lie down on the desk, or anywhere else he told her to. Onscreen, he saw she was now zooming in on the last person he wanted to see. Ido seemed to be having hysterics about something, yelling and hollering at someone who obviously didn't want to look at him either.

Vector helped himself to some more whisky. He was so tired of Chiren's bullshit that he couldn't even be bothered to tell her to get the camera off her pathetic ex and focus on Alita.

Chiren would pull herself together, Vector thought; she had as much at stake as he did.

Ido stared helplessly as Alita rolled onto the track. He tried calling out to her, but he couldn't even hear his own voice over the roar of turbines and engines.

They must have called out the toughest practice guys they had, Alita thought as she squeezed between two hulking cyborgs in the centre of the line-up. She smiled tentatively at them; they scowled back at her. Or maybe that was how really tough guys smiled. She gave a small, nervous laugh.

"Hey, guys, go easy on me, okay?"

"Oh, sure, kid," said the guy on her left. "We'll give you the cream-puff treatment." His name tag said "Antioch", and she wondered why she'd never heard of him. Or seen him on the track. In fact, she didn't remember any of these guys being in games she'd seen recently. The two guys down at the end in red and blue looked familiar, but she wasn't sure from where. Maybe the practice team didn't play much?

As she put her left wheel on the starting line, the internal phone in her helmet rang. If that was Hugo saying he couldn't make it, she'd kill him. "What?" she growled.

"Get out of there!" Ido yelled in her ear. "It's a set-up!"

"Players!" the announcer said ecstatically. "Ten-second warning. Hope you went before you left!"

"They're going to *kill* you!" Ido wailed.

Alita sneaked a glance left, then right. "Which ones?"

"All of them!" Ido cried.

One of the guys on Alita's right started up a device on the end of his arm: whirring blades instead of a hand. The name on his armour was "Stinger".

"Good to know," Alita said and broke the connection.

There was an enormous framework in front of her with a vertical row of lights. They began to flash one at a time, starting at the top with red and moving downwards to yellow.

The very last one flashed green and Alita felt her heart leap with excitement as she surged forward.

CHAPTER 21

During the weeks she had spent training with Hugo, Alita had learned a great deal about her Berserker body. She had to become accustomed to its adaptability. Once she got used to her body, she was more prepared to deal with the unexpected, which, according to Hugo, was what Motorball was all about.

This was why they put actual motors in the ball, Hugo explained; lots of little motors acted on its centre of gravity to make its trajectory unpredictable. Even if some of the motors malfunctioned, the ball's movements wouldn't be easy to anticipate. Plenty of rookie Paladins had learned that the hard way when the ball they thought they were about to get their hands on suddenly popped back at them so hard it cracked their helmet or knocked them out, or both.

The players, however, were a different story. People were full of surprises—but unlike a randomly bouncing Motorball, you could get to know your competitors.

When you were playing a game without teams, you had to assume that everybody was out to eat you for dinner, because they were. There was no way to see where everybody was at once, unless they were all lined up across the track and coming at you together, in which case, you were fast or you were toast. But that was pretty unlikely to happen. Players were all over the place, and you had to learn how to locate them without seeing them.

You gotta know how to listen, Hugo had told her. *When you're on the track, it might sound like just a bunch of machine noise, but it isn't. Every motor or turbine sounds a little different because of how a player moves as well as what kind of tech they go for. Some players accelerate then slow down repeatedly—zoom-brake, zoom-brake. The wear and tear that puts on a motor makes it sound different than, say, Jashugan's, because Jashugan uses things like steep banking on the track to slow down rather than stomping his brakes all the time.*

Then Hugo had talked about habits. *Everybody's got 'em, and a lot of guys don't even know it. Twice around the track will tell you a lot about your competition, even if you've never seen them before. Besides zoom-brake, there are guys who always swoop in front of you right after a banked turn. Then there are the tail-waggers—guys who tailgate you and keep faking coming up on one side, then the other, over and over again. Get away from them. They'll make you crazy.*

Hugo had showed her feints and fake-outs, get-outs and work-arounds, jump-ups and slide-unders. There was so much to think about, all kinds of strategy. But if you wanted to win on the track, Hugo said, you had to win in your head.

Alita had been amazed at all his knowledge and insight. He'd told her it was all just stuff he'd picked up hanging around crews and finding parts. But after her tryout was over, Alita was going to suggest he become a professional coach. He'd probably argue with her, but she was going to get through to him if she had to take his head off and pour in everything she knew by hand.

At present, however, she was certain that none of the scarred and beat-up thugs on the track with her tonight had ever been much for strategy or winning games in their heads. Hell, they weren't even playing the same game she was. She was here to play Motorball; they had come to play Murderball. And she was the ball.

Something else Hugo had said popped into her mind in her last half-second at the starting line: *No matter what you do, just be faster.*

Then the green light flashed, and she was faster.

Faster reaction time was one of the best things about the Berserker body; it was also her best chance of surviving the night.

The sound of Stinger's blades rose slightly as he swung them at Alita's head. At the same moment, she heard Antioch grunt with effort as he leaped for her. A human sound, even a grunt, had a completely different quality to the sound of a machine, and her Berserker hearing could pick it out from the cacophony around her, just as it could detect the infinitesimal rise in pitch that meant it was approaching.

Berserker reaction time put her three metres down the track before the rest of them got all their wheels past the starting line. A quick look over her shoulder was all she needed to know each player's position; she only had to listen to know when they moved. She hoped, for example, that the one whose name tag said "Gangsta"—whose legs formed a single big wheel and had smaller wheels running the lengths of his forearms—didn't really think he could sneak up on her, because he sounded like Hugo's gyro (which reminded her: she was going to kill Hugo).

Then there was Screwhead, the one with four arms. If having four arms was a real advantage, wouldn't she have been a champion by now? Her weapon of choice was a deadly-looking chain with multiple blades on one end, but Alita could picture her getting all four arms tangled up in it.

Another one, labelled Exploder, had two right arms and what looked like a small cannon on his left shoulder. He had wheels rather than legs, but they looked like they belonged on a baby carriage or maybe a tricycle. Even Stinger, with his double-threat blade-arms, had weird oval-shaped wheel-feet—the treads rolled around the stationary rims. Maybe the blade arms were supposed to distract attention from wheel-feet that looked like a malfunction waiting to happen.

And the two guys on the far end, identical except one was all in blue and the other in red—her borrowed gear looked to be in better shape than theirs. Taken altogether, the whole group looked like a bunch of mutant animals stampeding in slow motion.

But they weren't animals and they weren't in slow motion, either. Her Berserker body was pumping nutrients into her brain to accelerate her thought processes, but that wasn't going to last much longer. She had to remember everything was always happening fast and she always had to be faster.

When she broke the century—when her speed passed one hundred miles per hour—the mortar fired, snapping the Motorball into play. Alita heard the ball whistle through the air over her head before it hit the track several metres ahead of her, bounced once and flew five metres farther on, lurching from side to side, as if it were daring all of them to try catching it.

Alita didn't have to take another look over her shoulder to know the pack was gaining on her. Stinger was in the lead, waving his whirring blade-hand around. Time to show a little dominance, she decided, and pushed herself faster, keeping her eyes on the Motorball, observing the way it bounced. As she came to within three metres of it, she took a long leap of faith to the left: good guess. It bounded into her hands as if she had called it to herself. But just as she leaped for the ball, Stinger leaped for her.

"And the new kid, Alita, gets possession practically right off the snap!" yelled the announcer, on the verge of hysteria.

Alita smiled. If he thought that was exciting, he was going to wet his pants over her next move. Still airborne, she rotated her body around the ball, and then, a second before she touched down, drove the ball straight into Stinger's brutish face.

Stinger flipped backwards into the herd of murderers.

Four went down immediately, including the guy with one large wheel—Gangsta—and the guy with the nuts and bolts sticking up out of his head—Mace. *He* should have been called Screwhead, Alita thought, watching the carnage as she skated backwards.

Screwhead herself somehow managed to avoid going down in the pile-up, although she barely missed tripping over someone's loose arm sliding across the track. The thug in red wasn't as lucky. He jumped over the arm as it crossed his path but tripped as he landed and did an inadvertent cartwheel. Despite the fact that he was obviously no acrobat, he might have recovered if his fuel line hadn't ruptured. Sparks flying up off the track set him ablaze, turning him into a Catherine wheel of napalm. The crowd screamed ecstatically.

And it really was a crowd now, Alita saw; seats were filling up and more people were coming in all the time. Apparently word had got out that tonight's tryout was going to be a slaughter. Maybe it would be, Alita thought with a grin that would have scared Ido.

She turned her attention back to the track and everything slowed down again as her would-be murderers disentangled themselves from each other, got back on their feet, and aimed themselves at her. Two of them, Mace and another called Kumaza, pulled ahead of the pack with Exploder right behind them.

Mace was twirling a mace over his head. The dense metal club on the end of the chain was studded with thick, flat shards and circular saw blades, as well as spikes. It had to weigh at least as much as the Motorball itself, and Mace seemed to have no problem spinning it and skating at 100 mph. He might be unimaginative about his name but his balance was almost as good as hers. Almost; not quite.

Exploder was coming up on her other side—another less-than-creative type with pretty good balance. From this angle, his weapon looked a bit more like a jet engine than a cannon. Either way, he was carrying a hell of a big chip on his shoulder, Alita thought. The way he and Mace were positioning themselves relative to each other, it looked like they wanted to make an Alita sandwich.

Sorry, boys, that's not on the menu.

Time speeded up to normal. Alita saw the small change in the position of Mace's arm that meant he was going to let fly. She ducked just as Exploder blasted a fireball at her, or rather, where she had been. Mace ducked the fireball but his weapon slammed into Kumaza's head and they both went down, taking Exploder with them, sliding sideways across the track just as it began to curve.

Still holding the Motorball, Alita sprang up onto the outer railing, skating along the top so she could see more of the track as well as the stadium crowd, which had swelled to several hundred, with still more coming in. No one was booing her any more, although she knew a lot of the cheers were for the spectacular crashes. But she could work with that.

Alita came down off the railing into a position low enough that the Motorball scraped the track and threw up a flurry of sparks. The motors in the ball made it twitch in her grasp, as if it were trying to get away. She could sense the rage and desperation radiating from the killers behind her almost as clearly. Had they told Vector they'd leave her dead at the starting line? And how much was she worth anyway—100 K? 500 K? A whole million?

Hugo needed a million to get to Zalem. Would Vector offer that much for her? Somehow she didn't think so. She had a feeling that Vector, like most wealthy people, was a tightwad. It was probably why he'd hired this sad bunch to take her down, because he knew they'd work cheap. But that was okay. Even if he'd offered ten million, it wouldn't have mattered. Vector could buy them, but he couldn't buy her.

She heard Screwhead panting behind her. Alita slowed very slightly, letting her get almost within arm's reach, then leaped up into a spinning roundhouse kick, sending her flying into Gangsta, who rose up to knock her away into Exploder. Gangsta was upright long enough for Alita to deliver an open-hand blow to the chest, which put him flat on his back with his one large wheel spinning uselessly in the air and his motor making the kind of high-pitched whine that meant serious mechanical trouble.

Stinger suddenly drew even with her on her left. No doubt he thought that was more likely to be her weak side—except Berserkers didn't have weak sides. She was still grinning as her arm shot out and popped him before he could raise one bladed arm. He skidded sideways and Exploder skidded into him. *Get a room, you two*, Alita thought, laughing to herself as Screwhead swerved to avoid them and bashed into Antioch. Alita kept going, kept moving faster.

"A slow Tuesday night just got hotter than the playoffs,

folks!" sang the announcer, thrilled to have lucked into what would probably be the most memorable tryout of all time. "The fans have got themselves a new favourite to cheer for, an underdog with the face of an angel and a body built for battle!"

Yeah, sing my praises, Alita told him silently, beaming as the guy all in blue drew even with her. She sprang into the air, performed a showy body twist, and swung the ball into the back of his head. Head and body parted ways, the head soaring off the track while the body rolled on briefly before collapsing. Maybe that would go viral, Alita thought.

"We've been calling it Motorball," the announcer rhapsodised, "but in *her* hands, it's a *wrecking ball*!"

Someone kicked the guy's head back into the track, where it came to rest on its side, facing the oncoming pack of thugs.

"Aw crap," the head said, and then disappeared in a flurry of wheels and armoured legs while the crowd went insane.

Alita swivelled around to skate backwards and saw that the murderers were rolling towards her in a single line across the track. And Hugo had said that would never happen, she thought; she couldn't believe he was missing this.

Antioch pulled ahead and Alita marvelled at how his face and body communicated his every intention. He was planning to come straight towards her, feint right—his right—then left, and then lunge low. No wonder he'd never made it as a pro; she almost felt sorry for him, except he was the one who had promised her the cream-puff treatment. Well, she'd show him a cream-puff—

Then she was watching his body divide in two, the parts spraying bright-blue cyber-blood everywhere as they slid away from each other. Stinger moved into his place, his blades dripping with Antioch's cyber-blood.

That was some weapon he had there, Alita thought, but the guy himself was as dumb as a box of pig iron. He seemed to have forgotten what had happened the last time he'd tried to take the ball from her. But what the hell, if he wanted it that bad, she might as well give it to him.

Alita hurled the Motorball straight into his midsection. It knocked him backwards, but most of the other killers managed to avoid piling up on him. Alita noticed they also managed to avoid taking possession of the ball. Apparently no one felt the need to keep up the pretence that this was anything like a game.

"Hey, let's keep watching, folks, and maybe a little Motorball will break out in the middle of this street-fight," said the announcer with a nervous laugh. Poor guy, Alita thought—maybe he was finally getting the idea that this hot ticket wasn't a game after all. He probably didn't know how to call the action for Murderball.

Tough stuff, kid, and it only gets bloodier from here, so try to keep up.

The obstacle course ahead was called "the traps", Hugo had told her, and it could turn good luck into bad. The traps consisted of a transparent tube full of random problems—that was what Hugo had called them, problems—but not always the same ones from game to game. Sometimes they even changed things up during a single game.

The tube itself was the biggest problem because it limited

the range of movement. Being able to jump high wouldn't help her in the traps unless she fell into a really deep pit—and if she did, she'd have to get herself off the stakes at the bottom first. Reaction time would be even more crucial and so would flexibility—mental as well as physical.

Guys with big showy weapons were at a disadvantage in the traps unless they could retract them or somehow fold them away for easier manoeuvring. Alita grinned, thinking of Exploder, the tricycle with the giant chip on his shoulder, Gangsta with his big wheel, and the guy with the chainsaw arms who had done little except hang back and try not to get caught in any pile-ups. This might actually be entertaining.

Chainsaw arms was currently chasing her around pillars and potholes but he couldn't balance too well in tight quarters. Alita slowed up to let him take a swing at her; she dodged and his arm went into the pillar beside her, where it stuck, revved briefly, then died. He was trying to free himself by sawing the arm off when she side-kicked him, knocking him out. She lured another thug into a tar pit, jumping over it at the last moment when it was too late for him to do the same, then stuck a third to a ramp using his own nail-gun hand.

Exploder reappeared, much to her delight. It took her all of five seconds to get behind him, twist the fuel feed to maximum, and detonate him. Dodging shrapnel and body parts, she let the shock wave blow her towards the end of the tube. Just before she emerged, she heard the familiar whirr of spinning blades, the sound of Stinger cutting his way through the last few obstacles as well as a few of his competitors. Well, that was one way to get through an obstacle course.

The very last obstacle was actually outside the tube: an enormous metal spike with a deep groove in its surface that forced players to spiral up to the sharp point at the top. Alita knew Stinger was going to stay on her tail, intending to do to her what he'd done to Antioch. He wanted to make a big flashy kill. She powered her way up the spiral to the top where she tucked into a triple backwards somersault to land on the track.

Stinger tried to do the same, but acrobatic movement wasn't his forte; neither was physics. His blade-arms threw him off, and instead of flying through the air to the track, he belly-flopped onto the spike. Alita hoped that would go viral, too; she was pretty sure he'd never be able to do it again even if he tried. Not even if he *practised*.

She skated backwards slowly, watching to see who else would come out of the traps. Mace, Kumaza, and Chainsaw Arms appeared, followed by Screwhead, who bumped into them because they had all stopped to stare at Stinger trying to wiggle himself free. Then they turned to glower at her. Were they going to *scowl* her to death?

"Well?" Alita couldn't help laughing at them. "Did you guys come here for blood or quiet time? What're you waiting for?"

Stinger finally managed to heave himself off the spike, slid down to the track and rolled at her with his blades whirring, although the motor sounded a bit rough and overworked. He wasn't bleeding nearly as much as she'd have thought—he must have been packing sealant. *Did he even know that stuff was only temporary?*

Her phone rang.

"Ali, it's me! I got a big problem!" Hugo shouted.

He had a big problem? "Not a good time, Hugo," she growled, turning to skate forwards and accelerating.

"He's trying to *kill* me!" Hugo said.

Immediately, nothing else mattered. "*Who* is trying to kill you?" Alita asked, skating faster, widening the gap between herself and the killers.

"Zapan, the Hunter-Warrior! He killed Tanji!"

The sob in his voice sent a wave of fierce protectiveness and outrage through her. Tanji was part of her life with Hugo, sour face and all, not a mark for a Hunter-Warrior. She remembered what Hugo had said about Zapan when she'd first seen him: *Scanning for his mark. I wouldn't want to be* that *guy.*

If Zapan had killed Tanji, Hugo didn't stand a chance.

"Oh, shit, here he comes!" There were sounds of traffic and Hugo panting as he ran.

Alita turned to look at the killers behind her. They were lined up across the track again, with Stinger slightly ahead on the inside in case she had any thoughts about calling it quits and leaving the track. She wasn't supposed to get out of this alive, no matter what happened.

The hell with it—she was tired of this stupid game.

"Where are you?" she asked Hugo.

"Heading for the old cathedral," he said breathlessly.

"On my way. I'll meet you there."

Alita did a full turn, checking out her pursuers, then scanning the stadium until she found the area she wanted—no seats, no concessions, just plain wall.

Okay, you guys, this next move is a little something I call "Takin' It To The Streets". Alita kept her gaze fixed on the wall and went faster.

At first, people on the street thought a bomb had blown out part of the stadium. Debris sprayed in all directions for a half-block radius; a large chunk of cement and drywall crashed through a coffee-shop awning, scattering the people sitting underneath but without causing any serious injuries. Another large fragment landed in the middle of an intersection in front of a small gyro-lorry, precipitating a chain reaction of bumper-to-bumper collisions. Luckily, no one was seriously injured in this incident either. But those on the scene saw a young woman also land on the street nearby, hitting the ground hard enough to leave an indentation twenty centimetres deep. Seeing her armour and the number 99 on her shoulder, bystanders believed her to be a Motorball player caught in the explosion and thrown to her death.

Before anyone could check, however, the young woman picked herself up and skated off into the night as if she thought she were still on the Motorball track. Moments later, cyborgs also wearing armour poured out of the hole in the stadium and skated after her in pursuit.

Witnesses to this remarkable turn of events were divided as to how they felt. Many declared Motorball had obviously got out of hand, while others approved of this fresh new direction for a game that had shown signs of stagnating. A few others, believing they were hallucinating, went to the nearest emergency room to seek medication.

Alita zoomed around a corner and into a narrow alleyway just ahead of a skinny black truck and realised she'd made a mistake. The alley let out on another main road and she would almost certainly skate right into an ambush. But as skinny as the truck was, the alley was too narrow—not enough room for her to turn around and go back. Then, ten metres from the end, she saw the building on her left had a small recessed area. As soon as she reached it, she flattened herself against it and held her breath; the truck passed her with centimetres to spare and reached the end of the alley just in time to meet her killers and spoil their ambush.

Two of them bounced off the front bumper but the other two leaped up onto the cab and skated the length of the trailer. Alita was already speeding back the way she had come, looking for the turn she had missed. It was actually a space between two buildings, not even wide enough to be called a passageway. Not wide enough for her pursuers, either; she rolled through it sideways.

Hang on, Hugo. I'm coming.

Hugo knew every nook and cranny in Iron City, every hiding place, every place good for lying low. The problem was, Zapan did too. But Hugo had an additional problem: there was no way he could go on running flat out indefinitely. By contrast, cyborgs could run for days and they'd only have to stop if their legs fell off.

But worst of all was Zapan's hunting ability. The man was damned good, almost like one of McTeague's Hellhounds with their talented noses, keen hearing and sharp eyes. Hugo had tried going back to the upper level and Zapan had spotted him almost immediately. For some reason, the Hunter didn't come down to the lower level, either because the territory was too unfamiliar, or—more likely—he wanted to keep Hugo trapped below. There was nothing down here except abandoned buildings, the homeless, and some kind of strange Factory building with few windows and no doors, guarded by Centurians. *How long was Zapan going to keep this up?*

Zapan's words popped into his mind: *She thinks she can punk* me *and get away with it?*

The Hunter wasn't going to stop until he killed her, Hugo realised. As far as Zapan was concerned, everything began and ended with Alita's humiliating him. Nothing else mattered.

Hugo kept moving through the lower-level streets, staying in the shadows as much as possible. He had intended to find a way back up and double-back past the place where he'd found Tanji and Dif jacking the cyborg. But Zapan seemed to be a step ahead of him—maybe Zapan's hunting instinct told him Hugo would return there and he'd figured the odds on where Hugo was most likely to emerge. Or maybe he didn't have to do the math at all—maybe he had flunkies with night-vision goggles watching Hugo run around like a bug in a bottle.

He had to get out of here.

Hugo sheltered for a little while in the shadow of a set of stone steps leading to the upper level. They came out on a side street in a spot so obscured by the surrounding buildings that you couldn't find it unless you already knew it was there. A lot of black-market goods went up and down those stairs. Zapan would know that, but with any luck his flunkies had gone home for the night and he was still expecting Hugo to double-back to the scene of the crime.

Or not. It didn't matter. Hugo couldn't stand being down here a moment longer. The only chance he had of getting away from Zapan was to meet Alita at the cathedral.

He took a couple of steadying breaths and then climbed the steps, dropping low as he reached the top, and held still, listening for crazed cursing and death threats. But all he heard was traffic and the hurried footsteps of people on their way home. Hugo stood up slowly, wincing as his thigh muscles complained about all the running and crouching. He kneaded them briefly, working his fingers the way Tanji had showed him when he'd got a cramp during a pick-up game of Motorball.

The thought of Tanji made his throat tighten and his vision blur with tears. He had to move now or Zapan would find him just by following the sobs. A block away on his right, the main road was still busy although the traffic was starting to thin out as night-time segued to early morning. There wasn't much to his left but a few businesses closed for the night and, farther down, another Factory distribution centre with a shipment tube growing out of the roof. The graveyard shift would be clocking in soon to dutifully sort and categorise goods for shipment to Zalem. He had to risk the main road if he wanted to get to Alita.

Hugo moved quickly, sticking close to the buildings until he got to the corner, and paused to look up and down the main road before stepping out on the sidewalk. Nothing happened. He put up his hood, stuck his hands in his pockets and kept his gaze down to avoid making eye contact with anyone as he headed for the cathedral.

He managed to go an entire block before he heard Zapan's laugh.

"Got you now, you criminal!" Zapan yelled, standing directly across the street from him. People around him ducked and ran as he waved the Damascus Blade in the air. "You murderer, I'm gonna take your head!" Smiling evilly and pointing at him, Zapan was about to step off the sidewalk and cross the street when Hugo finally caught a break. Or more specifically, a bumper.

Hugo hadn't bumper-jumped for years but he didn't have time to wonder if he could still do it. Traffic was heavy enough that the driver didn't notice he had a passenger riding his front bumper; even better, no one ratted him out. All the good citizens were probably home in bed by now.

Hugo peeked around the side of the bus and for a

moment he was afraid he'd see Zapan grinning at him from the rear bumper. But for once, his luck held; Zapan was still standing on the sidewalk, turning around and around and looking pissed off.

Hugo's phone rang.

"I'm almost there," he said. "Almost."

"Got it," Alita said. She had reached the marketplace, which seemed to be very different late at night. People didn't notice very much that happened around them, no matter how weird or unsavoury, and they were even less inclined to help anyone.

She parkoured her way up to roof level, hoping her pursuers wouldn't be as skilled. To her dismay, a few followed her example with no trouble and shouted directions to the ones pacing her on the street. But she was still faster up here. Jumping from roof to roof was actually easier with wheel-feet because she could build up more momentum. She kept moving from building to building faster and faster, until finally she didn't hear them calling out her location to each other. Hoping she really had lost them, she rebounded from windowsills to drain pipes until she got to ground level—

—and found herself boxed into a dead end where they were all waiting for her. She hadn't lost them; they'd herded her. There were more of them now, several who hadn't been on the track, and they seemed to be organised into two groups, one led by Antioch who had somehow managed to staple himself back together, and one led by Screwhead. They surrounded her slowly, as if waiting for her to beg for her life.

Did they really think she would?

Stinger suddenly dropped down on her from somewhere overhead and started spinning his blades.

Alita threw him off, thinking absently that he wasn't as heavy as she'd thought. The moment she was on her feet again, Screwhead body-slammed into her, sending her crashing into the wall. The rest of Screwhead's gang piled on, forcing her to the ground with punches and kicks.

It was like being pelted with lots of little stones; Alita drove a wheel-foot into Screwhead's middle and she flew all the way across the alley to land on some overflowing trashcans. Alita sent the rest of her gang with her—*So you won't be lonely, bitch.* This discouraged them, and Antioch's gang as well. Antioch himself looked somewhat shamefaced as he backed off, even though he must have known those staples would never have held.

Then she heard the sound of spinning blades; one person *still* hadn't given up on trying to kill her. Alita groaned, catching Stinger as he tried to throw himself on top of her again. She slammed him down on the street, straddled him, and tore his head off.

"I do *not*—" She banged his head on the pavement. "—have time—" Another *bang*! "—for *this*!" *Bang, bang, bang-bang!*

If he didn't get the message now, he was too stupid to live, Alita thought. She dropped his head in a trashcan and took off for the cathedral.

CHAPTER 22

Hugo jumped off the bumper just as the bus started to turn right. He tucked, rolled and stayed on his belly, looking at the empty street straight ahead of him. The cathedral was only half a block away. With any luck, Alita would already be there. He was going to tell her everything; then they'd figure things out together. Hugo looked around and saw nothing but shadows. Maybe his luck was still holding, he thought as he got up and ran towards the cathedral.

Or he tried to run. It was more an uneven lope as his aching legs told him they'd had enough of his bullshit. His burning lungs agreed and his shoulder chimed in to remind him it was going to hurt a lot now that he was out of adrenaline. Hugo tried to focus on what he and Alita could do about the mess he was in. Doc Ido would help. He wouldn't be too happy to find out how Hugo had come by some of the parts he'd got for the clinic, but the doc would never believe he was a killer. If anyone could get him out of a false murder rap, it was Ido.

But first, he just wanted to see Alita. She wasn't here yet—he knew because he was almost at the entrance and if she'd been there, she'd have come running out and—

Abruptly he found himself on his back looking up at the dark sky. Something had hit him hard at the base of his throat. He was trying to sit up when he heard a familiar voice say, "Hey, where you goin', huh?"

Zapan loomed over him, holding his arm straight out to show Hugo how he'd clotheslined him. Hugo scuttled backwards from Zapan but the Hunter advanced on him, one hand on his sword, grinning with delight. He'd had his teeth re-done, Hugo realised. How crazy did a person have to be to get his teeth re-done while he was hunting a mark?

Hugo felt a solid wall behind him. He was out of room, out of time, and out of luck.

The Hunter was eyeing Hugo's neck avidly as he raised the Damascus Blade. But Zapan just stayed that way, holding the sword high in the hair, unable to complete the stroke, because a metal hand was gripping his arm. Zapan's chiselled jaw dropped as Alita ripped the sword out of his hand and flung it away.

Alita rolled to Hugo and knelt down beside him. She started to say something and then froze, staring past him in disbelief and horror.

Hugo raised himself up to follow her gaze. The motion detectors on the street had registered the presence of more than two people and activated the flatscreen mounted on the building across from the cathedral. It was the Factory's way of making sure everyone in Iron City could keep up with the latest news.

Tonight the latest news showed Hugo's face in glorious high definition and very much larger than life, unmistakable and unmissable. The caption scrolling sideways below it was equally clear:

Number 9107/HUGO—wanted for jacking and murder—bounty 30,000 credits.

There was a price on his head already.

For a moment, Hugo almost wished Alita had arrived too late to catch Zapan's arm. Except it would have put 30,000 credits in that bastard's pocket.

"Looks like your Hugo hasn't been entirely honest with you," Zapan said with fake concern, then laughed.

Alita was vaguely aware of Zapan saying something but it sounded too far away to make sense of. She turned from the screen to Hugo.

"Is it true?" she whispered.

"It's—you don't understand—"

Alita made a frustrated noise and drove her fist into the wall beside Hugo's head, letting her hand remain in the cracked indentation.

"I *never* killed anyone, *never*!" Hugo said desperately,

almost sobbing. "We only—we jacked *parts*. We paralysed cyborgs and stripped them for parts but *that's all*. We never—" He cut off and looked away from her. "I needed the money for Zalem. But I wanted to quit. I was trying to quit when—" He stopped and raised his eyes to her again. "I'm sorry," he whispered.

Mission accomplished, Zapan thought triumphantly, picking up his sword. Better yet, he'd got a two-for-one deal: he'd broken Hugo's heart as well as the girl's. Brute force execution was all well and good when it was just a bounty you were after, but when things got personal, there was nothing sweeter than devastating an enemy's soul. Criminals deserved to suffer as much as possible anyway, and he was just the Hunter-Warrior to dish it out.

"Step aside," he told the girl imperiously, "and let me do my job."

Zapan felt an explosion of pain as he hit something cold and hard. A cracking sound thundered from the point of impact behind him as Alita picked him up and held him against the stone of the cathedral with her forearm jammed against his throat. Her other hand was drawn back and flattened as blue light swirled and throbbed around it, a halo of unearthly fire.

"Touch him again," the girl warned in a voice that might have come from the dark depths of a bottomless pit, "and I'll kill you."

Not an empty threat, Zapan thought uneasily, watching

the blue glow. That looked an awful lot like a plasma weapon. How she could have got one, he had no idea. But he always had the code on his side: "Interference between a licensed Hunter-Warrior and a claimed kill is a violation of Factory Law and the Hunter's Code," Zapan informed her.

"He's *mine*!" she snapped.

"Oh, so *you're* claiming the bounty?" Zapan gave her his all-business, professional-to-professional smile, as if she weren't still holding him up against a wall by his neck. He felt her hesitate, and for a moment the pressure on his neck let up. Then it came back stronger than before.

"I had him first," she cried. "*You* are in violation!"

"Then make the kill, Hunter-Warrior," Zapan said, genial but still all business. "You have the licence. I've seen it myself." The blue glow around her hand was fading. She couldn't argue. "Become one of us."

Alita let him drop and turned back to her boyfriend, Hugo. Hugo the Magnificent, jacker and murderer extraordinaire. The kid was up off the ground now but he had his back to the wall, like he was too scared to move. What a coward. Not to mention ugly.

"You know there's no room in the Hunter's Code for love or mercy," Zapan went on. "But just because I know you're new to this, I'll make it easier for you." He stepped past her and lunged.

The Damascus Blade slid ten centimetres into Hugo's middle before it struck something solid, possibly his backbone although Zapan really hoped it was the wall behind him. What most people didn't know about stab wounds was that the real damage wasn't always from the blade going in. Quite often, what killed someone was yanking the blade out again. Especially from the gut. Zapan stood back, sword in hand, and watched Hugo crumple like a pile of rags.

And if that wasn't melodramatic enough, the tragic heroine scooped her doomed lover up in her arms and rushed into the cathedral with him. As if *that* would help either of them. Zapan looked down the street and saw the lights of approaching Centurians, responding to the message he'd sent them. Took them long enough, although their slow response had allowed him extra time for entertainment.

He was also happy to see his buddies coming along behind the Centurians. Good—he didn't want them to miss this next part, because it was going to be one hell of a show.

"Hey, Cupcake!" he called, wiping the Damascus Blade clean of blood. "You better finish him before I do!"

No answer. Well, she couldn't say he hadn't warned her.

Alita had never seen so much heart's-blood. It didn't seem possible that Hugo could lose so much and still be alive, and yet he was. But she didn't think he could last much longer.

"I have to get you to Ido," she said, holding him close so he wouldn't see how bloody her hands were.

Hugo turned his head to look at the lights flashing on the walls from outside. "Centurians," he said. "If you go out there with me still alive, they'll kill us both."

Alita's eyes welled with tears. "Oh, God, Hugo, what did you *do*?"

But he was looking past her up through a gap in the roof at a bright star in the sky. "Hey, you see that star up there?" He smiled and tried to lift his hand and point but couldn't manage it. "All my life, I wondered why all the other stars move across the sky but that one never does. I think I just figured it out." He gave a weak laugh. "I guess there's nothing like imminent death to focus the mind."

Alita looked from him to the star and back. "What do you think it is?"

"Zalem is *hanging* from it," he said with another feeble laugh. "That's what's been holding it up all these years—something big and far away. Maybe it's as big as Zalem—or bigger, even—way out in space."

"A star city," Alita said.

"Going to Zalem—it was never *just* about the promised land," Hugo said. "It was getting answers to so many questions."

"I need answers too," Alita told him. "I need to know what's in your heart—*right now.*"

Hugo gazed into her eyes. "I didn't kill that guy," he told her, and everything in her knew it was the truth. "But it doesn't matter. I tore people apart—for *money*. People like you."

"Where were you tonight?" Alita asked, her voice gentle.

"I went to stop the others, to tell them I quit." Pause. "Because I love you, Alita." He managed to lift his hand and touch her cheek. "I'd give up my dream for you."

Alita bent forward and pressed her lips to his, tenderly, lovingly. "*Never* give up your dream," she said and bent to kiss him again.

"*Never* give up your dream."

Hidden on the other side of a broken wall, Chiren stood very still with her face buried in her hands to keep herself from breaking down in sobs. It wasn't that she'd given up on her dream, she thought. Her dream had died and left her with nothing; nothing to dream, nothing to give up.

Unbidden, the memory of looking down at Iron City from Zalem with Ido rose up in her mind. It had been the night before they had been forced to leave. The dark landscape dotted with tiny lights had offered no hints as to what they could expect. It was simply unknown and, when she looked at it, she'd suddenly been unable to breathe as a hard lump of panic congealed in her chest and began spreading tendrils to every part of her. She had reached out blindly for Ido and he had gathered her into his arms so securely it damped down her panic.

"We'll be together," he said in a low, loving voice. "Nothing else matters."

And for a few hours, she'd believed that without a shred of doubt.

The cell phone on her wrist flashed. Vector's face appeared on the tiny screen. "Did you find them?" he demanded, impatient. Always demanding, always impatient, and she had nothing.

"No. They're gone," Chiren whispered and broke the connection. Then she picked up the case at her feet, stepped out from behind the wall and walked the short distance to where Alita was now rocking Hugo in her arms like a child.

"Don't die, Hugo. Please don't die," Alita begged. "You're so cold but don't die, okay? Please? Don't. *Don't*." She looked up at Chiren, showing no sign of recognition, only pain and loss and sorrow. "I'd give him *my life* if I could," Alita said.

Chiren knelt beside her and pushed her hair back from her face. She hadn't seen anyone so devastated and lost since the night she had walked out on Dyson. After her dream had died.

"Maybe you can," she said. "Alita."

It wasn't until close to dawn that the tragic heroine finally came out to play her final scene. Maybe she'd been praying, Zapan thought. The idea of a cyborg praying was as hilarious as that of a cyborg in love. Neither would do her any good now.

She stood squinting against the spotlights the Centurians had on her, clutching a backpack to herself. Zapan recognised it as Hugo's. Bless—she was sentimental. A sentimental cyborg who was in love and prayed. This was going to be more fun than three marks trying to get away on one gyro, and that one had been a *hoot*.

Zapan stepped forward and pointed at the girl. "You

have violated Factory Law and the Hunter's Code," he announced loudly.

A Centurian marched over to stand in front of him. "Where is the criminal Hugo, Bounty 9107?" it asked in its flat, mechanical voice.

The girl lowered the front of the backpack just enough to show Hugo's head. His eyes were closed and he looked peaceful. "Hugo is dead," she said dully.

Zapan's jaw dropped. The girl had actually done it! The other Hunters with him couldn't believe it either.

"I claim the kill," she added in the same lifeless tone. "Hunter-Warrior 26651."

"Damn," said a Hunter on Zapan's right. "She really did it. She killed him."

"Man, that is *hardass*," said someone else, sounding more uneasy than impressed.

Another Centurian scanned the head. "Claim confirmed," it said. "Case closed."

No, Zapan thought, something was off here. The girl had been completely in love with this jackass, and then suddenly kills him? Zapan knew women like that, and this cupcake wasn't one of them.

He lunged at her and tried to pull the backpack away. For less than half a second, he saw how the tubes of heart's-blood and cyber-blood ran from her partially open chest and disappeared under Hugo's chin. Then she raised the backpack to cover his head and pulled it closer to herself.

Zapan was baffled. How the hell could she have done that? It wasn't like she was any kind of a brain surgeon—

Then he spotted the tall woman sneaking out of the side

of the cathedral with a case in one hand. That was Victor's pet Tuner—the one he claimed could turn a chunk of scrap metal into a Second League champion. But what the hell was *she* doing here? And carrying a case that looked a lot like the one Doc Ido used to carry medical supplies—

The little *bitches—both* of them! "Oh, that's a real cute trick," Zapan yelled. "You think that's gonna fool anyone? Gimme that—" He made a grab at the girl's backpack; she shrank back from him as a Centurian rotated its gun turret in his direction.

"Hunter-Warrior Zapan, registration number F44-269," the Centurian said loudly. "Stealing another Hunter's bounty is against Factory Law and the Hunter's Code."

"Thank you," the girl said politely. She took a step towards Zapan and he automatically recoiled; she had a look on her little face that he didn't like one bit. He forced himself to stand his ground; he wasn't going to let anyone think a girl could make him flinch. Then she made some kind of gesture at him—no, not a gesture. That little cupcake had the Damascus Blade!

Zapan reached for her, intending to take his sword back, when a terrible pain exploded at his left temple. Something was on fire or burrowing under his skin and oh, God, now it was moving all around his face, across the top of his forehead at his hairline to his other temple, down the other side of his face, under his jawline, his chin, and coming up the other side and why the *hell* wasn't anyone trying to help him? Couldn't they see—

Something fell at his feet with an obscenely wet smack. Zapan looked down and saw his own face staring up at him. Except it had no eyes. His face had no eyes—

Because he had no face!

Screaming in pain and horror, Zapan turned to the other Hunters for help. But all they did was wave him off and back away, refusing to look at him, some of them even gagging. Meanwhile, the bitch who had done this to him was escaping with his Damascus Blade and no one was even *trying* to stop her. Were they all afraid of her because they thought she'd killed her own boyfriend for a bounty? Or was it that weird blue fire dancing along the length of the sword?

But she was just *a girl*, just a *stupid little girl*; any of them could take the sword away from her easy and give it back to him, the rightful owner. What kind of Hunter-Warriors would just stand by and let a girl walk off with a brother Hunter's weapon, especially after she'd just used it *to flay him alive*?

What kind of Hunter-Warriors wouldn't help one of their own save face? It was a very special face, too, not cheap plastic hackwork; it was expensive, worth more than all of those lame-assed so-called Hunters put together! They weren't his brother Hunters—they weren't even his friends. And now they were all walking away, like this was just another night in Iron City and he was just some faceless nobody.

CHAPTER 23

Alita had no idea how long she had been sitting on the bench outside the OR. Ten hours, ten days, ten centuries—she couldn't tell one period of time from any other. If she'd had to guess, she'd have gone with centuries. She would have waited that long for her Hugo. Ido said she was three hundred years old—what were a few more centuries between friends? As long as Hugo lived, she didn't care how long it took.

When she finally heard the OR door open, she bounced up in front of Ido, tears welling in her eyes, ready to spill down her cheeks.

"How— How is he?" she asked, afraid to raise her voice above a whisper.

Ido dabbed at her face with a soft cloth. "You can see for yourself. He's in Recovery now."

Alita dashed past him.

Even if the body wasn't a Berserker, it was A-grade, a composite that Ido had made himself, using the best parts and materials he could find. It was his own design, and when he had finished it, he had put it away carefully in cold storage, refusing to raid it for parts, no matter how depleted the clinic's inventory was. He'd had a hunch that someday this body would save a life, and when the time came, he didn't want anything missing.

Gerhad had been watching over Hugo since they'd wrapped up the cyber-surgery. In the past few weeks, they had done more embodying procedures than most reputable doctors did in a year. When things quieted down, Ido was going to suggest to Gerhad that she go for certification as a doctor—i.e., just take the test. She had enough experience in cyber-surgery to count as coursework.

Now she stepped aside with a smile as Alita went to Hugo's side. "He's good," Gerhad told her. "He's stable. No question, he'll be all right."

Alita touched Hugo's steel hand, so much like her own now. It wouldn't be as sensitive because it wasn't Urm technology, but it was the best work in Iron City, state of the art, top of the line. And maybe it wasn't such a bad thing that it wasn't as good as Alita's, Ido thought; the prospect of two Urm Berserkers running around together was a little scary.

"I'm sorry, Alita," Ido said. She looked up from Hugo, her expression mildly puzzled. "This city—eventually it finds a way to corrupt even the best of us and somehow the wrong people pay too dearly for other people's sins. Hugo didn't deserve what happened to him. Fortunately,

Chiren's surgical technique was brilliant—genius actually, rigging your circulatory system to include Hugo as part of your body. There's no brain damage at all. And that brilliant heart of yours was strong enough for both of you."

"Chiren knew how to do it," Alita said, smiling through her tears. "If it weren't for her, he'd be dead."

Ido had a sudden mental image of Chiren in the cathedral, helping Alita and Hugo, and his heart skipped a beat, the way it had when he'd seen Chiren holding their daughter, talking to her, playing with her, rocking her to sleep. Chiren's blue eyes hadn't been cold then, they'd been bright, full of life and love. During those years when Motorball had been the outlet for their talent, they had been busy and happy, creating champions for a game they both couldn't get enough of, and he had constructed a new body for their daughter, hoping to replace the one that wasn't strong enough.

But when the game had betrayed them and destroyed their beautiful girl, Chiren's heart had frozen and she had gone over to the kind of life that they'd promised themselves they'd never live.

Well, *he* had promised. He'd thought she had, too. But, to Chiren, life had broken its promise, rendering any promises she'd made null and void. As time passed, Ido had begun to wonder if there was something in Chiren that had always been drawn to the worst that Iron City had to offer, and losing their daughter had simply freed her to follow.

Either way, he'd thought the spirit of the woman he had loved had died with their little girl. But apparently, he was wrong—there was still a spark of his Chiren alive inside the ice queen.

"You had her heart in your hands—*in your hands!*—and you let her live." Vector came around his desk to grab Chiren by her upper arms and look into her face. "Why? Just tell me that. *Why?*"

She didn't try to twist away, didn't even yell at him for putting his hands on her when he was angry. Maybe she'd finally lost her mind. Entirely possible—she'd always been a little off. If he could sell Nova on the story that his Tuner had gone mad, and if Nova would give him a break for his past loyal service, he'd have Alita all boxed up and delivered within twenty-four hours. With whipped cream and a cherry on top.

"*Well?*" Vector gave Chiren a hard shake. "Do you even *know* why?"

Chiren was silent for so long he thought he was going to have to shake her a whole lot harder. Then she straightened up and looked him right in the eye.

"Because I'm a doctor. And a mother." She lifted her chin in defiance. "Somehow I'd forgotten that."

Vector pushed her away and threw his hands in the air. "And what the hell am I supposed to do with *that*?"

Chiren turned her back on him, on the view of Zalem, and on his enormous shiny desk. "I can't do this any more. It was one thing when it was just big stupid beasts fighting each other in the streets or on the Motorball track. But this—" She shook her head and walked towards the door. "I'm leaving."

"Chiren, *wait*!" It came out sounding more desperate than he'd have liked. She stopped, although she only turned her head a little instead of turning around.

"I understand now I can't keep you here any longer," Vector said slowly, doing sincere as if his life depended on it, because it probably did. "But if you're going to leave, don't you think it's time—past time, really—that you left for Zalem?"

Now she did turn around, and for a moment he wondered if she had seen the shadow behind the opaque glass of the door. But the way she was looking at him, her eyes too bright with tears of joy and her face alive with hope and gratitude, he knew she hadn't.

It had been hard, but Ido finally managed to get Alita out of the OR so Hugo could get some rest. She couldn't stop herself from talking to him, and if she kept it up, he would wake up too soon. Hugo needed all the rest he could get before he faced the world in this new and different body.

O brave new body, that has a Hugo in it.

Ido shook the thought away. His mind always generated nonsense when he was overtired. But sleep would have to wait; his patient was going to need him. Two patients, really—somehow he had to make Alita understand that what was normal, even exhilarating, for her would be traumatic for someone who'd been completely organic before waking up as a Total Replacement cyborg.

On the plus side, Hugo was young enough that his brain was still growing, so his central nervous system would probably adjust more easily to its new embodiment and accept it as natural. On the other hand, what had happened to his father would make it very difficult for Hugo to accept what had happened to him. And then there was what Ido would have to tell him about his grand dream of going to Zalem. He was going to take that hard—once he got Hugo to believe him, anyway. He was having a hard enough time convincing Alita of the truth.

"Vector was running a scam on Hugo," Ido said wearily. "I told you, if you're *born* on the ground, you *stay* on the ground—no exceptions, not for any amount of money. And the only way to get from down here to up there is to become Motorball Final Champion. That's it. You can*not* buy your way up there. No one can."

"How do you know that?" Alita said.

"Because *I'm* from Zalem," Ido said finally. "I was born there," He pointed at the small pale scar in the centre of his forehead. "I used to have the same mark Chiren has—the mark of Zalem. I removed it myself. Because our daughter wasn't perfect, because she was ill, Chiren and I were forced into exile with her down here. The magnificent floating city doesn't tolerate the weak, the sick, the defective. The man responsible is Nova, the Watcher behind the eyes. And because I fathered something imperfect, I couldn't go back up there if I wanted to."

Alita was staring at him wide-eyed and open-mouthed.

"And *that* is how I know Hugo was never going to get to Zalem. Hugo was conned. Vector's nothing more than a jumped-up con artist who doesn't care about anyone. He just strings them along with promises so they'll keep doing whatever he wants."

Alita peered at him with a searching look, as if she were trying to find some evidence in his face that he was wrong, even as her shoulders slumped and her eyes lost their brightness. She knew he was telling her the truth.

"I'm sorry," Ido added, wishing he were apologising for being wrong instead of right. He was about to say something else when there was a loud crash in the OR.

"*No!*" Hugo yelled. "*Nooooo, noooo!*"

Hugo had fallen off the table and was pulling IV lines and the nutrient tube out of his chest. Now he was struggling to his feet, still groggy despite his shock. Alita bit back tears; she had to help Hugo, not cry over him. But when she moved towards him, he backed away, waving her off with a wild movement that took out a shelf of beakers and equipment, sending broken glass, sensors and shattered bits of circuit board all over the floor.

"This was all for *nothing*?" Hugo cried, his cheeks wet with tears. "Everything I did, all the people I hurt—all for *nothing*?" He staggered to one side and knocked over a tray of surgical instruments, scattering calipers, retractors and scalpels. He kicked the tray across the room where it smashed into the far wall, dislocating a shelf of scanners and biochemical tracers, which fell on a freestanding cabinet below. The cabinet wobbled and tipped over with a terrible crashing sound of metal and glass.

Hugo didn't know his own strength, Alita realised. She had to calm him down.

"And now, *look* at me!" he sobbed, holding his metal hands out. "Look at what I've become—*look*! I used to make fun of them when I was ripping them apart—and now look at me!" He raised his metal hands and looked at them. "It's too perfect. It's exactly what I deserve."

As he dropped his hands and turned away, Alita wrapped him up in her arms. He was strong but he was no match for a Berserker. She hugged him tightly, keeping him still until Ido could sedate him. Hugo bristled when he felt the needle go into his neck, then slumped in Alita's arms.

"It will be better tomorrow," Ido promised gently.

Hugo raised his eyes and looked at Ido in despair. "What good is tomorrow to a dead man?"

"*I* see you," Alita told him as she carried him back to the table. "As long as we have each other, nothing else matters." She held his hand while Ido reconnected the IV lines and the nutrient feed. They hadn't broken, at least.

It wasn't supposed to be like this, she thought sadly. Only a few short weeks ago, he'd been helping her train for her big tryout. Her big tryout—what a joke *that* turned out be. Before that, he'd taken her out to the crashed spacecraft in the Badlands, to show her something that might help her with her memory. To help her, to help her—he'd done everything he could to help her. And in return, he'd been framed for murder and, for the grand finale, run through with a Hunter's sword. And he owed it all to her and her insistence on remembering her past.

"I wish I'd never found out who I was," Alita blurted suddenly. "It's only made everyone I love suffer! I'm sorry. I'm so sorry."

Ido turned her around to face him. "Don't you *ever* apologise for who you are," he said, his face intent and serious. "This is why you're here. You're the only one built for this."

She nodded, smearing away tears with the back of one metal hand. "And I have to face it all head on." Suddenly she caught sight of herself in the mirror over the sink. For a moment, she stood very still, feeling the Damascus Blade in her hand, feeling a purpose in herself that was slowly making itself clear to her.

Staring at her reflection, Alita became aware of a drop of water shimmering at the lip of the tap. It hung there for another second before it fell. The Damascus Blade was a bright streak in the air as she cut the drop in half.

"I want to thank you," Ido said as she turned back to him. "Because of you, I got to see my little girl grow into an exceptional woman. One who's going to save the world."

"Thank you, Father." Alita said as Ido dried her tears again. She leaned over and kissed Hugo gently on the forehead before she left.

❧

The Factory doors rumbled open. Alita stood with the daylight at her back, wondering how she must look to the Centurians lining the walls—a small silhouette standing in a rectangle of brightness. Something long and slightly curved extended down from her right hand, heat shimmers rippling in the air around it. Blue plasma cast no shadow but it was as real as anything—as real as the Damascus Blade, as real as she was and what she had come here to do.

"*Vectorrrrrrr!*" she roared.

The Centurians' gun turrets swivelled around to point at her. Her Berserker reaction time put her ten metres into the hall by the time they fired at the spot where she had been. Still firing, the guns swivelled again, shooting chunks out of the floor, the walls, the ceiling as they tried to get a fix on her. More Centurians stumped into the hallway, spraying the place with bullets and taking out other Centurians in the process. Someone had adjusted their programming from KILL-INTRUDER to KILL-INTRUDER-AT-ALL-COSTS, and Alita was pretty sure she knew who that was.

Unhurt, she vaulted onto the back of one of the reinforcements and plunged her plasma hand into its brain case, causing it to freeze. The others registered her location but she had already leaped away as they shot the frozen Centurian into scrap. She bounced up beside another, sliced off its gun with the Damascus Blade and dragged it along with her.

"Violation! Violation!" A deckman came down off the bounty platform and rolled towards her.

Oh, come on—seriously? It really was no more than a tin can, and not a very good one. Alita used the Centurian's gun to blow it to pieces.

Past the bounty platform, she saw a bank of three elevators. Two went no higher than the floor where Vector's office and penthouse suite were located. The third stopped on the level below, where there was maintenance access.

Vector had already been waiting several hours for dispatch to pick up the cabinet in his office and send it up to Zalem when the alert came in from Security. The cyborg girl his hired thugs had failed to kill, Alita, was coming up the front steps, and she was obviously loaded for bear. After the past couple of days, he wasn't in the mood for any more of her steel-assed bullshit and he'd set the Centurians to "Overkill". After they obliterated her, he intended to send whatever was left up in a plastic bag to the Watcher. If Nova wanted her heart so bad, he could piece it back together like a jigsaw puzzle.

Vector was pretty sure the Centurians would close Alita's case before she got as far as the bounty platform. But the gunfire went on and on and Vector began to get annoyed. It was one thing for a gang of hired killers to screw up—it wasn't like any of them were geniuses. But Centurians had big guns, a perfect aim, and they couldn't be outsmarted or distracted in a limited space like the entry hall.

When the sound of gunfire finally died away, Vector stabbed the intercom key.

"Security, report!" he barked. "Did you get her?"

He waited for someone to babble apologies for the noise, but there was no response.

"Security, dammit, report!"

Still nothing. Someone was definitely going to die before the day was out. He was trying to decide who and how many when his skylight exploded.

Shards of glass rained down on him, cutting his face and hands, sticking in his hair and clothing. He tried to brush himself off and ended up pushing the glass even deeper into his skin. A whole bunch of people were going to die for this, Vector thought, momentarily blind with rage. The stupid skylight was supposed to be shatterproof, made with the same kind of glass they used in Zalem. Obviously someone had swapped out the good stuff and left him with Iron City crap while making themselves a fortune on the black market. When he found out who, he was going to kill them so hard it would wipe out everyone in a six-block radius—

Then he saw her in the middle of the room, and all thought ceased.

Alita assumed a fighter's stance: knees slightly bent, hands up to protect her face as she glowered at him. Like she felt she mattered to him—like she mattered *at all*. She looked around, straightened up and walked over to his desk. "You were never going to send Hugo to Zalem," she accused him, her big eyes as dark as her voice. "Were you?"

"I *always* keep my promises to send people up," he said, but he could tell she didn't buy that. What the hell— the girl wasn't getting out of his room alive; it wouldn't matter if she knew. "Like Dr Chiren here," Vector added, gesturing vaguely at the cabinet in the corner of his office. Alita looked at where he gestured, then back at him with a puzzled expression.

Vector walked over to the cabinet and rapped his knuckles on it, but the girl still didn't get it. He shrugged and deactivated the seal so he could open the front. If dispatch came now, they could just wait a few minutes, he thought, as a little vapour snaked out of the refrigerated interior. As long as he didn't leave the door open too long, nothing would spoil. A minute or two would probably do it. Alita wouldn't be able to distinguish any of Chiren's packaged internal organs from the mystery meat they sold in the market, and she probably wouldn't recognise Chiren's hands, as lovely as they were. But he was sure she'd know those blue eyes. They were packaged separately in transparent containers and secured side by side, to indicate they were a set. They were as beautiful and as cold as they had ever been. Literally cold.

"If dispatch ever get their asses in gear, she'll go up with the rest of tonight's shipment." Vector gave the girl another few seconds to be thoroughly horrified before he closed the cabinet up and reactivated the seal. "Who the hell knows what the boss does with any of this." He rapped his knuckles on the case again. "And *that* is the only way anyone *ever* gets to Zalem."

Vector smiled, seeing the shadow through the opaque glass in the door behind Alita. This was going to be good.

Alita saw Vector start to duck just as the door crashed inwards. Berserker reaction time let her protect her face from the various fragments, which bounced harmlessly off her body. But the grind-cutter didn't bounce. It sliced through her side and she fell to the floor, holding the wound as bright-blue cyber-blood poured out between her fingers.

"I knew you would not wait for your fate to find you," Grewishka said, towering over her in ugly triumph.

Then he vanished.

They were under attack.

Zalem was under attack. The wind was screaming past her ears as the supply tube she was climbing with the rest of her squad shivered and rocked—not much, but enough to make it tricky to hang on. They were up pretty high but they still had some distance to go. Gelda was leading them, urging them upwards, reminding them every metre, every centimetre, every millimetre was a gain.

At this height, they had to be ready for the bladed rings that appeared without warning and slid down along the supply tubes. These were the floating city's defence against any ground-dwellers foolish enough to think they could simply climb to a better life in a better place, neither of which they had any right to. Alita and her squad had already fired on a few with plasma rifles and shoulder-mounted missile launchers, blowing them into fragments that went spinning off into the void.

The squad had just destroyed another one when the side of the tube blew out.

Earth and sky slewed crazily as Alita clung to the tube,

dragging herself forward until she was clinging to the jagged, still-hot edge of the hole. The wind was quickly drying splashes of heart's-blood and cyber-blood on the tube and on the parts of dead and dying cyborgs still stuck to the metal.

Her whole squad was gone, she realised. *Now* what was she supposed to do?

A hand reached down and clamped onto her wrist. Alita looked up to see Gelda's torn face, bleeding blue in some spots, seeping red in others.

"You know Zalem's defences!" Gelda shouted at her over the wind. *"Finish the mission!"*

Finish the mission—

Grewishka was back, looming over her. Under her fingers, Alita felt the wound in her side closing up, healing itself, and she knew it wasn't just temporary sealant.

How about that? She got to her feet.

"I know who you are," she said to Grewishka, her voice low and dangerous. "You're a child of the underworld, taken to live up here as a slave. And I'm just an insignificant girl." As she spoke, she felt a sudden profound pity for Grewishka, for the utter tragedy of the life he had been forced to live. "Die knowing this—the people who did this terrible thing to you will suffer. I'll *make* them suffer."

Grewishka laughed at her and she found it in herself to pity him even more. Chiren had rebuilt him into something like a walking truck. His thick arms and bulky shoulders were vaguely suggestive of a gorilla but there was no life in them, only machinery. His torso was a distinct triangle, made so his lower body could be attached easily. His thick metal legs were shaped like a human's, but such exaggerated musculature didn't exist organically; his feet were more like a Centurian's.

And all of this was topped off with the last vestige of his humanity. His head and face were protected by his over-built shoulders. To Alita, however, it looked less like protection and more like the machinery was swallowing him.

The body was no good for anything except killing— killing *her*, to be precise. Grewishka had become nothing more than a Centurian with more metal and less purpose.

"My master Nova is *so* eager to meet you," Grewishka said. "Allow me to introduce you!"

The intake doors on Alita's arm opened with a discreet hushed noise as they drew air in. Blue fire blossomed on her hand, flowed over the pommel of the Damascus Blade and ran along its length like a living thing.

Sneering, Grewishka pointed and his grind-cutter flew out from his hand. There was a blinding flash of blue light and then the grind-cutter was writhing impotently on Vector's shiny marble floor.

The cyborg bellowed with rage and fired all the rest of his grind-cutters at once. Alita leaped into the air, performing a whirling dance with the brilliant blue flames, moving too fast for Grewishka's brute eyes to follow. But afterwards he had no trouble seeing the other four grind-cutters dying on the floor like headless snakes.

Grewishka raised both fists and charged at her. She

dodged him effortlessly and one fist demolished one of Vector's absurdly ostentatious pillars, leaving a pile of rubble below the ragged piece of stone hanging down from the ceiling like a weird stalactite.

Time slowed as she somersaulted over Grewishka's head. In his bewildered, upturned face, she caught the barest hint of the innocent he'd never really been, before she dropped straight down, driving the Damascus Blade so that it bisected him from top to bottom. Alita landed on one knee with her back to the monster, not wanting to see the two pieces fall away from each other.

This city—eventually it finds a way to corrupt even the best people.

Ido had said that, and she had told him the problem wasn't the streets or anything else in the city, but up above. There was no pleasure in knowing she was right, she thought as she got to her feet and turned to Vector, who was cowering behind his desk.

"No, no, wait!" he pleaded, backing away from her as she moved towards him. "Please, just wait—" He tripped on nothing and fell on his expensive ass. Alita walked around the desk, watching him try to scuttle away from her like a bug. She raised her arm and drew it back so the point of the Damascus Blade was aimed at his left eye.

"Speak," she commanded.

"Sure, what do you want me to say? I'll say anything, tell you anything," Vector babbled. He was backed up against another of his stupid classical-knock-off pillars. "Anything, just tell me what to say—"

"Not *you*," Alita said. "*Him.*"

Vector had a fraction of a second to look terrified before his eyes went dead and his face lost all expression.

"So we finally meet, Alita," he said in a calm, inhuman voice.

"Nova." The name felt like a profanity.

"May I?" asked the Watcher, making a small gesture at the space between them. When she didn't move, he shrugged, got to his feet, and made a business of smoothing Vector's clothing and brushing off any remaining bits of glass, ignoring the cuts and scratches they left on Vector's skin.

"Where are you?" Alita asked.

"Home, as we speak. Feet up. Very comfortable." He glanced out of the window at the floating city, then moved past her to sit Vector's body on the edge of the desk. He was looking at her with what she realised was supposed to be a mischievous grin. But implanted optics didn't twinkle, and neither did Vector's dead eyes.

"Well, my girl, you've certainly exceeded all expectations, mine included," he said. As if he were complimenting a small child on their homework. "Killing my champion Grewishka—most impressive! And turning a selfish creature like Chiren to your side—I never saw *that* coming. You're definitely more interesting to me alive than dead. And we're from the same place, which in these hard and perilous times makes us practically *family*."

She waited, her sword ready and unwavering.

"You can go ahead and walk out of here and the Factory will not stop you." The Watcher made Vector wink at her—a neat yet nauseating trick for someone who hadn't had eyelids in centuries. "*This* time."

"I don't need *your* permission to live," she said evenly.

"Ah, but others might." He chuckled. "Your precious Dr Ido, for example. And what about your beloved Hugo? Yes, I know he's still alive. Although not for long—we'll track him down." Nova laughed again. "I've found the best way to enjoy immortality is to watch others die."

Fury surged through her. She gave Vector's body a hard shove that put him flat on his back on the desk with his legs dangling, then raised the Damascus Blade with both hands. All at once the Watcher vanished and it was just Vector on the desk, looking terrified.

"Please, *don't!*" he begged. "I'll do anything! I'll make you a champion in the Game. You're good. The crowd loves you! I'll give you anything you want, just *please don't kill me!*"

And then as Alita was staring at him in uncertainty, the Watcher was back. "See? No character. None whatsoever."

In answer, Alita drove the Damascus Blade through the centre of his chest, pinning him to the wood.

"Then you'll enjoy losing your puppet," Alita said.

Nova lifted Vector's head to look at the sword sticking out of him. "That does look fatal," he agreed. "Well, no matter. Vector was getting tiresome." He coughed; heart's-blood leaked from his mouth and he began to tremble. But still the Watcher kept his eyes clear and focused. "Oh, Alita, you poor child. Everything you've gone through and still no answers."

"And you've just made the biggest mistake of your life," Alita said matter-of-factly.

"What would that be?" asked the Watcher, as if indulging a clever but insolent child.

"You let me live."

Nova made Vector smile, exposing blood-soaked teeth. "Then adieu, until our next meeting. And remember—" He was losing his hold on the last shreds of Vector's life. "*I see everything.*"

He was gone. Alita pulled the Damascus Blade free, letting Vector's body slide to the floor. She stared at his corpse, but there was no pity in her for the man who had lied so egregiously to Hugo, to Chiren, and to all the other sad, lost souls who'd thought they could get out of Iron City in one piece.

Her phone rang, making her jump. For a moment she was afraid it was *him*, with one last word. But her relief at hearing Ido's voice was short-lived.

"Factory enforcers came looking for Hugo," he told her. "Somehow they found out he'd been kept alive. I sneaked Hugo out of here but they've sealed the city. The Factory's determined to find him."

"Do you know where he went?" Alita asked.

"He—oh, God, Alita, he's trying to go up."

Y'know, if I were as strong as you, I'd climb that tube to Zalem right now.

Alita ran to the window and looked out, scanning each of the spider-leg supply tubes until she made out a tiny figure working his way upwards to the flying city he thought was heaven. Only because he didn't know what really lived there.

You know Zalem's defences—

CHAPTER 24

Finish the mission.

Gelda's voice echoed in Alita's head as she made her way up the supply tube after Hugo. The sense memory of the climb she'd made with her squad seemed to echo the same way in her body. She went faster this time; it wasn't easy but it wasn't as hard as before.

It would be more difficult for Hugo. The increased strength and coordination of his cyborg body would have made the first part of the climb easy. But as he went higher, it would become more of an effort for him to hang on in the wind. To withstand the forces of wind and rain, all very tall structures need some give to them, but the supply tubes had a lot more than most, something that wasn't obvious from ground level.

Finish the mission.

Alita knew she could do that; she always had. She couldn't remember the missions themselves but she knew she had finished all of them, and she would finish this one, too.

It was after the first third of the length of the supply tube that Hugo would have begun to struggle. Even hardcore adrenaline junkies willing to gamble that Centurians would be too busy to show up and shoot them down had never gone higher and never, despite their claims, scratched their initials into the tube. They couldn't have—they'd have needed both hands to hang onto the bucking, swaying pipe.

If they actually *had* gone higher, however, they'd have found themselves in real trouble. The middle stretch of every tube had sensors to detect pressure and movements produced by someone engaged in purposeful climbing. The sensors would then trigger the bladed rings, sending them down towards would-be trespassers. They were virtually impossible to avoid, and the only way to get rid of them was to destroy them. Few climbers were strong enough to carry weapons that powerful. Even if they were, there was still the possibility of being blown to smithereens by a mine left over from the War. Even a squad of Berserkers could get chewed up and spit out.

Anyone foolhardy enough to try scaling a supply tube usually attracted a Centurian before going any higher than twenty feet. The Centurian would invite the daredevil to dismount under penalty of law, allowing thirty seconds for compliance. After that there was no further warning before the penalty of law kicked in.

Hugo had picked the one time in the history of Iron City when, thanks to the spectacular snafu of Vector's "Overkill" command, there were no Centurians available to shoot him down. The handful of still-functioning Centurians were aware that Vector's life-signs had ceased, and were currently on standby, awaiting orders from his successor.

Alita realised that Hugo had made his choice when he was unaware of all this, that this option was the only one he had left.

"Hugo!"

At first, he thought his ears were playing tricks on him again. When the wind had started to pick up, Hugo had thought he'd heard voices calling to him—first Tanji's, then Doc Ido's, even Vector's. But he hadn't heard Alita's until just now. Clinging to the tube, he twisted his head around to find it was no trick; she was really there, her beautiful face serious as she pulled herself towards him.

"You have to come down!" she shouted. "You can't stay up here! *We* can't stay up here!"

"This is the only way!" he called back to her. "I'll never make it out of this city alive!"

Alita moved a little closer. "Zalem isn't heaven, Hugo!"

"It has to be!" he told her.

"But you don't even know what's up there!" she replied.

Hugo looked down over the long, snaking supply tube to the ground below. "It doesn't matter."

"Don't you do this!" Alita shouted, and he saw her eyes were welling with tears. "Don't you dare leave me behind—" she looked past him towards Zalem with pure hatred in her face. "For *that*!"

Hugo shook his head emphatically. "I'm trying to set you free!"

"Please—*please* listen to me, Hugo! I've been here already—I mean, *here*, in this spot—and it's right where Nova wants us! Nova's the Watcher behind the eyes and he's using you to get to me! We have to go back down *now*!"

Hugo shook his head. "If I go back down there, I'm dead! Don't you understand that?"

"I can fight them off!" Alita was almost close enough to touch him. "We can make a run for the Badlands. They'll never follow us!"

The Badlands; Hugo thought of the day he'd taken her to the Urm ship (with Koyomi and Tanji, and for a moment the memory of his friend was a knife in his heart). He looked past her, down the length of the supply tube, and then up to where it disappeared into a low-hanging cloud. What was the Badlands or any other place compared to a city in the sky?

"We belong up there!" he called to Alita.

Alita shook her head vehemently. "We don't belong *anywhere*! You and I are the same, Hugo. You're the only one who sees *me*, and I'm the only one who knows you for who you really are!" Her eyes welled with tears, not because of the wind, and it occurred to Hugo that he was always making her cry.

"We'll always be on the run!" he called to her.

"We'll be *together*!" she yelled. "Please, come back down with me so we can go home—wherever that is—*together*!"

The love shining in her face was wide, deep and unconditional, and he finally understood that without it he had nothing. Hugo stretched out his arm to her.

Alita moved up a little more and reached for him. "We can go home," she said, straining to touch him.

I almost threw away the only thing of value in my life, Hugo thought as his heart filled with every feeling he had ever wanted.

The hideous roar and clang from above startled him so much he almost lost his grip on the tube. He looked up to see a horrific circle of metal burst through the cloud and bear down on him in a halo of spinning teeth.

This time, she had no squad, no plasma rifle, no missile launcher. Alita reached for Hugo, intending to leap over the ring, and found that somehow she was already in his arms and *he* was lifting *her* over the bladed ring. Their combined weight should be enough to keep them from being blown away, she thought, and aimed herself so they would touch down on the tube again together. Always together.

Except something had gone badly, terribly, horribly wrong—Hugo was suddenly so light, he almost flew out into empty space. From the chest down, his body had been chewed away, and heart's-blood and cyber-blood streamed out from him on the wind. Berserker reaction time let her catch his hand just in time.

With her other hand, she drove the Damascus Blade into the supply tube as an anchor, and there they stayed.

"Hold on, Hugo, please!"

Hugo looked up at her. She was beautiful even like this, clinging to the side of a supply tube with the wind blowing her hair every which way while she strained to save him. He would have gladly held on for as long as she wanted him to—an hour, a year, a thousand years— except his arm wasn't going to last another minute. The ring had chomped him good, killing every connection in his cyber-body. His arm was going to come apart before he could even bleed to death.

Show's over, thank you and good night.

"I love you, Hugo!"

He realised that Alita was trying to pull him up and shift him onto her back. It wasn't going to work. He was going to let her down again and this time he couldn't help it.

"I'm glad I had the chance to know you. To love you," Hugo told her. His arm came apart. "Goodbye—"

She shot away from him at high speed. Still, Hugo went on looking into her eyes even after he couldn't see her any more.

Hugo's face was dreamy as he fell away from her, as if he were flying off to somewhere beautiful, like the Zalem he'd always believed in, and not falling to his death in a place he'd spent his life trying to escape.

Or as if she'd find him waiting for her at the cathedral, so they could climb the tower and look up at Zalem and the bright, unmoving star.

As if his arm hadn't fallen to pieces in her grip.

As if he hadn't been chewed up by a machine made by a man who needed the suffering of others to relieve the terrible boredom of his immortality.

Alita threw back her head and screamed defiance and rage and loss at the sky and everything in it.

CHAPTER 25

Nova heard her.

Chrome optics weren't his only enhancements, and there had been many upgrades since the young battle prodigy had first spotted him watching her spar with her sensei Gelda in the zero-g sphere.

That hadn't been the first time he had watched her, nor the last. He had kept track of her over the years—the centuries—and when she had finally fallen, he'd thought she had met her end.

In hindsight, he should have known better. Gelda herself had said it: this girl, this Alita as she was known now, would never give up, never stop. *Never. Stop.*

And after Dyson Ido had lifted her out of the trash pile, she never had. She had opened her eyes in a completely different world, with only a few fragmented memories of her life, but she was still who and what she had always been: the warrior who would never give up, never stop. This was bound to bring a great deal of suffering to everyone around her.

But the best, most entertaining, part was that she had no idea. She was completely unaware that she caused more suffering by persevering than she would have by giving up. Resignation was merely constant, ongoing misery that never waxed or waned, a treadmill where people were not so much alive as they were simply waiting to be dead. But then she had come along, shaking everything up, making people believe there was more to life. And there was—just not for them. When they realised that, their pain was ineffable.

Immortality was definitely less boring with her in the picture.

The uncaring stars travelled the same courses they always had through the darkness, except for the brightest one, which never moved. That wasn't *strictly* true, of course. The star never moved relative to any observers on Earth, in Iron City, or the Badlands, or in the one city still floating above the surface of the Earth, where observers' feet never touched the ground.

The residents of Zalem enjoyed the prolonged sunsets and sunrises that came with their elevated status. They also soared above the low-lying clouds characteristic of local weather conditions so they saw the stars more often, and many of them had become stargazers. Their interest was more about appreciating beauty rather than technical astronomy or astrophysics. Why the brightest star in the night sky never moved wasn't something that concerned them. Nor did they feel compelled to investigate the bright beam of light that ran from the centre of the city up into the sky where, somewhere out in space, it ended at that very same bright star. The beam was only visible at night, and it was most easily seen from the edge of Zalem. The people in Iron City couldn't see it at all, which was just as well. They might start asking questions they'd never get answers to. No one in Zalem knew why the beam of light was there or what was on the other end, and it really didn't concern them. They were all too busy with their own pursuits and amusements.

The man in the silvery suit watched the very end of the sunset from his usual spot on the observation deck at the edge of Zalem. He knew how important things like aesthetics, beauty and amusements were to maintaining a stable society, suspended in the air or otherwise. Currently, the most popular amusement in Zalem was Iron City Motorball. The people just couldn't get enough of it. Bread and circuses; it had ever been thus; and as above, so below. Iron City couldn't get enough Motorball either, especially now.

His own taste in amusement had evolved to include a lot of abstract concepts and conditions over the course of his long life. Fortunately, cyborgs provided entertainment that went well beyond their bashing each other to pieces. It was incredible how cyborgs that were more machine than organic flesh could spend most of their waking hours *emoting*. The tragic death scene he had enjoyed thanks to his enhanced sight and hearing—*that* had been exceptional. The cyborg girl who saved her boyfriend's life by turning him into the thing he was most afraid of becoming, which was, in fact, exactly what his one true love happened to be—oh, the drama, the humanity! And her scream of anguish at the end!

Better yet, she was *still* screaming, with everything she did, with every fibre of her being. It was a different kind of screaming, not audible to the ear, perceptible only to those with a true appreciation of human nature, who knew that it was the nature of humans to suffer. Now *that* was entertainment.

Tonight he was using his enhanced hearing to listen to the Motorball stadium announcer wax rhapsodic about tonight's game.

"The Second League waited for a long time for a new hero, someone they could follow, someone worth cheering for, who would never let them down! Well, I'd say they found their hero in a rookie who came out of nowhere! In the first five games of the season, her point record has been *outstanding*, a record-breaker—ask anyone, they'll tell you! There isn't a soul in Iron City who doesn't know this little beauty's name!"

The man at the railing smiled. A smile which, on his face, was terrifying, without warmth or humour or humanity, an expression of pleasure taken in the kinds of things that should never happen, or even be imagined.

He hoped the little heroine remembered what he'd told

her: that he saw everything. He wondered how long it would take before she understood that all of it, bread and circus, belonged to him and, being part of the circus, so did she.

These days, the pads and armour she strapped on were custom-made for her by Ido and Gerhad, with a little help from a walking toolbox of a man named Ed, who would say, "You're welcome," whether you thanked him or not. All of it was beautiful and it fitted not only her body but her style of movement, with preternaturally responsive nano-sensors that reinforced the material at points of impact. Wearing it made her feel invincible without slowing her down.

"—her team's facing a pretty tough line-up tonight," the announcer was saying in a tone that suggested he was tickled to death about this and all of life in general. "With Skamasakus *and* Massiter traded to the Vipers to shore up their offensive game, our girl will have her work cut out for her—"

Alita tuned him out and had a look at the Damascus Blade strapped to her forearm. Every time she used it, she did her best to be worthy of it. It had never let her down. She popped on her helmet; the feel of the lining adjusting to the contours of her head was Ido's doing. It was like getting an extra hug from her father before every game.

She revved her wheels, did a quick burn-out and whispered *Hugo* to herself before she left the locker room and headed for the pit lane. Sell-out crowd again tonight, and she thought she could hear every single one of them individually as well as together.

"She's new, she's white-hot and she's captured all our hearts!" enthused the announcer. "If anyone's got a chance of becoming First Champion, it's Iron City's very own sweetheart, number ninety-nine, the Battle Angel herself—*Alita*!"

The cheering seemed to make the whole stadium vibrate, all the way down to the track beneath her wheels. She raised her hands to acknowledge the crowd and looked to where Ido and Gerhad were sitting in their usual seats. Then she slid the Damascus Blade down into her grasp and turned to point it straight at Zalem. Blue flame danced around her hand and along the length of the sword to flare at the tip.

So you see everything, Watcher? Then see this: I have declared war on you and war is the one thing I'm even better at than Motorball. I was made for war and I will not stop, I will not give up, and I will not be defeated. I will finish the mission: I will come for you and I will break you and throw the pieces off the edge of Zalem, to land in the trash pile below. Where you belong. Because I will not stand by in the presence of evil.

Ten thousand fans screamed their approval of the angel who dared to challenge heaven, loving her defiant strength, giving themselves to it, and embracing it as their own.

ACKNOWLEDGEMENTS

My thanks to: Ella Chappell, for being the kind of editor every writer wants to work with; Joshua Izzo and Adrienne Ogle at Lightstorm for helping me see the world of Iron City and Alita, and for their encouraging words; Amanda Hemingway for ongoing support and friendship; my amazing, brilliant son Robert Fenner, who makes me proud every day of his life, and his lovely and talented girlfriend, Justyna Burzynska, who is quite the Battle Angel herself; Jo "Mutha Hydra" Playford, who has come to our rescue so many times, and Colin Harris, a true friend for many years; George RR Martin and Parris Phipps, for more than I can say; and Mic Cheetham and Simon Kavanaugh, my absolutely indispensable agents.

ABOUT THE AUTHOR

Pat Cadigan is a science fiction, fantasy and horror writer, three-time winner of the Locus Award, two-time winner of the Arthur C. Clarke Award, and one-time winner of the Hugo Award. She wrote *Lost in Space: Promised Land*, novelisations of two episodes of *The Twilight Zone*, the *Cellular* novelisation, and the novelisation and sequel to *Jason X*. In addition to being the author of the novelization of *Alita: Battle Angel*, Pat is also author of the official prequel novel, *Iron City*.

For more fantastic fiction, author events,
competitions, limited editions and more

Visit our website
titanbooks.com

Like us on Facebook
facebook.com/titanbooks

Follow us on Twitter
@TitanBooks

Email us
readerfeedback@titanemail.com